THE TAMING OF TRUDI

'Scared?' he said.

'Yes. What happens next?'

'You'll see. I expect you will take champagne?'

'Yes, please,' I gasped, my corset almost unbearably tight.

Peter snapped his fingers. At a bound, the coffee table – a nude, crouching girl – sprang into life. She rose to her feet, breasts wobbling, and her naked, gel-slimed body padded into the kitchen. The cane-stripes on her buttocks quivered as she passed me.

By the same author:

MEMOIRS OF A CORNISH GOVERNESS
THE GOVERNESS AT ST AGATHA'S
THE GOVERNESS ABROAD
THE HOUSE OF MALDONA
THE ISLAND OF MALDONA
THE CASTLE OF MALDONA
PRIVATE MEMOIRS OF A KENTISH
   HEADMISTRESS
THE CORRECTION OF AN ESSEX MAID
THE SCHOOLING OF STELLA
MISS RATTAN'S LESSON
THE DISCIPLINE OF NURSE RIDING
THE SUBMISSION OF STELLA
THE TRAINING OF AN ENGLISH GENTLEMAN
CONFESSIONS OF AN ENGLISH SLAVE
SANDRA'S NEW SCHOOL
POLICE LADIES
PEEPING AT PAMELA
SOLDIER GIRLS
NURSES ENSLAVED
CAGED!

THE TAMING OF TRUDI

Yolanda Celbridge

Nexus

This book is a work of fiction.
In real life, make sure you practise safe sex.

First published in 2002 by
Nexus
Thames Wharf Studios
Rainville Road
London W6 9HA

Typeset by TW Typesetting, Plymouth, Devon

Printed and bound by
Clays Ltd, St Ives PLC

ISBN 0 352 33673 0

Contents

1	Barefoot Girl	1
2	Set for Spanking	17
3	First Blossoms	30
4	Pair Bond	44
5	Skinny-Whipping	57
6	Damaged Meat	71
7	Full-Hair Beaver	87
8	Plaything	102
9	Voyeurs	120
10	Slutmaster	137
11	Bondsmaiden	153
12	The Dungeon	170
13	Housebroken Girls	185
14	Nevada Popcorn	200
15	The Cost	213
16	Juniper Berry	230

1

Barefoot Girl

My name is Trudi Fahr, and I am a female submissive. I am 22 years old. It will become clear in my narrative, I hope, just what a submissive is, how a girl can tell she is one, and what she might choose to do with the knowledge. Coming to submission is not to be rushed. It's like painting a picture. You start at the beginning and develop at your own pace, often understanding what appears on your canvas only after it's there. Two years ago, I could not have written this because I'd have been eaten up with shame. Sometimes, I awake at night, sweating in fear, at my shame. But you harden. I've hardened, although deep down I hate myself for it, and hate how others have hurt my body, and to punish them and myself too I want them to hurt me even more. I'm that wildest of animals, a tamed girl.

That is being a submissive: wanting to be shamed and hurt – beaten, specifically, with a rod or whip, on bare skin. Submissives masturbate a lot, because our behinds can never be beaten as much as we'd like, and there are only so many limbs that can be wrapped or shackled in bondage. So, we have to imagine. I'm playing with myself now, as I write: finger on my clitoris, and stroking my pussy, which is juicing at the thought of beatings I've taken and shall take, bare-ass and squirming, as my skin reddens under a cane. Most women are

1

submissives by nature, and have to serve the male, in everyday life, one way or another. I guess there are few married women whose men haven't paddled their ass, in a playful spanking, for some pretend misdemeanour, but for most, that's as far as it goes. American men can be very childish – I mean, calling themselves a 'tit man' or 'leg man' or 'ass man' as if women were just so many centrefolds or chunks of meat. Women are the same, only we tend to focus on the butt, which is a round-about way of saying the cock. Cock size is what we like. 'Check the cute buns!' That cry will get girls' heads turning, and the sexiest men are always those with pert, muscled asses, so I understand why so many men are 'ass men' when it comes to females. Buns, though, come way behind the most important thing.

Never mind feminism and power dressing and stuff – those are just for women pretending to have cocks. Really, we worship the cock, and are at the very *least* fascinated by its symbol, the whip or the cane. Yet, most girls don't feel the need to go the whole nine yards. Our clothing is submissive enough, if you think about it: all those straps and buttons and zippers and high heels, and slinky, sexy uncomfortable things, which are really a kind of bondage. Making a guy's breakfast or slinging his clothes in the washer is pretty submissive, too, especially if you have to ignore unfamiliar hairs sticking to the crotch of his jeans.

It is no mystery why I, and those like me, should choose to make ourselves real slaves, allowing men – *or* other women – to enslave us. Usually, enslavement begins with that playful spanking, and progresses to full slavery. At a certain point, the sex of the enslaver doesn't matter, it is the shame and the pain which count. *They identify us.* A mistress can be almost as effective as a master; indeed, it is sometimes more shameful to be enslaved by a lesbian, who really despises you. Maybe we subs are compelling *them,* male or female, to enslave *us?* Certainly, there are plenty of male subs, and sometimes the hunkiest jocks turn out to want their ass paddled by some Amazon – a role which my physique suggests. Generally, I despise male subs, although a naked male whipped turns me on – it's just that he mustn't *want* it as I do. Some of the best masters are little wiry guys with massive dicks; preferably with big balls, too. Big balls, full of cream and power . . . I'm a greedy girl.

I am writing my story for other girls, to help them understand themselves, and I'll begin the story proper with an account of my first spanking, when my real life began. First, however, I shall give some details of my life before my submission. They are necessarily few, and only to serve the purposes of my personal story. I had my upbringing in small-town America, with kind parents, in a comfortable home. The Fahrs came from Germany, and my full name is Daniela Gertrud (no 'e') Fahr. Trudi suits me fine. My father was a doctor, now retired, and I had a liberal upbringing, excellent grades at school, with no family disputes or rebellions on my part. I was smart, read a lot and liked my own company, but not so much as to make me an outsider. I'm reasonably good-looking, and kind of athletic, which helps. I declined being cheerleader for the high-school football team in favour of my friend Cher Baxter, who wanted it more. I mean, it was the biggest thing in her life, apart from a condo in Palm Beach. (Bitchy? Yeah.) What was the biggest thing in mine? (I'm not being gross!) Coming to submission, obviously.

I'm five foot ten in height, with a big, pear-shaped bottom, long, well-muscled legs, and large breasts, 42s, if you're a stickler for detail, with a C cup, and to sugar the pie, my hair is blonde – yes, an all-American centrefold, although without the airbrushed, sanitised pubic hair. I have a very thick, wide fleece between my legs – I mean, a real jungle, if that's not too crude,

3

which I never trim. That is, I never mess with it. When the mood takes, I shave completely, otherwise I leave the jungle intact, no ditsy half-measures. It goes over my belly, and hangs low between my thighs, hiding my pussy lips, if I want it to, although they're generally pretty swollen and visible – like now! My vulva is one of the rosebud kind, rather than the long slit some girls have, and it fits neatly, in its entirety, into a mouth, opened wide enough to pleasure me in that way, although the lips, which are quite thick, get kind of squashed up around my clitoris, which is fun! I don't trim or shave my armpits, either, so I guess no amount of airbrushing would make me a centrefold, despite my tits and ass (crude!). I very occasionally depilate my legs, but normally they have just a film of gossamer down, which is better than nude. But I'm very careful never to touch an actual pubic, as opposed to leg hair, except with shampoo, or baby oil, or hairspray, which I sometimes use for photos! Pubic hair is surprisingly versatile – at least, mine is. With oil, I can brush it into a silky mane, like head hair; backcombed and sprayed, it stands up like a garden of golden roses. I'm proud of my fleece.

I mention my German ancestry because it is relevant. I never went to Europe when all my friends were back-packing because my folks never went either. The place in Germany we came from, Königsberg, doesn't exist any more, that is, as part of Germany – it's now in Russia. My father always said I was free to travel the world, but that travelling in your mind is sometimes best. The thing about Königsberg taught me that places can change, and people too: nothing is for ever, or immutable. If I'd been born a short distance north of an imaginary line on a map, I wouldn't even be an American. I'd still be a sub, though – that cuts across all lines, as it were.

I don't wish to make a big thing out of my figure and looks, because stereotyped beauty can be a hindrance to a girl – attracting undesirables and scaring off men she really likes. Being a fulfilled female sub is not about looks, but attitude. I dated in much the usual way, lost my virginity at 16, in much the usual way – sneakily, while baby-sitting at a neighbour's, and with less than expected ecstasy. It was with a boy named Don Funicello – Italian, very macho, leather jacket ... He was efficient, if brutal. Strike that – *because* brutal. We shared a Four Seasons pizza – Don smelled of pizza, even in daylight! – and he wanted to push a slice of pizza up my pussy, and eat it, so I let him. We'd had some wine, though I drink alcohol sparingly. He didn't lick my clitoris, though – I don't think he knew where it was. When he'd eaten the pizza, with extra topping of my pussy oil, he slid his cock in and fucked me, with my palms cupping his ass. It didn't last long – just a few ramming strokes. We weren't naked – I wasn't wearing panties, which helped, just a denim skirt, which went up pretty smoothly – but I managed to come (I'll get to that later), and I was so pleased I masturbated in the toilet afterwards, with my pussy still sore. Generations ago, girls used to lose their virginity in the back seat of a car, at a drive-in movie or something, and I guess boys did too, but cars were bigger then. It's a funny thing about American men – a lot of them really do prefer to keep their pants half on for The Event, as though some gunslinger is going to sneak up on them, or they mustn't miss the Dow Jones, or just feel less guilty than if they were bare-ass.

I had a few more boyfriends, again in the usual way, although practice in masturbation made the sex part more fulfilling. My parents were pretty good. Sometimes I feared letting them down by not being rebellious, like a proper teenager, and maybe they felt guilty for giving me no cause. I was an only child, which suited me fine, but I would stage pretend tantrums, just to give my dad the opportunity to be dad-like, and he would dutifully respond by pretending to be angry. He never smacked or spanked me. The only thing he got mildly annoyed about was the weather, which in New England, apart from summer and early fall, ranges from hard, to very hard. He would purse his lips and cluck over the weather forecasts, although you always knew there were going to be snowfalls, or gusts, or whatever. I figure that's why he came back to New England, to have the weather to cluck about. In LA, the weather's always the same, which makes life kind of dreamlike.

My home town could have been anywhere in Middle America, but it was Plattsburgh, on Lake Champlain, in the state of New York. On the other side of the lake was Burlington, Vermont. A lot of my friends were itching to get away from Plattsburgh and go to New York City, or even just to Burlington, but not me. I was quite happy wandering barefoot in the woods, or swimming nude in the lake, and just assumed that one day I would go to New York City to study, but was in no hurry. We went to New York on shopping weekends, so I was always familiar with Manhattan. In Plattsburgh, the nearest big city is in fact Montreal, 50 miles away, and in another country, Canada, where they speak French. It seemed very exotic to hear a foreign language so far from Miami or LA or El Paso. In Plattsburgh, Montreal was where you went for fun.

My only eccentricity, which genuinely worried my dad the doctor, was that I am a barefoot. That is, ever since I can remember, I went barefoot most of the time. That sounds weird, but it is surprising how little harm a barefoot comes to. Plattsburgh, like most of New England, is very clean, without trash on the streets. I like to feel the grass or stone under my bare soles, and since our family had lived in New England for so many generations, I felt the earth was on my side, so to speak. I politely wore shoes to school, but after class I would kick off my shoes and socks, or, later, stockings, as I didn't want to get them dirty or holed. It sounds funny for a girl sub, no stranger to the most agonising forms of bondage, to say she doesn't care too much about clothes, but it's the truth. My folks had no taboos about nudity, but didn't make a big thing of it. At home, I walked around nude, if I wanted, or just in a towel. Mom had to remind me to wear a bra outside, as my breasts were always firm enough to stay up without one. So were hers, although it would have been rude to remind her. I oohed over fashions like any other girl, but it was peer pressure, mostly. I was always happy naked. Often I didn't even bother with panties. I liked air on my bare.

In my late teens, I started skinny-dipping at one or other cove on the lake, sometimes alone, more often with my friend Elle, but that is scarcely eccentric in rural America. There are plenty of places secluded by thickets or brush. Elle wouldn't join me in winter, when the water was frozen, but giggled from the safety of her fur coat while chomping on a mayo-slathered corn dog, as I stripped off to the raw, scampered across the snow, and cracked open the ice, before plunging under. I would spend a good 20 minutes in the freezing lake, swimming vigorously, and cracking another hole in the ice, the further and further I got from the shore, just to worry Elle, and she would give my shivering-blue nude body a big hug when I made it, dripping, back to our car. I loved coming up for air, all alone and nude, with my audience of snow-draped beech and oak and maple and birch trees – I didn't yet realise how blessed my home town was, in its abundance of birch – and, way across the lake, the slumbering, snow-shrouded Vermont shore, and felt how wonderfully, awesomely *big* America is. Americans travel a lot around America, but flying isn't travelling. Californians call the space between New York and LA as 'the great overfly'. You have to drive, on and on, through day and night, with the miles piling up on the odometer, to feel the awe. Even in a sleepy corner like Plattsburgh, people can occasionally tune in to the higher reality – to which corporal punishment is a short cut. I mean, you can be sitting in some restaurant, looking at your car under the snowflakes, and it suddenly hits you, *Hey, I don't have to be here* – I could just drive straight to Mexico! Many feel such moments of higher consciousness but few act on it, just as few act on the impulse to submission. Girls regularly fucked remain unspanked and unfulfilled, but not knowing why. Few think, *Hey, I don't have to be here* . . .

It felt so good as the warmth seeped back into my body when I got home after a winter nude swim, that I went straight to the bathroom to masturbate, thrilled by the sheer physical beauty of being *me*. I never went skinny-dipping with boys, who are surprisingly silly or prudish about nudity. I mean, either they hit on you, or go shy when they get a hard-on – *or* when they fail to get one. Elle and I would furiously sunbathe in the nude! We wanted an all-over tan, but, like good girls, took care to use lots of sun blocker, and the northern sun never quite made us the California brown we wanted. Dad gave me a sports car for my 17th birthday, and I drove barefoot, which seemed an LA thing to do.

When I say my sex life was the usual thing, I mean I experienced nothing, as far as I know, that my girl-friends did not also experience. Giddy passions, pillows soaked with jilted tears, my own vengeful mockery of some rejected boy – I had my fair share of it all, but at the same time was aware that I was acting a role. I suspect we all were. I wanted something more. I remember looking at Elle's bare behind the first time we sunbathed nude – it was all smeared white with cream that hadn't been fully absorbed – and she let me rub the cream into her skin. As I rubbed her bare ass, I kept getting flashes of how she would look, spanked, and what it would feel like to spank her. I was so astonished at my thought, and so curious as to where such a strange idea had come from – I mean, something that was just a fantasy could actually occur in the flesh, there and then – that I never said or did anything about it at that stage. It didn't occur to me that she might well have felt the same about my own derrière, for she was just as eager to rub my sun cream in. We were both pretty well-developed behind – they say that like attracts like. As I was to learn, one of the good things about being girls is that we can appreciate each other's bodies dispassionately – I won't say without envy! – and touch each other. Men worry their chests aren't hairy, or their muscles big, or something – and as for touching, that's a no-no. Girlfriends can be intimate without being sexual, and those of us with ripe derrières, and understanding what cute buns are really for, can have spanking friendships! Just as we can swim together in the nude, for fun.

Girls are more aware of *simple* physical gratification than men, who so often make such a big thing out of it. So few men make good masters, because they care too much. A good master is not necessarily one who despises the slave-girl he whips, gratifying though that can be, but one indifferent to her pain, and whose interest is control of the girl as object. A successful sub is one who comes to see *herself as an object*, from outside, which is why, in some of the scenes I shall describe, I shall refer to myself as 'she' or 'Trudi'. I can masturbate to climax, watching a video of myself, screaming and writhing in the direst bondage, under whip, and despise the masked female on the screen, who happened to be me. A really good master makes a girl hate her submission, but beg for more, and harsher. He understands her addiction to pain, shame and helplessness. I am an addict. I tremble before every thrashing, even though I crave it. A single cane-stroke on my bare behind can make me come, yet I hate pain. Really and truly.

I should add one little detail about my parents, though I think everyone has an inner nature, independent of nurturing, and I'm wary of all the pseudo-psychological explanations for people's behavior. You are what you are. Anyway, once, when I was about 11 or 12 years old, they had one of their rare arguments, or, I should say, differences of opinion. Mom always seemed too cheerful to argue with my dad. It was to do with me – about my bedtime, I think. My mom always set great store by the book on childcare, and on that occasion quoted it to dad, who said, without raising his voice, that she perhaps set too much store by it. My mom said, half-joking, that she believed he was jealous of another doctor. Dad raised his eyebrows and stared at mom, then nodded, and said he and mom had something to attend to upstairs, and when mom seemed about to comment, he said it couldn't wait. I saw her lip tremble, and she swallowed, closing her eyes for an instant, but she obeyed him and went upstairs. He left me watching my TV programme while he followed her. It was some stupid cop show, with lots of noise, but over the TV, I began to hear a drier, more rhythmic noise, like two coconut shells clapped together. Tap, tap, tap, tap, it went. Then I thought I heard mom's voice, sighing, but I didn't really pay too much attention. Afterwards, she came down all red in the face, and beaming, and said that dad was right, and knew best.

That was the first time I noticed such an event, but looking back to my earlier years, I realised it happened quite a lot – the mild disagreement, dad's raised eyebrow, and the trip upstairs. That was the first time I definitely heard the tap-tapping sound, though. It occurred a few more times, until I was in my pre-teens, and then I never heard it happen again. Mom was as cheerful as ever, so I reckoned they waited until I was

10

out for one of their sessions. Looking back, I see it plainly: mom was so cheerful because my dad the doctor spanked her regularly. I suppose it must have been on the bare, for once a woman is into serious spanking, there is no other way. I'm not arguing for heredity but after, relating that, I can scarcely argue against it, either.

So, my story starts with my first proper spanking. As you'll see, I was prepared for it, knew what it meant, and knew that I wanted it, even though my role in the scene demanded I pretend otherwise. Prepared as I was, I was still scared, but that first spanking on the bare opened up a whole new world to me. It is a world most girls only dream of, and if they do, then it's with a shudder, not knowing that their shudder is one of longing. They never reach their desire, because they won't look at it clearly. That is why they are unhappy. When I felt a man's hand first crack on my exposed rear, and felt the awful smarting as he spanked me, I suddenly knew the truth. My pussy knew the truth before my brain, for I was juicing up between my legs. Then I understood that spanking was what I had longed for all my life. I wriggled and squealed, and all my squirming just made him spank me harder, and I felt the glow spreading up my spine, through my belly and my loins, as my bare ass burned. It was only a hand-spanking, but I wanted him to spank harder, and for ever. I knew then that I wanted much more than spanking. I didn't have the words for it, but I felt what I was – a submissive, a 'sub', a natural slave, in search of a master. It's the shame, the helplessness, the wriggling of her bare ass – ultimate indignity! – that sets a girl free.

We've all seen movies where prisoners, slaves or seafarers are whipped on their bare backs. They always made me horny, but a little guilty. Sometimes you see women being whipped – not full nudity, or anything, but discreet, leaving lots to the imagination – and how I imagined things! I thought of myself as a serving-girl

11

in colonial times, stripped to my shift, or completely nude; shamed and jeered by a bunch of males, as some brute of an overseer, or English officer, striped my bare back with his whip, and *then* – when I was already screaming and sobbing in agony – larruped my bare ass with a hickory stick or springy officer's cane. That – the bare-ass punishment – was what really brought me off. Whipping on the naked back is painful, and humiliating, and, strangely, quite an effort, as it knocks the breath from you, and a willing sub has to brace herself, arching her back to meet her chastiser's whip. But caning on the bare buttocks is special, because a girl is totally helpless, and all she can do is wriggle, and scream or whimper. It was one of my first masturbation fantasies; like most teenage girls, I masturbated a lot. I still do. All girls do, but they don't like to talk about it.

As time went on, I added to the fantasy: I would be tied up, or chained and gagged, held over a fire that singed my pubic hairs, even stripped naked, tarred and feathered, and made to ride a rail while I was whipped. That was a punishment for whores, in the old west. They had to ride a rail, with their whole weight supported by the pole biting into their vulva. It's very painful; believe me, I know. However, I felt guilty the first time I masturbated to orgasm over that fantasy, because it seemed wrong to relish a whipped bottom, even if the bottom was my own. To punish myself, I play-whipped my own bare behind with a leather belt, folded in two. It didn't hurt enough to punish me, but made me juice more, and of course masturbate as a result, so I wasn't sure if whipping myself was punishment *for*, or encouragement *of,* my masturbation fantasy! I devoured all sorts of books, and discovered references to what was called 'flagellation', that is, whipping and caning of the bare skin; most importantly, I read of persons caned on their buttocks. The nudity of the portion caned is important, although a beating on

12

the panties stretched tight, or even a flimsy basque or teddy, can hurt as much as one on the bare, if only by extra strokes. Yet, to be flogged on the bare is so juicy and shameful, with not a shred of clothing or dignity left to the beaten girl. At that time, I was aware of 'hazing' in fraternities at men's colleges, where novices had to bare up for spanking with a table-tennis or baseball bat. It seemed to me rather dubious, and still does – merely a parody of flagellation, and in poor taste.

However, it was thrilling to read of disciplinary methods used mostly, but not only, on boys, and which involved use of a thin rod or cane on the buttocks either partially exposed, in undershorts or panties, or else completely bare. Schools and institutions in Europe accepted that kind of severity, often schools of a religious or military nature, and corporal punishment – 'thrashing', 'flogging' and so on – appeared quite casually in the pages of centuries ago, as though young men and women saw nothing untoward in a bare-bottom thrashing with a cane, or, worse still, a birch. The birch – just writing the word makes me tingle, and my pussy juice – is the most divine and awesomely beautiful of flogging instruments. I read of navvies in former centuries, of prison whippings on the bare back with the cat-o'-nine-tails, and of slave plantations, where male and female slaves were flogged. However barbaric such practices were, they still undeniably excite even the most timid or repressed women. I fantasised often about being a princess in chains, naked and whipped in some oriental slave bazaar. All girls do, I guess. In fact, probably the most repressed adult women are the *most* fascinated. My interest came to focus on the punishment of the naked buttocks, specifically. My masturbation fantasies centered on the *gluteus maximus*.

I was a wicked harlot, in some puritanical New England town, stripped and bent over a spanking-stool on the common, for a public caning by the muscular blacksmith. He would stripe my bare buttocks again and again with a hickory or maple switch, and I would scream and wriggle, but could never escape from the clamps that bound my wrists and ankles, nor the halter round my neck. Or I would be the same harlot, nude and harnessed like a horse, with a bit to gag me, and obliged to squat with my face in the dirt. I found my climax more intense if I was not just a whipped girl, but *wrongfully* shamed – it was the blacksmith himself, or even the hypocritical preacher, some Cotton Mather type with an insatiable cock, who had fucked me with his truly monstrous organ! It was all the more exciting a fantasy, because nature has gifted, or burdened, me with an unusually narrow vaginal passage. I always seek masters large of cock, so that fucking hurts as well as delights. Size *is* important.

As a variation, I imagined myself as the person administering the punishment: the wronged victim taking revenge on her seducer. I watched his firm, hard-muscled ass squirming faster and faster under my cane-strokes, and the bruises blotching and darkening, until his bare skin was all puffy and blue. I would apply the fantasy to some boy at school that I liked, and imagined myself in total control, my caning of his bare ass educing him to a whimpering jelly. That fantasy too was oddly exciting, but a teaser, to be kept in reserve. I was mentally testing myself. For a deliciously slow build-up, masturbating faster and faster to an intense orgasm, with my teeth grinding, it was always *my* bare ass that was caned.

When I masturbated, I found myself caressing not just my clitoris and nipples – the 'usual way' again! – but also stroking my rump, and fingering my anus, getting half a finger or a whole thumb up my anal shaft and wriggling on it while I rubbed my clitoris. For preference, I would slap myself on the bare buttocks and come very quickly after a few spanks, but I never dared do it very hard, as I was afraid the familiar tap-tap would carry through the house, and, of course, my mom and dad would know it! I experimented with the back of a hairbrush, slapping myself until my skin reddened, but again, I was embarrassed at making a noise, and, in truth, I didn't like the pain. I wondered why I dreamed of being whipped or caned on the bare bottom when even those clumsy experiments were not agreeable. Later, I understood that shame, humiliation and obedience must accompany the desired whipping of a girl's skin.

More girls are like me than anyone knows. Don't ask *why!* If you ask why, you'll never know. We adore the sting of the cane on our bare bottoms, that's all. It's almost as much for what it means – *obedience* – as for the thrilling shock of a cane on the naked skin, and the stimulation of the 'secondary erogenous zone' of the buttocks. Secondary, indeed! Only a male could have made *that* up. Most women are submissive in real life, without even being aware. They burden themseves with chores and worries and furniture and *things* – female clothing itself a form, or symbol, of bondage, with straps and buttons and hooks and zippers, high heels that render you helpless to run, and all the more delicious for it. True subs go that extra mile, with corsets tighter than tight, heels higher than high . . .

I wondered what sadism meant, and read some of the Marquis de Sade, then Sacher-Masoch, who wanted to be whipped and enslaved by a dominant woman. Sade uses erotic language to argue that nature doesn't care whether we are good or bad, and neither rewards virtue nor punishes vice, so that we might as well be wicked if it suits. Sacher-Masoch pleads for his 'Venus in Furs' to punish him for being male – I hope the poor wimp got to meet her. Both men are too self-conscious in what they do, or propose. Dominance and submission aren't about punishment or reward, but about self-awareness.

A female submissive does not, in fact, submit to anything. She resists! Every thrashing is new seduction, new surrender, new shame. She *is* submission, and she loves to hate herself for it. A cock can lie, but never a cane. Must pause to masturbate! I'm all wet now.

2

Set for Spanking

Usually, we went up in a gang, but this was the first time I had visited Montreal on my own. I drove up one Saturday in July, shortly after my 18th birthday, barefoot, of course, in my new car. I had a place at NYU for the fall semester, and was taking things easy that summer, though most of my friends were away in Europe, backpacking. At that time, I was still seeing a boy, not Don, but another one, James, whom I really liked, in a friendly, someone-to-talk-to way. We dated every weekend and always had sex, but for me it was really a chore I had to do in order to enjoy his company, which I did. For orgasmic pleasure, I masturbated, and didn't yet dare mention my fantasies to any boy. I guess I still thought nice New England girls didn't have fantasies. We went bowling or skating, or just for walks, and I was beginning to feel that the sex was a chore for him, too. My tight crack never juiced very much for him, and although his cock wasn't so big, it hurt as it went in, even with KY jelly, which I felt was a bit gross, as I knew it was really for anal sex, which I couldn't imagine any girl enjoying.

We did it missionary position, without deep penetration, and I couldn't bring myself to give him oral sex, which most American males are obsessed with. It's a power thing for them, but he was too polite to insist.

How green I was! Don, the cock monster, never even mentioned oral, he was in so much of a hurry to get 'it' into my beaver. He even called it 'beavering', which is not even right – beavering is when a girl masturbates for a man to watch. James and I were friends, but Don was different – an animal with a truly large cock. He hurt me when he fucked me that first time, and I cried out, but he made me come, so I associated coming with pain: another part of the painting. Don dropped me, or I dropped him, after we had used each other's bodies for a while, to mutual satisfaction – my pussy's pain at his ramming, which brought me off, with or without the help of my fingers – and the limits of his, or my, imagination. I have to admit that Don continued to figure in my masturbation fantasies. Sometimes he was an Italian pirate, whipping my bare back at the main mast . . . I closed my eyes and imagined that, sometimes, when James was friendly-fucking me, with me tickling my clit. Why are Italian boys always called Donnie or Vinnie? Umberto, there's a respectable-sounding Italian name, but I guess 'Umbie' wouldn't sound macho enough.

Going to Montreal that Saturday was for adventure, although, like a good girl, I pretended otherwise. I got to the city about 11 in the morning, and went to the Latin quarter, near the university, where they have all these artsy cafes, doing their best to be like Paris. I got an espresso, and sat in the sun at an outside table with a flowery parasol. I promised myself a high-calorie lunch, then an art gallery or two, shopping in the rue St Catherine, perhaps a movie, and be home before midnight. It didn't work out that way. I should have known. It was the way I dressed, of course. Girls always know, yet don't know, what signals they send. I had on a red top, just a cotton shirt that had belonged to Don, and the first two buttons were undone, so a peeker could see I had no bra. Because it was a roomy man's shirt, I felt bralessness was permitted, under the rules of teasing. My ass, though, was another matter.

I wore my favourite skin-tight white jeans, which I had to roll on rather than climb into. They really clung to my bottom, and were very tight in my crack – tight jeans or panties give any girl a nice tingle between her legs when she walks. I was aware of the attention those bun-squeezers drew. Plus, I had the shirt tucked into the jeans, not loose and floppy in the casual student fashion, but with a slight overhang, so you could see every contour of my ass. It was obvious to an onlooker though, just possibly, not to innocent me, that I was drawing attention to my bottom rather than my breasts, as I could equally have chosen a combination of a tight top and uplift bra, but baggy jeans.

I had no panties on, and the fabric of my jeans was stretched so tightly it was almost translucent. Just then I had my fleece completely shaved which, as I mentioned, I've done from time to time ever since I first sprouted, since extreme bushiness 'down there' occasionally makes me curious to try the opposite. Sometimes, a barefoot girl wants to get rid of that big thick fur coat. People think a jungly bush is sexy, and it is – Don certainly agreed, as his stiff cock kind of ploughed through my undergrowth – but it's a lot of trouble if you have hairs hanging well below the lips of your pussy, as I do. You have to wash thoroughly every time you go to the bathroom, or your hairs get smelly. Most girls trim their pubis, but for me, it's all or nothing: jungle or baby's bottom. After Don and I drifted apart, I shaved off my whole fleece. It took an hour.

I had tucked the shirt tail not fully in, which would have looked untidy on my buttocks, but just far enough down to touch the crack of my ass, and show my bare globes, making it clear I *wasn't* wearing panties. I was barefoot, of course, with unvarnished toenails. I left my hair long, so that it dangled inside my shirt around my breasts, and I kept having to scoop it back. Believe me, the effect was entirely unconscious on my part – my subconscious was in charge. All the guys were looking at me, except for this one guy, who wasn't really looking at anything, but staring, as though into a mirror which wasn't actually there. He was about 30, I guessed, and good-looking, but not striking – a soft, boyish face, and compact body, like those movie actors who seem taller than they are, because they are proportioned right. He had mousy hair in need of a trim, and gold-rimmed eyeglasses. On that hot day, when everyone else was casual, he wore a conservative blue suit, white shirt and dark blue necktie.

He sat with a really stunning woman, maybe a few years older than me, who was very sexy and vampish – long black hair, slightly olive skin, long bare legs, which she kept crossing and uncrossing to show a string or thong that didn't cover much of her abundant pubic hair, big breasts and ass, the breasts braless and jutting under a tight white T-shirt, and a mini-skirt that was little more than a rag, fastened with a safety pin, with bare feet like my own. She had that fabulous sort of sulky, sluttish look that I imagined Parisian intellectuals had. I felt awkward all of a sudden, a busty blonde Plattsburgh German, among all these svelte sophisticates! A girl just about my age approached the guy and pushed an autograph book in front of him, which he signed very politely, without any swank.

The girl had chestnut hair, a wisp of a lemon-coloured skirt, and a blouse with only the bottom two buttons fastened – no bra, no panties, like me, and hair down to her waist – and, with her autograph, got a French-style handshake, which was so *cool*. I wondered what the guy's attraction could be to women, because I felt it too. It was as though he was attractive simply because women *were* attracted. He had an aura of control, which I must admit turned me on. Women are

20

always attracted to men who have power over lots of women, because we think that if he fucks us, we'll gain some of his power. It's a mystical thing, almost. He shifted slightly, and I caught sight of his bulge under his pants. It was hard not to catch sight of it – I at once thought of Don, who was puny by comparison. That cock looked massive, as though all his strength was in the snake at his crotch. He saw me watching, and smiled at me.

I blushed, but couldn't turn my eyes away. He beckoned me! He put out his hand, lazily, and made a 'come here' gesture, with his fingers curled under his knuckles, which managed to be regal, but not rude. He said nothing. I got to my feet, picked up my coffee cup and walked over to his table. He looked at me politely, almost amused, while the woman gave a big smile, without showing her teeth. I sat down, expecting someone to say something, but no one did. I sipped my coffee, feeling increasingly awkward, as his eyes travelled up and down my body. He nodded to the beautiful woman beside him, who spoke.

'My husband would like to paint your portrait,' she said. He had said nothing that I could hear.

His name was Marc Robichault, and he was some kind of famous painter, and had exhibitions in New York and Europe. His wife's name was Helena. She said that I had a classic face, with a good skull and cheekbones – as though I was some horse or something. He looked right into my eyes as I said who I was and where I came from, and I knew he was really looking at another part of me, and felt myself redden, as I unconsciously shifted my buttocks. Helena laughed. She took a book out of her purse and gave it to me. It was the catalogue of a recent exhibition of Marc's, all portraits of women and girls, some full-length, in formal society gowns, and one or two in pretty summer dresses, which were the nearest they got to erotic. Marc said that

21

if I cared to visit their apartment, which was about a mile away in the old quarter of Montreal, he could take some photographs and work from those. Posing was arduous, in fact, a job for professionals. He didn't propose to pay me, as an unpaid model was 'keener', but nor did he wish to inconvenience me, as I lived so far away.

'Marc paints commissions, for the vainglorious,' Helena said. 'He wastes his talent. However, he makes some *good* portraits for sale, or to keep.'

Marc seemed to accept her put-down as casually as it was made. I said I was flattered, which I was.

'I don't have any expensive gowns,' I said.

'Perhaps you'd feel more comfortable in a summer dress, then,' said Helena. 'That is, if Marc decides to paint you full length.'

'Whatever you think, Helena,' said Marc mildly, but without taking his eyes off me, or rather, my haunches and ass.

I became acutely embarrassed about my lack of panties – I thought the whole street was looking at my crotch – then told myself I was just imagining things. I looked up again, and gulped the rest of my coffee, and saw that only Marc was looking at me there, and I didn't mind that. What I did mind, and I felt annoyed with myself for minding, was that his bulge didn't seem to grow any larger as he watched me. Don would be stiff as an elm, right in his pants, if I so much as crossed my legs, or let him peek between my breasts, which I suppose was one of the reasons I went with him. No girl can say she isn't flattered when a guy gets hard for her, or deny she's disappointed if he doesn't – if she's flaunting her stuff, I mean. Helena was looking, too, at the curves of my butt, and they let me stand up, before they did.

We drove down to their apartment in my car, with Marc sitting in the front and Helena in the back. I could see her in the rear-view mirror, and she had let her skirt ride all the way up, with her thighs parted, just enough to cradle her hand between her legs. Her fingers rested in her crotch, patting her pubic mound, as though her pussy was an animal to be comforted. I sensed I'd found the adventure I'd been pretending not to seek, though I wasn't sure what it would be. I imagined it would be sexual, obviously. I had flashes of Don, and his cock ramming my tight pussy, hurting me, just as I imagined Marc's massive snake, so docile beside me, would cleave my pouch; I saw Elle's body, nude by the lakeside, with her big firm ass all shiny with water, melding into Helena's body, which I felt instinctively I was going to see in the raw. Suddenly, I didn't mind how hazardous my adventure was going to be. I thought it best to play innocent, which I was.

Their apartment was big and airy, all white, with a view of the river and all the granite-grey buildings of Old Montreal. I don't remember it much, to be honest – you never really remember a scene, only what happened there. It could have been anywhere. A *scene* – that's what we call it – for corporal punishment has a special essence or aura, that a submissive can feel, as I felt it then, though without yet being aware what made me tingle so. Spanking takes a girl into a world beyond this one. There were some portraits on the wall, including a full-length one of Helena. She was in the nude, and painted from the rear. She had her head turned, with her lips in an angry pout, rather than smiling, and she was straddling the very sofa on which I now sat, facing her portrait over the fireplace. The cheeks of her ass were thrust up, and blushed quite a deep pink, over her olive skin, which at first I thought was a trick of the light, until I felt my heart race. That pink, and her grimace, could only mean one thing: that the model for the portrait, Marc's wife, had just been spanked on her bare bottom. And I was sitting on their davenport, delicately drinking my coffee, pretending I didn't notice, while they seemed so accustomed to their furnishings as not to notice my embarrassment, and excitement.

We started talking about my bare feet, and Helena's, and she said she liked to go barefoot, but wasn't a full barefoot like me, and was fascinated. Being a barefoot is always a great conversation-starter. Helena served a lunch of sandwiches and salads, which we ate on our knees. We talked for what seemed like hours, as the sun waned, and the rays lengthened on that pink spanked bottom of Helena in her portrait. I was enthralled, only gradually realising that they were learning all about me, while I was learning the minimum about them: Marc was from Montreal itself, and spoke English without accent, while Helena came from Quebec City, where it seemed they spoke only French. Helena sat perfectly still, like a tigress, but rubbed her thighs together in a constant, slinky motion. I told them about skinny-dipping with Elle in Lake Champlain, and how ... *interesting* it was to rub sun cream into her bare ass, and all about Don, and James, and how Don always smelled of pizza. They both gave the impression they were far too polite to find that amusing, so I added that he was ... *big*. Marc raised one eyebrow, while Helena winked at me, licking her teeth.

'Quite an *abruti*,' she purred. 'Did he bite you on your neck, or perhaps on your derrière? Even *slap* your derrière? Some males do.'

I fingered my neck, for hickeys long gone, and blushed.

'Maybe,' I said. 'Yes, Don bit my neck, when he came ... I liked it. He didn't slap my bottom or anything.'

'You liked the size of his penis?' she purred.

'Why, yes. I guess so.'

'You guess so!' said Helena. 'Why, I *hate* the size of Marc's. Don't tell me you haven't been drawn by that

24

bulge, Trudi. It hurts me, every time . . .' She paused, to lick her teeth. '*Wherever* the monstrous thing goes . . .'

'Don't you think Helena was unfair, telling a complete stranger that I wasted my talent?' said Marc, suddenly.

'I don't know,' I said. 'I mean, *I'm* a complete stranger.'

Plattsburgh, and the innocent air of Lake Champlain, seemed so far away, in this city apartment, shimmering with cool, perfumed promise. Outside, on the river, floated ships from Thunder Bay, or Duluth, which seemed to have made the pilgrimage from those mysterious places, right in the middle of the continent, to witness my own initiation. New Englanders are parochial: we stay in the snow and the rain, and the glorious red maple leaves in the fall make it seem worthwhile. But we know there are other worlds on our continent, intimidating ones. There's Florida down south, hot and humid and gangster-ridden, and gunslinging Texas and Arizona, and laid-back California on our farthest shore, a whole mysterious world of western ease, the flipside of our colonial primness. A rusty hulk from Thunder Bay, certainly not western, and anything but exotic, none the less seemed like brute force, invading my New England haven.

'Surely no stranger by now,' said Helena. 'And I wasn't just unfair to Marc, I was rude. It was rude, also, to pry into your personal life with your *pizzaesque* friend.'

She put her hand on my knee, with a gentle, exploring pressure. As she did so, her breasts began to quiver, and her thighs clamped tight. Her buttocks shifted under their flimsy cover.

'It is a fault of mine,' she said.

'A beautiful *slut* has *no* faults,' drawled Marc. 'Apart from demands for attention, which can be . . . dealt with.'

25

'Trudi,' Helena said, 'we've talked about everything, except your posing for Marc – and my portrait, that you've stared at the whole time.'

'Oh!' I said. 'I didn't mean to be rude. It is a lovely portrait.'

'I'm the rude one,' said Helena, 'and I get what I deserve when I am rude. That's why my ass is pink in the painting. Marc tames me with a spanking on the bare, before every session.'

She said it quite casually, as though a spanked pink ass was no more than a colour of nail polish.

'It is our game,' said Marc. 'Lots of women need their backsides tickled. I hope you're not shocked, Trudi.'

I said I wasn't shocked, with all the cool I could muster, despite the tingle up my spine, and the throbbing in my clit. *Spanking . . . on the bare!* Those magical words will make any girl-sub wet, and I could feel the moisture seeping at my pussy. Marc's words seemed to anger Helena.

'A game!' she spat. 'It is more than a game. No woman craves *games*. If you knew how my bottom smarts, every time *he* . . .'

'Helena!' snapped Marc. 'Don't embarrass our guest. I invited her to pose for some photographs of her *face* . . .'

Helena hung her head right down on her breasts, and squeezed my thigh. She looked up, and her eyes were moist.

'Oh, I'm sorry,' she said. 'Truly sorry.'

'That's not good enough, Helena,' Marc said very quietly, but with menace; then, to me, 'I must apologise, Trudi. My wife's vanity obliges me to keep one of her portraits in our lounge, when it should really stay in private. But perhaps she's right. Let's proceed to the photographs – that is, unless you've changed your mind.'

'No!' I cried, too fast, my urgency betraying my excitement. 'You have *other* portraits of Helena, like this one? In the same . . . style?'

'Meaning, in the nude, and with the marks of punishment?'

I blushed!

'Yes,' I murmured, 'I guess so. It's new . . . *Different.*'

Marc nodded.

'There are other portraits,' he said.

'I am vain,' Helena whispered.

'Hey, if you've got it, flaunt it,' I replied, 'and you're beautiful, Helena. You have a fabulous body. I'd *love* to – *May* I please see more?'

'Oh! Don't encourage her,' Marc drawled.

'Please? If it would be no trouble?' I said.

'Very well, Trudi. But no more compliments. She's already committed enough *errors.*'

'Enough for what?' I said, as if I hadn't guessed.

'Why, for the bare-bottom spanking she'll get after you've gone,' Marc murmured. 'Helena is one of those *bitches* who needs to be *shamed* – her pride quashed, yet her beauty stimulated, by slaps to her naked buttocks. She knows what she deserves, *don't you, slut?*'

'Yes,' whispered Helena, her head hung.

I stood up, with my own derrière a few inches from Helena's face, trying to look liberal, shocked and excited all at once. I didn't need to act.

'I'm no angel,' I said. 'I've been bad, you know, and been spanked for it, too.' That was true, even though I'd spanked my own bottom. 'So, if she's been bad,' I continued, trying to sound impish and not let my voice tremble, 'then surely she should be punished straight away? I'm sure that would be your normal routine, and I wouldn't wish to disturb that. You've been kind enough to invite me to pose, and if you extended your kindness to letting me watch, quietly, as Helena took – *you* know, her normal spanking – I might make a . . . a brighter model.'

That speech was the best I could do, without begging to watch Helena being spanked! I could feel my slit all slithery against the tight crotch of my jeans. I was juicing heavily, and was terrified of the big wet stain that must now be forming where my pussy lips bulged against the fabric, yet I didn't dare look down to inspect. There was silence. Both looked at me. I rubbed my lips, feeling increasingly nervous and embarrassed. Helena stood beside me, and, without looking at me, unpinned her rag of a mini-skirt, letting it slide to the floor. Her loins were naked, save for a leather G-string, studded on both sides and pressed between the lips of her pouch and the crack of her ass, biting her waist. Her ass was magnificent, two perfect jutting pears of taut flesh. The nipples, on big firm breasts that quivered just a little, thrust up very prominent and erect under her T-shirt – I could see why she was vain. Her skin was raw at her pussy and the soft inner thighs, where the leather had rubbed her. It must hurt awfully, I thought.

'You have neglected to clean our guest's footwear,' said Marc, smiling. '*And* my own.'

I wasn't wearing footwear. Helena squatted, with her bared buttocks high, and began to lick my feet. I endured the tickling sensation in silence, even as she made sure her tongue got into every cheesy crevice, and she swallowed and licked my big toes, whole. I felt turned on by this abrupt, amazing act of submission, and I imagined myself the same, only obliged to lick a *man's* feet. My slit was squelching with come at that thought. When she had licked my feet clean, she licked Marc's shoes, both soles and uppers. That made my pussy wetter. He did not allow her to rinse her mouth, but asked me what I would like next.

'Yes! Please *tell* my husband what you would *like,* Trudi,' Helena said, her scarlet face staring numbly in front of her, but with waist twisted, to lift and part her buttocks to my view. 'Address him, not me.'

Another silence. I felt tingles, like mice running up and down my spine, and my clitoris was throbbing.

There was a definite wet patch on my jeans, at my pussy, that I was sure could be seen.

'Marc, if it would please you and Helena, I'd like to stay, and . . . watch, as you spank your wife's bare bottom,' I blurted.

He nodded.

I swallowed, then, feeling bolder, I thrust my breasts and ass out.

'First, I'd like to see these other paintings of her, spanked,' I said. 'I've never seen anything like it before.'

Marc smiled.

'You find bare-bottom spanking exciting,' he said. 'Bare feet, bare bottom.'

'No!' I cried, then, 'Yes, I'm curious, and excited, too,' shocked at how simple it was to tell the truth.

My cunt was juicing but I didn't care if my jeans were stained with come; I wanted them to see, as, no doubt, they did. I looked from suave Marc to his slut wife, her big teats quivering, and nipples erect, with a slime of come seeping from her own leather-buckled pussy. I knew, and they knew, that before my visit ended, my own bare bottom would be red with spanks.

'Very well,' Marc said, purring. 'We shall go to my studio, and you may look. When we return, Helena's spanking shall then take place, where you were sitting, Trudi. After you witness the punishment, you may pose for me. I do hope you aren't as demanding as she is.'

3

First Blossoms

Marc ordered Helena to go before us, turn on the lights and make herself ready. Moments later, we followed, entering a softly lit studio, high-ceilinged like a loft, with the crisp tang of paint and the equipment of a painter; there was a video setup as well. On three walls, there were black and white photographs of nude females, singly, or in groups, and often in elaborate bondage (though I was unfamiliar with the term, at that time), all of them undergoing, or conniving in, another's chastisement on the bare. The end wall was covered in portraits, beneath which stood a single wooden pillar, standing upright and about five feet high. I gasped, for its purpose was obvious, and I began to tremble. I thought of all the times I had masturbated, thinking of my nude body strapped to such a post, and whipped raw. Helena was nude, kneeling with her face pressed to the post, and her wrists crossed behind her, in the cleft of her buttocks. Around her neck hung flaps of Velcro affixed to the post, and on the small of her back, she had placed a Velcro cuff, ready to be fastened. Without a word, Marc cuffed her neck to the post, and her hands behind her back. He smiled at me.

'Despite Helena's pretensions of grandeur, it *is* a game,' he said. 'It tames her, though she often begs me to replace Velcro straps with ones less comfortable.'

'*Please,* Marc,' Helena whimpered. 'For our guest . . .'

'If our guest agrees,' he said, raising an eyebrow at me.

I gulped, then nodded, yes.

'Stronger bonds for my poor wife?' he drawled. 'That would please you, Trudi?'

My pussy was wet. I said it would be very interesting.

'Interest is not the same as pleasure,' he replied.

'Yes!' I blurted. 'It would please me!'

I watched as Marc removed the Velcro cuffs and bound Helena in thick black rubber straps, which bit into her naked flesh. The moons of her ass gleamed in the soft lighting, and I thought at once that by their sassy posture, they positively begged to be spanked. I felt the juice, seeping from my cunt, quicken to a stream, and my nipples, already stiff, were like rocks. I longed to masturbate. Helena's bondage was obviously a foretaste of her spanking shame – her buttocks were 'presented ripe' (as we call it), but would require her spanker to stoop low, or himself kneel. Unless, it occurred to me, that bottom took *more* than spanking. A biker's heavy leather belt, studded, like her G-string, lay coiled on the floor bedside her. Perhaps Marc was going to thrash her ass with it, instead of – or as well as – spanking her.

The studio floor was polished bare board, save for the area around the post, which was unsanded. Helena's soles cupped the undercheeks of her ass, raised from the floor but nevertheless with ugly splinters wedged in her knees and calves. Her eyes were closed, and her breath came harsh and rhythmic, as though she were in a mystic trance. Her whole nude body was covered in goose-bumps, and quivered. I was quite giddy with excitement, and had to focus hard on the paintings, which only intensified my trembling. I was not so innocent – I knew my own buttocks would play a role in their game, if I chose, but wasn't certain my body, and my desire, would even give me the choice, if things reached the point of no return. The knowledge, that I might be helpless to avoid my own chastisement, made my cunt gush with come.

The paintings showed Helena's naked bottom. I mean, they showed the rest of her, too, sometimes in a crouch, so that her breasts hung bare, like the dugs of some farm beast, but the focus of portraiture was in every case the buttocks. Sometimes she straddled a leather couch like the one on which I had recently sat, either bent right over, or standing with her back arched and legs splayed; sometimes she was standing with her arms and legs curled, unbound, around the present whipping post. Or she perched, with her belly balanced on the flat top of the post, her arms and feet roped together beneath her dangling breasts. Her face was in profile, sometimes entirely hidden by her hair, with her head hanging low, as if in exhaustion. In those particular frames, her spanked bottom was at its reddest. Some pictures showed her bound by hands, feet and neck, to pegs in the floor, in a cluster of ropes flattening her breasts and biting her cunt, with her face masked, or her mouth gagged, and always with the bare buttocks as focus. I asked Marc how many spanks were in an average spanking.

'There is no average spanking, Trudi,' he answered.

'That one, then,' I said, pointing to a canvas where Helena's bottom was so blotched with spanks that her skin looked about to burst.

'Two thousand, perhaps,' Marc answered.

He took my breath away. Two thousand blows to the bare ass!

'Maybe three,' he shrugged. 'It's time-consuming. A spanking mustn't be hurried. You start softly, to warm the nates, and relax the victim; then, the spanks become harder, until her ass is crimson and the bruises hard, and the spanking is part of her, and she begs for it not to stop. It is hard, and painful, you realise, Trudi.'

'I'll bet!' I said, whistling.

'I mean,' he added, 'for the chastiser. A spanking of three thousand might last several hours.'

'Marc,' I said, 'this isn't a game, is it? It's something deeper and . . . sinister.'

'Is it?' he said. 'Some games are quite rough, Trudi. I notice you haven't wished to absent yourself. Well, now you've seen Helena's normal posing session.'

'Show her the other pictures, if you dare,' hissed Helena.

Marc frowned, in unfeigned anger.

'*You* give *me* orders! You have gone beyond the bounds of politeness,' he said. 'There will be an additional beating.'

There was menace in the studio now and my pussy juiced hard, as I became aware that this was no game. Marc stooped, picked up the biker's belt, and thrust it between her legs, sliding it hard between her gash flaps as she moaned and wriggled. He withdrew the belt, glistening with his wife's come, rubbed it and put a finger to his tongue. He uncoiled the belt, and stroked its tip down Helena's trembling spine. I was trembling too, and my pussy was soaking.

'Are you going to whip her, Marc?' I murmured.

'That is what *she* wants,' he answered. 'She wants her bare ass whipped raw, which is no more than her job, as artist's model. I want her *truly* shamed, for our guest.'

Marc fastened an extra rubber thong to bind her ankles, then released her neck from the post but left her wrists bound behind her back. He ordered her to follow us back to the salon, at a crawl. I turned to watch Helena bumping and shuffling, with tears in her eyes, as, wrists and ankles bound, she negotiated the stairway, banging her bare breasts and her face on the floor and walls. She made her painful progress upwards to where we stood awaiting her. Marc tapped one hand with the belt folded in two, the gleaming sharp studs pointing outwards.

'You impudent, lazy slut,' he said. 'You are disgusting. You embarrass our guest.'

I was beyond polite protest, fascinated and appalled by the hobbled woman, inching in bondage towards us. I felt an almost uncontrollable urge to masturbate. I looked at Marc's crotch, and saw not the slightest stirring at a spectacle that should have excited any male; then, down at my own, and, sure enough, there was a tell-tale dark stain on the white cloth, where the juice seeping from my gash was spreading fast.

'This . . . this is some game!' I chirped. Marc ignored me.

When Helena finally reached the top of the stairs, her face and tits bruised from her stumbling, Marc stuck the belt into her mouth, placing it lengthways so that she looked like a dog, or bitch, with a bone for her master. She was to carry it like that to the salon, scene of her chastisement. I touched myself between my legs and felt an electric buzz at my clitoris. I thought neither of the pair was looking, and began to gently rub myself there, resisting the urge to moan, as electricity tingled in my wet cunt-pouch and my belly. I was juicing more and more as I masturbated, following Helena's big bare ass, as she in turn followed her master. Wow, I thought, not one spank given, and already I'm masturbating, and going to come any second! Gulping, I removed my hand from my vulval area as we re-entered the salon.

Marc placed a footstool below the couch and ordered his wife to hoist herself and kneel on it, balancing herself with her buttocks raised and spread, as her ankle bonds would permit. She was to press her face down in the couch cushion while she took her spanking, but keeping the folded belt between her teeth. Helena was openly sobbing, her body convulsed and trembling, but

34

she obeyed her master without question. Marc never raised his voice, but gave his orders as though organising a place setting at table. Helena's bottom faced me, the pink dark slit of her gash covered in a jungle of moist pubic hair, her slit's ooze actually dripping from the fleece that dangled – like my own when unshaven – well below the outer folds of her labia. Her face was buried under her mane, with the tips of the belt peeping on either side of her jaw. To hold her buttocks high for their spanking, she folded her body almost in half, with her tits squashed against her thighs.

Smack!

Without warning, Marc slapped his palm on her bare nates, though it was more of a slap than a spank. He repeated it over 40 times, with her bottom pinking slightly, and clenching tighter and tighter, as each blow struck her flesh. She was obliged to balance precariously on the narrow footstool, and ground her face into the cushions to steady herself. Marc paused.

'That was a warm-up,' he said to me, smiling. 'A spanking must be delivered carefully, in stages, Trudi. One does not strike the hardest blows at first, but keeps them for later. You will see that just as the object thinks her spanking can get no harder, it does. The initial smacking is to dilate the blood vessels and relax the gluteal nerves, in preparation for harder and harder spanks, which bring the subject to her plateau of pain – the point where pain and pleasure are not to be distinguished, and the subject craves further spanking.'

Helena snuffled and sobbed, her crying muffled by the cushion. She didn't sound like someone craving. Her ass was two flans, glowing pink, but her inner thighs glistened, wet with the juice trickling from the swollen lips of her gash.

Smack! Smack! Smack!

Marc recommenced the spanking, his blows much harder, and I couldn't help myself: I just had to

35

masturbate. Placing myself behind him, I reached between my thighs and began to rub my engorged clitoris. I didn't care if he saw the pool of wet between my legs.

Smack! Smack! Smack!

'Mmm . . .'

I masturbated quite vigorously, but it shocked me how far gone I already was. My cunt was flowing with come, and shivers of pleasure convulsed my belly and spine as I masturbated my throbbing hard clit. I saw Helena's quivering pink flans shudder under her husband's spanks, and had a fleeting image of my own mom spanked bare-ass by my dad, then replaced it with the fantasy – which, I knew, *must* come true – of my own naked bottom, spanked by this man with the cobra in his pants, ready, once I was gushing come, and helpless, to . . . to penetrate my vulva, or even my very anus. That thought made me wild with fear and shame and brute lust. To be *butt-fucked* by that monstrous cock! *Oh . . .!* I rocked on the balls of my bare feet, my' toes clutching the carpet, as a shuddering orgasm flooded my loins and belly. I just had time to whip away my trembling fingers, slimy from the cunt juice that soaked my pants, before Marc turned to ask me what I had said.

'Mmm . . .' I said, or rather gasped. 'It is fascinating, Marc, yes – really fascinating.'

He smiled, and returned to his work.

Smack! Smack! Smack!

Helena's buttocks were turning brighter and brighter red, and were beginning to swell with puffy blotches. She no longer sobbed, but wailed into her cushion at each set of rapid spanks.

Smack! Smack! Smack!

'Uhh . . . *Uhhh!*'

As the spanking continued, Helena's moans became deeper, turning to gurgling howls that could have been of agony, or pleasure, or both. Marc delivered the spanking with a practised swing, achieving maximum impact, with the momentum of his whole arm swung from the shoulder, and a fluid twisting of his torso. I couldn't keep my hand away from my now-soaking crotch; my willpower had gone, and I was caressing my bare nipples inside my shirt, having unfastened two more buttons, so that almost the whole of my tits were bare. I masturbated continuously, pinching both nipples, and with my fingers pushing inside my cunt through the wet pants cloth. My thumb rubbed hard on my erect clit as I watched Helena's bare bottom spanked from red to deepest crimson, wriggling and squirming, as her whole trussed body struggled to keep her balance on the spanking stool. I lost count of the spanks, and of my total of comes. Each spank to Helena's bare ass seemed like a little orgasm in my own pussy.

It was dark in the salon, lit by only the glow of streetlights, when Marc stopped spanking his wife. The whole of her thighs glistened in the pale light, with the stream from her pussy like lava from a volcano, and the stool a lake of come beneath her vulva. Marc reached down and took the belt from between her teeth.

'One thousand spanks,' he murmured. 'She should be warm for the strap.'

One thousand spanks! I couldn't believe it! I had watched a naked woman *tortured,* and had masturbated almost to fainting. It could have been me . . . *Oh!* How I *wanted* it to be me! Marc lifted the studded belt to arm's height, over Helena's quivering bare ass globes, already bruised crimson from spanks, with some bruises darkening to purple. Her voice was a choked whimper.

'No . . . no . . . please . . .'

Thwap! Thwap! Thwap!

'*Ahh!*'

Helena reacted at once, screaming, as three strokes of the belt lashed her puffy bare bottom, laying dark, deep weals above the general blotchiness of the spanked skin.

The indentations of the belt's silver studs were clearly visible, pockmarking her ass.

Thwap! Thwap! Thwap!

'*Ahhh! No! Ahhh!*'

My pussy flowed with juice; I touched my throbbing clitoris just once, and came, and this time Marc clearly saw me. He said nothing, but smiled as he continued to thrash his wife's naked buttocks.

Thwap! Thwap! Thwap!

Her come flowed down the backs of her thighs, and her rubber cuffs were soaked in her juice. At his own crotch, Marc's bulge was like a tree beneath his pants. It was bigger than I remembered Don's, and the thought of what that monstrous cock might do to my narrow slit, or – *no, don't even think about it!* – my *anus,* made me masturbate harder. At that time, even the idea of butt-fucking was terrifying, but then, I didn't know its giddy delight. That moment when a man has a girl's cunt swimming in come, then moves to her anus bud, to tickle it with his fingernails, or his tongue – probing, teasing, tickling, getting inside, like a rolled flower petal – then the shock, as she feels his glans, his actual *cock,* slipping into her asshole, to about an inch! The insistent sweet pressure, the pain, the resistance, her ass cheeks spreading, welcoming her penetration without knowing it, then the rush of pleasure and pain, as her sphincter gives way, and the hard cock-meat penetrates her to the root, filling her as she's longed to be filled . . . I'm getting ahead of myself again. *Rats! I have to pause to masturbate. You deserve a spanking, Trudi Fahr!* Anyway . . .

'I hope you'll take my erection as a compliment, Trudi,' Marc said. 'I neither gain nor seek pleasure from thrashing a female, least of all this slut. Your own obvious pleasure, though, is satisfying.'

He flicked his wrist, and the belt took his wife vertically, right in her perineum and the flaps of her gash. It stroked her erect clitoris, standing plainly amid the wet pink cunt folds, and she howled. He whipped her vulva again, and again.

Thwap! Thwap! Thwap!

The dry, slithering crack of the strap in her vulval folds made Helena squirm, as juice gushed from her gaping, churning cunt.

'*Ahh!*' she screamed.

Marc returned to lashing her croup, moving quite methodically from the top buttocks to the undermeat, with vigorous slaps to each haunch, bruising more cruelly than the fleshier substance of the main buttocks. Her screams subsided to a sobbing, choking moan, rising in a crescendo as his strokes grew faster and harder, until her voice became a whine, breaking into staccato yelps, as come flowed in a glistening torrent from her cunt flaps, and her whole body joined her buttocks in convulsive shuddering, as she orgasmed. That was the moment I masturbated myself to my strongest, most intense orgasm, and closed my eyes, moaning aloud, not caring who saw or heard. I was in that space beyond space that a spanking scene induces.

'What . . .?' I cried, before Helena's hand clamped my jaws and forced my head down into the cushion, still warm from her own.

I was bent across the back of the sofa with the top biting my belly. Helena was strong, and I could not wriggle much as I felt her fingers fumble with my jeans, unfasten and roll them down. I even conspired to help her bare me, by kicking them off, and leaving my legs and buttocks naked. I did not resist as she removed my shirt, leaving me nude. This was it. This was the adventure.

'Buttocks *begging* for colour,' Marc murmured. 'And a shaven pussy. How *defiantly* lovely . . .'

'No . . .!' I cried feebly. 'I'm not ready . . .'

We all knew I was. No more words were needed. I thrust up my bare ass, spreading the cheeks, so that my

wet cunt and my twitching little ass bud were fully
exposed, in shame. Helena held me down, while Marc
spanked me. Smack! Smack! Smack! My fesses smarted
and wriggled as the skin burned under his spanks. Tears
blurred my eyes. Smack! Smack! Smack! I could feel the
clenching and squirming of my spanked bare buttocks,
crying at what I must *look* like, so exposed, with my
swollen cunt lips bare and gushing shameful fluid . . .
and knowing I wanted them to look.

'*Ah! Wait . . . No!*' I sobbed. '*Please, wait . . .!*'

My heart raced, and my ass cheeks clenched tight, as
if that could stop the awful smarting of my spanked
skin.

'You no longer have a choice,' Helena hissed, and at
those words, my gash juiced powerfully, and my come
tickled my quivering inside thighs, around my pussy
lips.

Smack! Smack! Smack!

'*Ah . . . Ah . . .*'

Smack! Smack! Smack!

'*Ohh!*'

This was no warm-up, but a full bare-bottom spanking. Helena pinned my head in the cushion, but I
twisted, and saw her masturbating with her free hand,
with Marc's spanking arm a flashing presence behind
her in the gloomy light. I felt my pussy open up with a
flood of come, as my ass glowed under my first ever
bare-ass spanking, my first *ever* spanking: by a male,
ruthless beneath his suave exterior, and my body held
down by his voluptuous pervert of a wife. My come
gushed more copiously, as I discerned that he had
unzipped, and, while he spanked me, his huge stiff cock
thrust between his wife's buttocks, plunged right to his
balls: he fucked her from behind, his hips slapping the
weals of her bare ass, as he spanked my own. My ass
danced, feeling as though red hot coals were caressing
my skin, and his palm thudding on my gluteus sent a

tingle up my spine and into my pulsing clit, which my wriggling loins rubbed against the soaked linen cloth on top of the sofa.

Smack! Smack! Smack!

'*Ah . . .! No, please . . .*'

Smack! Smack! Smack!

'Ahh! *Ahh!*'

I can't begin to describe my excitement. Helpless, spanked on the bare . . . I could have gotten free, but my moans and pitiful sobs convinced even me that I was helpless. Helena's own sobs of pleasure, as that massive tool rammed her, made me rub my clitoris harder on my spanking chair.

'Oh . . . *Oh!* Yes, Master! Fuck me harder! Do me! Oh, *yes . . .*' Helena squealed. '*Fuck my ass!*'

Her fingers clutched my jaw, and, instinctively, I opened my mouth and enclosed them, which seemed to turn her on as much as it did me. Sucking my tormentress's fingers, and grinding my erect clitoris into the chair back, while the male spanked my bare ass, I twisted my face, wet with tears, and saw that Marc's giant tool was ramming his wife's *anus*. Her grin – teeth bared in a rictus of power, fury, and desire – was terrifying, and I climaxed at once, in an orgasm so intense that I went into a dream for a few seconds. When I opened my eyes, I was still bent over the chair, with Helena and Marc standing, looking at me with their arms folded. Beside them stood the beautiful teenage girl who had asked for Marc's autograph in the cafe. Slowly, I got up, blushing, yet still tingling in the afterglow of orgasm, as they laughed at my fumbling efforts to get my jeans on. Naked, with my pants round my knees, I stood with my hands on my hips and faced them.

'Very funny,' I sad, as glacially as I could, allowing my voice to choke in a sob.

'Don't worry about your photographs, Trudi,' Marc said. 'Yvette, here –' He put his arm round the teenager, and fingered her bare breast inside her shirt '– has already filmed everything.'

'You set me up!' I stammered.

'Yes,' purred Helena. 'We needed an innocent for our scene. Yvette is way beyond innocent, but I sensed that you, Trudi, are just at the cusp. Am I right? You enjoyed my spanking – and *needed* your own?'

'Yes, damn you,' I said.

I bit my lip.

'Can I come and see you again? I still have some paintings to see . . .' I whispered.

Marc gave me Helena's studded G-string, still moist and smelly from her cunt.

'Call first,' he said. 'And when you come, wear this as your loin-string for your journey. Don't try and cheat, for I'll know exactly how raw your pussy and thighs should look.'

He placed a wide strip of sticking plaster across my shaven mons.

'What . . .?'

'Don't remove that. I shall do so, on your next visit. You'll find it exceedingly painful, as the new hairs are ripped from your skin.'

Grimacing, I pulled my new loin-string over the sticking plaster, then managed to get the jeans up and zipped. The string's studs already hurt my tender cunt basin.

'I might change my mind,' I whimpered, rubbing my ass through my jeans. 'You really made me smart! How many spanks did I take?'

'One thousand two hundred and thirty roses,' he said. 'A bouquet of red blossoms.'

My spanked skin was hardening, like cardboard, and very painful, with a dull, throbbing smart. I was appalled at my shame; hated myself and my buttocks that had submitted so uncomplainingly to torture yet felt glorious and proud at having taken so much.

42

'You won't change your mind,' said Marc. 'Your buttocks are only at the beginning of their submission. There is the strap . . .'

'More than the strap,' added Helena.

Yvette suddenly raised her flimsy lemon skirt and showed me her naked buttocks criss-crossed with blue weals, etched deep with age. Those marks were not from mere spanking, not even from thrashing with a biker's studded belt.

'*Much* more,' said the girl my own age.

4

Pair Bond

I drove home in darkness, alternately seething with rage and pausing in righteous indignation, passing one hand behind me to feel the bruises on my ass. I ran my fingers up and down my pants rear, to feel the hardening spanked skin beneath which only made my pussy juice. The studded G-string hurt horribly, and the sticky plaster made my pubic hillock itch. The US customs guy asked me if I was OK when my hand trembled as I showed him my driver's licence, and I smiled and said it was a woman's thing, meaning my period. That's enough to terrify most men, so he waved me on. I could have had a trunkload of rocket launchers, for all he knew. I had to stop twice, to masturbate, in the parking lot of a comfort station, and a third time I felt the need to come so intensely that I diddled myself while I was driving, with my hand down the open front of my jeans. I used the studs of my loinstring to excite my clitoris. In the parking lots, I had one hand on my clit, which was erect, and throbbing hard, and the other feeling my skin all ridged and puffy with bruises from the spanking. I didn't need fantasy – my bottom was fantasy come true. In fact, a true sub knows her bottom, and its every weal, and what made it, and when. Orgasm, like thirst, is a hard thing to remember, but a whipping is never forgotten, and you can replay the memory to infinity.

Marc had called my bruises blossoms, or roses, but the roses of a bare-ass beating don't wither.

Masturbating cleared my head. Before I brought myself off, I was furious, asking myself how these complete strangers had dared to treat me like a plaything, and how I had been so crazy as to let them. But after masturbating twice, I understood my anger, as though the come that slopped my diddling fingers was the fluid of my wrath and my longing. I wanted to be more than a plaything. Even that early in the game, I realised it was too serious to be a game. That was why my third session of diddling, while moving on the freeway, couldn't wait, and each masturbation, each orgasm, was more intense. I began by simply rubbing my clitoris, but by that third time, I was drenched in sweat, and had three fingers inside my soaking slit, with my thumb pounding my clit as though it was a wrestler to be subdued.

Having no panties but a hurtful leather string, and the thrill that I wore it *on command,* made the task easier and more tempting, I admit. I fantasised about the customs guy hauling me inside for strip-searching, and being embarrassed and alarmed, then turned on, when I coolly showed him my plastered bare mound, and then putting me over his knee for a long, hard, really *vicious* spanking on the bare. And then . . . I shuddered as I came, imagining him fucking me, but parting the cheeks of my spanked bottom to push his monstrous tool, like Marc's, *right up my asshole.* It was really a hideous thought, but I couldn't forget the look of . . . power, pain, ecstasy, *revenge,* on Helena's face, when Marc's cock penetrated her anus.

Spanking wasn't enough. I *did* want more, and the thought of that more made me wet. The bruises didn't last long – even deep subs sometimes insist on being beaten with a paddle or flat object rather than a cane or a whip, which leave marks. But I guess a true sub should have nothing to conceal. I waited two days, to be sure my skin was no longer blotchy, and masturbated every time I checked my ass in the mirror, which was often. I tore off the sticky tape – did it *ever* hurt! – and stopped wearing the studded loin-string. I figured that if I saw Marc again, he'd whip me for insolence, so I would be the winner. It was probably his plan, anyway. Meanwhile, every so often, I scampered to my bedroom, lowered my panties and peeked at my spanked moons. I always rubbed my clitoris while I traced the furrows and swellings. I didn't always bring myself off, even though I got myself very wet – I was beginning to like teasing myself. I had some ideas about Elle, and teased myself, wondering what she would do, how far she would go, how far I wanted her to go.

My masturbation fantasies involved the usual whipping or caning on my bare, but now, the haughty English lord, or down and dirty redneck blacksmith, or other power figure – a customs man, I concluded, was too wimpy, even though a male in uniform is an automatic turn-on to a sub – would bugger me into the bargain, after my whipping. I went to the supermarket and bought two pounds of zucchini, trembling as I paid, even though I had put a lot of other stuff in the basket, like nail polish, and magazines, and tortilla chips, that I didn't need, or even like. I felt the zucchini, big as small cucumbers, were a big neon sign, blinking on and off, and saying to the checkout girl, 'This is going into her beaver!' Several were as big as Don's cock, I thought, which meant pretty big, and certainly built for slit-strain, let alone anal penetration . . .!

Back home, I locked myself in the bathroom, turned on the shower, stripped off the clingfilm, along with my clothes, washed the zucchini, and towelled the little dildos dry. Then I coated each one in Vaseline. KY jelly would have been better, but buying a cucumber *and* a tube of KY jelly in the same basket . . .! I would have

46

imploded. I thought the shower was a good idea, as it would be messy, but of course it isn't messy at all. Your anus obligingly cleans up after itself – at least, a girl's does. I squatted nude, over the toilet, with my asscheeks as far as I could spread them, and began to apply the Vaseline to my anus hole. My finger smeared the hole with goo, and I felt my cheeks clench, involuntarily, as a lovely sexy tickle darted up my spine. I could feel my pussy beginning to juice, so I fingered myself in the slit, brushing my stiffening cookie (which is what *really cool* girls used to call our clits!), till I had a good smear of my own come, which I added to the Vaseline on my anal opening.

I selected one of the largest fruits and put it to my cunt lips. My pouch was well oiled, so the tube slid in with little hindrance, though I still had to push, clenching my pouch walls to give that lovely illuson of being invaded. I got the zucchini fully inside my cunt, and began to thrust in and out, while thumbing my cookie at the same time, until I could scarcely hold on to the fruit's smooth skin, it was so wet with my come. All the time, I was applying dollops of come to my butthole. My whole vulval region was bathed in come, and I could hear little plip-plops, even above the spray of the shower, as it dripped into the toilet bowl.

I fantasised about being whipped, *at the same time* as I took a fucking, but even that fabulous dream didn't seem right – I mean, being cunt-fucked didn't seem quite shameful enough. I sifted through the pile of shiny little green tubes, looking for one that would not be too painful as a butt-plug, but I was so horny, and about to come, and my clit throbbed so hard, I thought, What the hell – I nuzzled my come-wet anal bud with the tip of the cock-size zucchini, already shiny and lubricated with my pussy juice. I was really drooling, with saliva dripping on my chin, and falling on to the points of my nipples, and I didn't bother to lick it away, I was so excited. I slid the fruit a little way into my anus crack, which widened easily, and gave me the most delicious tickly sensation. Heartened, I pushed harder, and had to stop myself yelping, for suddenly it hurt. Panting, I held the tube in place, relaxing my sphincter, and, little by little, my asshole widened to accommodate her new visitor.

Would it go *all* the way in? I pushed some more and grimaced again as pain flooded me, but held it there, my hands trembling and awash in come from my gushing pussy. I rubbed come into my spanking welts, rubbing my fingers all over the slithery ridged surface of my cheeks, as my clitty throbbed to bursting. I trembled violently, pushed harder and harder at my dildo, until I thought I'd split in two. The pain was unbelievable, but so was the gorgeous sense of fullness, and the promise of greater pleasure, if only – *if only* – my ass would relax enough to get it all the way up me. And as I pushed, suddenly there was a sort of rush, and a slither, as if my asshole had just put her hands up and said, 'OK!', because the fruit penetrated my anus fully, I mean, right to the root, and I hugged it in place, filling my *whole*! I panted so hard in exultation and relief that I scarcely noticed I was on the brink of coming. Just one cautious thrust up and down, though, and I felt my clitty, my tits, my whole body tingle and shiver and glow, in the onset of climax. As fast as I could, I rammed my asshole with the new toy, faster and faster, feeling my orgasm build up, twitching and fluttering in my belly and my swollen throbbing clit, until I just expoded. I kept on buggering myself, gasping, until the last spasms had ebbed, leaving me with an utterly new, and utterly lovely, secret. I had just been butt-fucked, for the first time! My asshole ached most painfully for the whole day afterwards. I loved it.

On the third day after Montreal, a Tuesday, Elle and I went to the lake and swam, and I thought she glanced rather a lot at my butt, but she didn't say anything. I wondered if my spanks showed that much, or maybe my butthole was raw and expanded from my self-penetration. I looked quite openly at hers, wondering how *she* would like a trip to Montreal. I was curious about how Marc was going to portray me, if he had any intention of doing so. Before I visited Marc and Helena again – *if* I did – I wanted to be more comfortable in my new role. Where to start? My boyfriend James, obviously, except that when he'd called, I'd stalled him. I was still so blitzed by my bruised buttocks *and* asshole, and the way I'd so easily, *shamefully,* accepted Marc's spanking, that straight sex seemed vapid.

I could call Don, of course. He would do anything for a fuck, and would probably like spanking or whipping me, but would have none of the subtlety necessary to make a girl really shiver. He would probably sulk, as the end of our relationship had put a dent in his macho image, but a good sub can turn male vanity to her advantage, and his resentment would have put more zest into his whipping of me. But he probably wouldn't butt-fuck me, as many Latin males recoil at any hint of gayness. James might recoil too, not because his maleness was threatened but because it wasn't very Lutheran ... I was thinking all that while Elle and I were sunbathing after our skinny-dip, and I sighed. Elle asked me what I was sighing about. Her real name wasn't Elle, by the way, it was Vonda Skidelski, but I think she was embarrassed about being Polish, and anyway, 'Elle' sounds better than 'Skid', as the dorkier boys used to call her if they felt mean when she blew them off.

'Oh, nothing,' I said.

'Come on,' said Elle. 'It's your ass, isn't it?'

'My *what?*'

'You're twisting, so I don't see your ass. It looks kind of pink. Have you got heat rash?'

I decided to tell Elle a half-truth, to test her.

'I was thinking of James,' I said.

'When are you seeing him again? He's an improvement on that animal Don, if you don't mind me being nosy.'

Elle had a steady boyfriend named Daryl, who was – I felt guilty for thinking – pretty much the same dutiful, dependable arm-candy as James.

'I don't know,' I said carefully. 'My last date got kind of heavy.'

'James? Heavy?'

Elle sat up, and poised her chin in her palm, not minding the dangle of her big breasts. I ritually made her promise not to tell, and she ritually promised – *sure, Elle* – and I told her, after much sighing and pouting and heavy breathing, that I had been spanked on my bare buttocks. I was telling only the truth!

'Really? Wow! *James . . .!*'

I couldn't tell if she was shocked or delighted. She asked me how I could let James be such a *brute,* although I hadn't said it *was* him.

'I just let it happen,' I said.

'Don't tell me you enjoyed it!'

'I must have, I guess,' I said.

'Well! Here, let me see . . .'

Elle put her face inches from my bottom and inspected me. I could have sworn she sniffed when her nose was near my bruised ass bud.

'You must have taken it quite hard.'

'Am I damaged?'

'Just red.'

She stroked my bare ass.

'You poor baby . . .' she said.

'It wasn't like that, Elle,' I retorted. 'It was kind of fun.'

'I wouldn't let Daryl . . .'

'Wouldn't you?' I said, suddenly twisting, and landing a spank on Elle's own bare, right across the centre of her big bare rump.

50

'Oh! That hurt!' she cried.

'Then I mustn't do it again.'

'Hey, I didn't say that, Trudi,' Elle said.

She knelt in a crouch, resting her chin on two fists, to stare at the lake. Her posture presented both cheeks of her bare, raised and spread. My pulse quickened.

'What are you *doing*, Elle?' I said.

'What do you mean, what am I doing? I'm looking at the lake, is all. Isn't it pretty? The water so pure, and the trees so green . . . just for us, Trudi.'

I put my hand on her bare ass, and felt her stiffen, but she let me stroke the globes. They were big and firm, like her breasts. She had a good body. My spank had left red fingermarks on her skin.

'Anyone would think you were asking to be spanked,' I said. 'That's the position.'

'Oh, *is* it? *The* position? My, we have come a long way, Miss Fahr,' she said, not looking at me. 'Maybe I'm just curious – that was quite a slice you gave me. Does it show?'

'Yes. Did it hurt?'

'I'm not sure,' Elle said, parting her cheeks a little more, and thrusting her ass up, like a puppy begging. 'I'm not sure at all . . . It was kind of nice, in a funny way.'

Smack! I landed another spank, right in the same place; her buttocks jerked, clenching, and she gave a little moan.

'Was *that* nice?'

All she did was gasp, not looking up. Smack! I spanked her again, leaving pink fingermarks on her naked skin, and she spread her bare fesses wide and high.

'Was *that* nice?'

She wouldn't answer. Smack! I spanked her hard, right in the crack of her ass, and she whinnied.

'Yes . . .' she moaned. 'Just a little . . .'

The cleft of Elle's bare buttocks was dusted with powdery sand from the cove, and it began to dislodge as I spanked her. She jerked at each spank, and made little whimpering noises. Her buttocks reddened very fast, or else I must have spanked them quite hard. I was careful to follow Marc's advice about warming up the gluteal nerves with a mild spanking, then increasing the force of the beating. By about my 50th spank, I was really belting Elle, and she was gasping. I couldn't help being turned on, and my pussy was moist, mainly because I fantasised it was my own bare ass being spanked. That's how I rationalised girl-on-girl spanking. I felt I was doing Elle a friendly favour, which, as it turned out, I was. I spanked her in quite a slow rhythm, figuring five-second pauses would make her feel at ease, and maybe wish to talk, but for a while she said nothing, and her bare flans quivered after each spank, as if impatient for the next.

'Sometimes I wish Daryl would do that,' she whispered. 'Spank my ass, show me who's boss.'

'Be more of a man?' I said.

Smack!

'*Oh!* That *hurt!* He's an OK fuck, but . . .'

'But you want something more.'

Smack!

'*Ahh!* I guess so.'

'We all do, Elle,' I said.

Smack! Smack! Smack!

'*Ohh! Ohh . . .!*'

'Hurt you?'

'*Yes!* Don't stop . . .!'

My own pussy was juicing, but Elle's was a torrent, with a gush of come down the quivering insides of her thighs. Her gash lips were all swollen and dark, and glistened, all wet with her come. I told her to masturbate if she wanted, as I knew how she felt.

Smack! Smack!

'*Ohh!* Trudi! I'm not like *that* . . .'

Smack!

'Nor am I. We're friends, Elle. You're imagining Daryl's spanking you.'

'Yes.'

'I'm just helping you with the stinging part.'

Smack! Smack! Smack!

'*OOH!*'

'So it's all right to masturbate,' I said. 'I'll diddle too. We're pair bonding, that's all . . .'

Purring in pleasure, Elle began to masturbate, with her fingers darting between her thighs, bringing her off almost at once, with little squeaks and gasps of joyful surprise. I joined her, diddling fast, as I spanked her red, glowing cheeks, squirming and bare, beneath my own juicing pussy, with droplets of my come splattering her blotchy pink bruises. My fingers worked gently on my cookie, and as Elle's sighs of climax died down, my own erupted, and my belly fluttered, with my own cunt gushing juice in a really good, mammoth come. I had spanked her for ten or twelve minutes, with well over a hundred spanks. Afterwards, she joined me in the lake to pee, a kind of female bonding ritual, and said the cool water on her spanked behind was blissful.

'I needed that, Trudi. I don't know why. Thank you,' she said as we peed, our golden liquids floating together to form a cloud. 'I never dreamed that spanking could . . . could bring me off so fast. Normally, I'm a slow comer. But you diddled too, didn't you? Spanking me, and seeing my ass squirm? What a sight!'

'What are friends for?' I replied. 'I enjoyed the workout – and the sight made *me* come.'

'Would you . . . spank me again, if I asked?'

'Yes,' I said. 'But I hope Daryl's up to the task. I mean, you've proved you can take it.'

'That was my big worry. When I saw your red cheeks, I sort of guessed what had happened, and all of a sudden I knew I wanted it, too. We're both lucky, not being scared of what we want. I'd spank you, Trudi, if ever you needed me to.'

'I'll hold you to that,' I said.

We towelled each other dry. My fingers played on the red skin of her spanked ass, and her face blushed the same colour. She stroked my behind.

'I hope so,' Elle whispered.

We subs are devious. I knew Elle would work on Daryl, by telling him James had spanked me. James and Daryl were friends, and they'd josh about it in the locker room, and . . . it all worked out even better than I intended. How did I know to spank Elle that time, know instinctively that she wanted to be spanked? Look in the mirror, girl-sub. Not at face or titties, but ass. Run your hands over your haunches, as you look at your globes of flesh. The crevice between, a sweet furred slit. Touch yourself, make yourself wet, looking at your ass. Brush the skin with your fingers, let your nails caress, then bite, your anal pucker and vaginal lips. Now slap your buttocks, because you are naughty. Again. Again. They are clenching, in anticipation of each spank. Back to your cleft now. Your pouch should be moist. Get a finger just inside, and rub the inner surface of your slit. Withdraw, and do the same with the anus pucker. Stick your finger in, an inch or so. You'll find the hole widens for it. Squeeze your finger with your anus. Tickle your asshole. Now spank yourself again. Watch your skin redden as your slaps get harder. Your gash is dripping now and it's time to do what you long to. Touch your throbbing clitty. Feel the tingle in your spine and your belly heave. Spank your bare buttocks harder and faster, see how beautifully the flans quiver and clench. Pause, to nip your clitty with your thumb and forefinger as you spank yourself, watch your juice dripping from your wet swollen gash lips. Get that finger all the way up your anal passage, and give your greasy, tight, lovely hole a proper reaming. Look at your bare, spanked buttocks, the most beautiful globes in the world. Come.

Elle was an ass-worshipper, like me. That's how I knew I should spank her. Men worship girls, but they also love cars and cameras and other stupid toys, and that's why girls get jealous of such things – until we realise that a male can only love something he possesses. That's why he must worship our bodies, by owning them outright, even, or most importantly, inflicting pain on them: the logic of submission is love. Girls are really in love with their own bodies – we have the world inside us, and males are just the givers of sperm, and wielders of the rod. The female buttocks are the most beautiful things in creation, so firm and smooth and ripe and silky, all at the same time, twin worlds of softness and pain and beauty, and so a girl can easily love her own fesses, or another girl's. Especially when every nerve tingles under spanking, and those girl-fesses really come alive. Things sometimes sound gross in English – I mean, our words for the most beautiful part of a girl's body: buns, ass, fanny, butt. One thing I learned in Montreal, from Marc and Helena, was that things sound nicer in French. Your ass is your *cul*, pronounced cool – isn't that sweet? Buttocks are *fesses*, which sounds more elegant. So, I'm going to use those words in this narrative, if I feel elegant . . .

The double date fixed for myself and James, with Elle and Daryl, had me tingling with excitement. A double date for teens who aren't fucking is a way of overcoming shyness and maybe starts fucking. To those who fuck already, it means some sort of game-playing, like swapping partners. You have to be ready for anything on a 'mature' double date, especially this one, where spanking was on the agenda – at least, my, and, I imagined, Elle's agenda. Daryl would have to be provoked, somehow, into spanking Elle, and my little untruth had to be exposed. I had implied to Elle that James had spanked me, when – hopefully to James's anger – it had been another guy, a *foreigner* yet! I wanted James to get mad, and *really* spank me. Oh, what a tangled web we weave! Subs love weaving webs.

5

Skinny-Whipping

Our double date was set for Friday. Elle and I hoped to persuade our males to join us, after the usual date-type things, for some moonlight skinny-dipping, then let nature take its course. If that meant partner-swapping, then we both understood by little hints, asides and outright giggles that it was up to the stamina of the boys, and that we poor girls were so easily tempted . . .! We both understood that for a spanking scene we needed an excuse to bare our bottoms as a prelude to action, and skinny-dipping was the perfect excuse.

First, we were to have drinks, dinner, then a movie. Before I showered and dressed, I spanked myself hard with my hairbrush, so my ass would be as red as Elle's, which I knew would still be a little puffy from my lakeside spanking three days previously. There was also the distinct possibility that she'd have tested her own hairbrush in the meantime. I didn't masturbate, which was hard, as I was juicing heavily, but I wanted to remain super-horny. My anus was still sensitive from a new session with the zucchini, right after I parted from Elle. I had diddled, giving myself another cornholing, while recalling her spanking in every detail, and adding the fantasy that I was striping her bare ass with a sheaf of those birch twigs that grow so profusely around Lake Champlain. The fantasy flipped over, as I orgasmed, so that it was *my* bare croup writhing under *her* birch branches.

Before our Friday date, I gave my fesses over a hundred whacks with the flat of my hairbrush, until they were smarting terribly, but lovely and red and puffy. At any scene, a spanked bottom is a good conversation-starter, and at the scene I planned, it was meant to inspire further spanking. I took an ice-cold shower, then slipped on a little black party dress, in voile cotton, so short it just about covered my derrière cheeks and practically showed my beaver: no stockings or underwear. The front showed most of my breasts, too, with their strapless tan. I loved that dress, because its shortness gave me every excuse to be constantly tugging it down, ostensibly covering myself modestly, but really to draw attention to the parts being covered. Girls are allowed to do that. I was barefoot, and drove to the restaurant with the top of my sports car down. My car had a stick shift, so my skirt rode up, and it would have been pointless to tug it down so I left my pubis and haunches on view, with the wind caressing my newly stubbled, perfectly tan hillock, and my quim lips, which drew some gapes at stoplights. I had to squirm a lot, because my bare ass was sweaty on the car seat, and it smarted from the spanking I'd given myself, so I kept shifting my bare thighs and bottom to get comfortable.

The movie, drinks and dinner were fine. Daryl, whom I had seen from a distance, was indeed like James: cool, but not too cool, polite, but not too polite, horny without drooling. Both boys were good-looking, and Elle and I fell into a routine of alternately flirting with our own, then the other's boy. By flirting, I mean touching, exposing flesh, then hiding it again, all those little things which are supposed to turn boys on, and do. We went to the bathroom together, and without my asking, Elle at once lowered her jeans and showed me her bare ass. It was scarlet and well ridged.

'This morning,' she whispered, 'a hundred with a hairbrush before breakfast, and a hundred after.' We both giggled, but Elle pouted when I coyly refused to moon her in return, saying she'd already peeked quite enough at my butt.

It was a fine summer's night, so everyone agreed to some fresh air and a few bottles of wine at our lakeside cove. I drove James in my car, while Elle drove Daryl in his, as the boys had taken more wine than either girl. We got some bottles of California champagne as an excuse for the trip, though neither Elle nor I drank much alcohol. James, perfect gentleman, stroked my thigh while I drove, but didn't try to get at my beaver. Well, he knew we would fuck later, so there was no testosterone urgency, and a lady with a fingered pussy is a serious road hazard. We got to the cove shortly after midnight, and there was a wonderful moon, with all the stars lovely in a velvet sky. As I got out of the car, instead of opening the door I vaulted over it, allowing my dress to ride way up over my waist and show James my full bare moons. I glanced back and relished the stunned, lustful look on his face. My ass was still scarlet from my self-spanking with the hairbrush.

'Trudi! What . . .?' he began, and I gave him my most mischievous grin.

'What do you mean, "What?"' I said, coyly.

'Your ass . . .'

'You've seen it before.'

'Not all red!'

'Wait till you see Elle's,' I murmured.

We clustered by the shore, while the boys popped champagne corks. James was more horny than puzzled by now, and stared at Elle's ass as though her designer jeans would melt. We drank from little plastic non-designer cups. Being a barefoot, I took the lead, being able to wade right into the water without any need to take off shoes. I went in up to my thighs, with the water lapping at the hem of my dress. Daryl said I must be careful not to wet my dress, so I dramatically lifted it up, with my bare beaver facing them, right to my titties. Everybody cheered, then cheered more when I said they were too chicken to skinny-dip, pulled my dress right over my head, took it off, and threw it so that it landed on Daryl's face. I could see James was jealous, which suited me, and I knew he must be wondering if it was Daryl who had spanked me. Elle promptly began to strip. She had no underthings, just jeans and a white silk halter top which was tied round her breasts in a bow. Nude, she handed her clothes to Daryl, and ordered him to fold them neatly.

One of the games you can play with men is that no man ever likes to put down the drink he's holding. It's a sort of primitive caveman thing: he imagines some other caveman will steal it. The same applies to any girl he has his arm around. So you can always throw things at a man, and he'll duck or catch them rather than put his drink, or girl, down. Elle wore high-heeled gold lamé sandals, sort of outrageous kitsch, and she lifted her legs right up to kick them off one by one, so that each landed on James's crotch, which by now had a satisfactory swelling. She didn't hide her spanked bottom, but wiggled it at Daryl. It was lovely and red and puffy in the starlight, and he gaped.

'What *happened,* Elle?' he spluttered, but she was splashing beside me in the water before he could grab her.

'Hey, Trudi –' James began, frowning.

Daryl was as puzzled by Elle's spanked fesses as James was by my own: who had spanked whom, or who was the deceiver? My web woven . . .

'You've got to catch us, guys, to find out,' I sang, and started swimming so that my own spanked ass gleamed wet under the moonlight.

By now both boys had seen both girls' reddened fesses, and both desired an explanation. They stripped

60

off, sheepishly, the way men do, both turning to hide their semi-stiff cocks from each other. I saw that Daryl was as big as James, which was pretty big, though at that time I thought nothing could beat Donkey Don's. 'Donkey', that was his nickname in the locker room. The boys ran, whooping, into the water, and followed us. By now, Elle and I were a good way out, and treading water, and it was Elle's turn to be puzzled and/or angry.

'How did your butt get so red, Trudi?' she said. 'Did James spank you? I thought *I* was to spank you . . .'

I shook my head.

'You've been seeing another boy?'

I shook my head again, but pointedly gave a big smile at her boyfriend Daryl, who was gaining on James in the race to reach us. Elle paled.

'N-not *Daryl . . .?*' she stammered.

'Ask him,' I said, and dived, to emerge several yards away and continue out towards the centre of the lake.

I was the best swimmer, and now I had two nude boys and a nude girl pursuing nude me, jealous of what they imagined. Like a good sub, I was directing the scene that would lead to my own punishment. I let them catch up with me, but eluded them when they tried to grab me. I was slippery as an eel, and my laughter made them all the more furious, precisely because they didn't know why they were furious or whom to be furious at. Normally, jealous boys will start swinging at each other, which is gross, but spanking was completely alien to the boys, and the etiquette of spanks, submission and dominance so new to Elle, that they could only squeak in puzzled exasperation. I slipped away from them, sticking my fesses in the air and my head under the water, and waggled my scarlet cheeks at them, then struck out for the shore. Panting, we all stood, the others glowering at me, and the boys with full erections, I noticed. Well, a girl can't help noticing. I licked my

61

lips, with my eyes flicking from one cock to the other. Both were tempting. I juiced more, imagining the hard cocks would magically grow to rods big enough to thrash my bare behind.

'What has been going on, Trudi?' James asked.

'Same question for you, Elle,' said Daryl.

Elle became my uneasy ally. Faced by two erect cavemen, a girl needs allies. She put her arm around my waist and let her palm slip into the crack of my ass, then cover my buttocks. I didn't stop her from stroking my derrière, but began to do the same to her, so that the boys could see.

'Well, we've both been spanked,' she said. 'I think that's obvious.'

'You girls spanked each other?' James said.

'Elle never spanked me,' I replied.

'James ought to know,' Elle said.

'Obviously, he doesn't,' I murmured. 'Maybe you should ask Daryl.'

'Wait a minute . . .' said Daryl.

'Guys,' I said, 'we have a difficult situation. One, who spanked *me,* and two, who spanked *Elle?* Are you going to confess, Elle?'

Elle's ass shivered under my touch. I had my thumb on her anus button, and was poking it gently inside. I felt moisture seep from her gash.

'Should I?' she whispered.

'Nobody is going to believe anybody in this situation,' I said, 'so the best way to find out is the truth game.'

Both males were throbbingly erect, and I could see their attention might wander at the sight of two pussies juicing. They might even forgive us! An erect male will forgive a female anything, just to put his cock in her wet pouch . . . or her mouth. That was another reason I pleased James – I gave him good head. I liked doing it, because it meant I could kneel, with thighs apart, in submission, and I used to masturbate as I sucked him, which made him come fast. I made sure to swallow every drop of his come. It is a myth that sperm tastes nasty. It doesn't really taste of anything. Some women just want to think it tastes nasty because they correctly associate swallowing with submission. It's all in the mind, plus which it has a lot of protein and no calories. My tongue has always known how to caress a man's glans, which is a skill some women instinctively have. Oral sex is one way a girl can show submission, but I wanted to see if James was man enough to thrash me. I plucked a couple of juicy rods from a tree, and slashed the air.

Vip! Vip!

'Truth by ordeal,' I said, my voice as still as the waters of the lake. 'Two girls, beaten to confess . . . real New England colonial.'

James, Daryl and Elle shivered. Conscious that I had full control of the scene, I handed a rod to each boy. Both inspected the canes, as though they had never seen a tree branch before. They were springy young sapling canes, about three feet long, with creamy green flesh where I had broken them. Three feet is an interesting length for a wooden rod, for it hasn't many other uses, being too short, or too long, other than for caning flesh. I chose a suitable rock on the beach, and bent over it, with my fesses raised and my thighs parted, so that everyone could see my naked quim, with the lips open, and into my wet red pouch. My whipping-rock adjoined a second, and I invited Elle to join me in presenting her naked croup for thrashing.

'Now wait a minute . . .' she stammered. 'I mean, OK, a *hand-spanking*, but, Trudi . . . with *that?*'

She pointed at the rod which Daryl was flexing as he eyed the big bare plums of her ass.

'The truth game is voluntary,' I said rather coldly. '*I'll* play, even if you won't, though a contest is more fun.'

'A *whipping* contest?'

'That's right,' I said, in a more friendly tone. 'Strokes on the bare ass, under the moon, until the first girl begs for her beating to stop, and must confess. It could be after the first stroke – it could be before the rod has even touched your skin. One way or another, the secret of our red asses will come out. Isn't it so *gothic . . .?*'

I knew Elle liked to read those ditsy gothic horror tales, by weird women from Mississippi or someplace.

'So, the loser must confess. What is the winner's prize?' she said, moving already to take up position, her cheeks already quivering with goose-bumps, and her eyes glazed; I could see a seep of oily moisture under her fat cunt-mound, and its jungle of tangled wet hairs.

'*Choice of cock,*' I hissed.

The only sounds were the lapping of the lake, and the rasping breath of my nude companions. Both boys had hard-ons to bursting.

'Anyone have a problem with that?'

I heard only the whispering of the lake, and the hoarse breathing of the two males, with their cocks straining stiff. I briskly ordered Daryl to cane me and James to cane Elle. No one argued. Even I was surprised by the success of my delicious onslaught. Looking sheepish, then determined, the two males raised their canes.

Vip! Vip!

'*Yikes!*'

The first two strokes landed almost simultaneously on our bare behinds, and Elle let out a yelp. I felt my cheeks clench, as Daryl dealt a really strong whop right to my middle fesses. It stung hard, like a red-hot sword, and that was only the first of what I hoped would be many, if I could endure what I longed – *lusted!* – to endure. I can't say I wasn't scared – I was – for this was no mere spanking but a proper thrashing with supple wooden rods. However, my pussy was sopping wet, and I felt come trickling down my inner thighs. I knew both boys could see it sparkle in the moonlight. My clitty and nipples throbbed stiff at my very first bare-ass caning! *Way to go . . .!*

'It's better if you clamp your teeth, Elle,' I gasped, although the searing pain of that stroke on my bare had made my gorge rise. 'Squealing doesn't help.' *(Liar, liar, pants on fire!)*

Vip! Vip! I felt Daryl's cane sear my buttocks, the cut slicing right across both cheeks, and couldn't help grunting and clenching my fesses very tight.

'*That* won't help,' Daryl said.

I looked round, through eyes misting with tears, and saw both boys had big, fierce grins. Vip! Vip!

'*Ahh . . .!*' Elle shrieked, ignoring my advice.

Her bare fesses squirmed madly, and I saw her puffy weals drawn by the cane. It was young green wood, very springy, and hard on bare skin. Vip! Vip! My own breath started coming in harsh gasps, and my ass squirmed, clenching automatically, as the strokes rained on both our helpless bare behinds. We both clutched our rocks of submission, with tears streaming down our faces, looking at each other half in defiance, and half for moral support. Neither of us opened her mouth to form the word 'stop'.

Vip! Vip! Vip! Vip! Both boys caned as though they had been doing it all their lives. Maybe they had, for all I knew. I must ask Elle, one day, if we ever meet again for another scene, which, in the world of submissive girls, is not at all unlikely . . . Anyway, I lost count of the strokes at the 12th. My ass was one glowing bare fireball, the pain melting through my naked skin like acid. My gash was flowing with come, and my clit throbbed, every lash of the wood on my bare making my belly contract, twitching, and sending tingling shockwaves up my spine and clitoral nerve centre, until my clitty seemed to throb hard enough to explode. I began to rub my cunt on the bare rock, which was slimy with my come. It hurt, as I wanted it to. I rubbed harder, masturbating on the rock, until my belly was fluttering, juice cascaded from my twitching cunt flaps, and I *did* explode, almost fainting in the intensity of my orgasm.

'*No more!*' I screamed, lying. 'No . . .! No . . .! *Please!*'

Both panting, the boys stopped caning us, much to my disappointment. Elle was sobbing, in little choked gasps, but I saw her own rock was a lake of come beneath her juicing pussy. Her bare ass gleamed with deliciously puffy red welts under the moon, as I was sure mine did. I wriggled it, and looked at James with pleading eyes.

'I didn't know Daryl would *do me so hard,*' I whined, sobbing, in little choked gasps, as pathetically as I could.

'Seems you've lost, Trudi,' James said, with a new, unexpected brutality in his voice, 'so Elle has the choice of cocks, while you confess. And if you think Daryl whipped you hard, just wait till *I* punish you.'

'*Ohh* . . .' I moaned, almost coming again on the spot.

'I think the bitch *deserves* punishment,' said Elle. 'Real punishment.'

'Now, wait! OK,' I sobbed, 'I mean, I'll confess. It's just a game that's gotten a little out of hand . . . I didn't realise a beating would hurt so much. I thought it would just be like a paddling . . . but, oh! It *hurts!*'

I did confess. Not about Marc and Helena in Montreal, but about nude bathing with Elle, and my spanking her on the bare, being vague, and sobbing to skate over the fact that we hadn't actually had lesbian sex but making sure, from my hesitations, that no other inference could be drawn. Elle was speechless with anger. I begged them to believe that my scarlet fesses came from my very own hairbrush, and that I was just horny for spanking and didn't know why. The more I told the truth, the less the boys believed me. That's

66

another thing about men. They always believe a girl when she lies, but not when she's telling the truth.

'So,' drawled Daryl, 'sweet little Elle likes making it with girls? Who was the bull dyke, and who the femme?'

'And my girl likes her ass paddled! They *both* need another tickling,' said James. 'Not a game, this time.'

'No!' wailed Elle. 'It wasn't like that! Oh, *you!*' she squealed at me. 'Don't you guys see it's her *game?* Making me *want* spanking, then setting up this . . . this *scenario,* so that we are all jealous of each other? *She's* the one needing a lesson!'

Right on cue, I burst into tears.

'You bitch!' I sobbed. 'You *begged* me to spank you, and . . . after what Don did to my ass . . . so *hard* . . . God, *I* needed it, too!'

'You've been seeing *Don!*' James spat. 'You whore!'

Elle leapt on me and clawed my breasts, but the boys restrained her, only so that they could leap on me more. I found my titties and quim pressed against my come-slopped rock, with Elle straddling my neck between her thighs, and her own gash seeping juice on my back and down my wriggling spine. I felt my wrists bound behind my back with a creeper, and each ankle roped to a tree stump, spreading my thighs far apart. I was helpless. Now my thrashing began in earnest.

Vip! Vip! Vip! Vip!

'You bitch!'

'Ahh . . .! Oh, God, no! Please!'

James was thrashing me now, harder than Daryl, and I screamed in genuine agony as the cane seared my already flaming bare ass. My cheeks clenched and squirmed, greasy with my come, sand particles rubbing into my raw welts.

Vip! Vip! Vip! Vippedy-Vip!

'Ahhh . . .!'

I smelled cock, sweaty and hard; my scream was stifled by Daryl's glans pushing all the way to the back of my throat.

'Tongue him, bitch,' James snarled. 'I guess you've tongued everybody else in town.'

I was frightened, for I'd forgotten how mean men can be, with lust for revenge overcoming rivalry. I began to fellate Daryl, with Elle's come trickling down my hair and neck, as she masturbated. Daryl's back was arched, and he was chewing her titties as I fellated him, with my tongue licking the sensitive apex of the glans. He groaned hoarsely. Vip! Vip! Vip! Vip! I couldn't scream, as my mouth bulged with Daryl's cock. My whole body shook as each stroke striped my raw bare ass. I was giddy with the power of my submission. I sucked and licked Daryl's cock, until, suddenly, my caning stopped. I felt James's hard, throbbing tool ram between my wet gash lips, to fill my slit. I shuddered, for although my narrow channel was used to him, and was wetter and juicier than it had been for ages, his cock really hurt as it penetrated me, and I stifled a scream, deep in my throat, as his glans began to pound my womb-neck.

As I tongued Daryl, feeling his cock tremble in the first sign of his spasm, James fucked me from behind, hand-spanking my bare globes, already raw from caning. I was so wet that he was able to withdraw his cock almost entirely, right to his glans tip, then plunge it in fully at every thrust. I rubbed my tingling clit against the rock as he fucked me, and my orgasm started as soon as I felt his spunk spurt. I squeezed his cock with my slit walls, as hard as I could. I felt Daryl's first spurt of cream hit the back of my throat as James's copious spermload bubbled from my cunt lips, down my inner thighs. Elle groaned, drooling, as Daryl's teat-biting and her masturbation of her clitty brought her off.

Things got blurred after that. I remember sucking James off while Daryl fucked me from behind and Elle spanked me, then steeled herself to cane me, although she wasn't very good at caning, with her strokes too hesitant and girly. I've never really appreciated being thrashed by a novice, especially another girl – although it's better than a hairbrush – when I *really need* bare-fesse attention. She gave me about a dozen cuts, I think. I was relieved when the boys resumed my thrashing, and they both whipped me so hard, it drove the breath from my lungs. My teats were heaving like pumps as those rods striped my bare ass.

Vip! Vip! Vip! Vip!

'*Uhhh . . .*'

All I could hear was the swishing of the canes, and my own harsh breath. All I could feel was my heart pounding, and the white-hot smart of each cane-stroke on my bare skin. The rest of the world had gone away, save for Elle beside me. She was down on all fours taking it from behind, from James, then from Daryl, then I was sucking their cocks, slimy with her come-juice . . . The important thing was, at no time was I anything but helpless, at the mercy of two males, with stiff cocks and angry canes. I honestly can't remember how many times I orgasmed during that night of thrashing. I almost fainted with pain and ecstasy. Both boys were dripping with sweat when they finally stopped my caning. I must have taken over 100 strokes on the bare. When I was freed, I at once crouched in the dirt and licked Daryl's feet, then my own boyfriend's. I openly masturbated as I licked their grimy toes, and I saved my come for James, twisting my hips so that my pussy dripped all over his feet, and then licking my own juice from him. Elle was on all fours, sucking Daryl's cock, while I masturbated – beavering! – for them all to see. I licked James's balls after I had cleaned his feet, and he fucked me again, from behind, pushing my face into the dirt, while Elle swallowed Daryl's come; he slapped her quivering moons as she fellated him.

We partied, or orgied, till dawn. My ass burned like fire; I remember Elle taking the lead in caning me at one point while both boys held me down, and my cunt gushed wildly at *that* thrill. She was vicious, her wand slicing me again and again in my soaking pussy, or on my tender ass bud, as well as the top buttocks and haunches, where the skin is tender and the pain greater. So much for not being lesbian, I thought, as the tears poured down my cheeks, and I had to chew a clump of lakeweed to stop myself screaming. Maybe she was avenging herself for her own desires . . . just as the boys were punishing me because each thought I'd fucked around, with Elle, or Don – who cared? Just as long as they were mad enough to larrup me! I couldn't stop juicing, or coming, and pissed myself more than once as my bottom squirmed under the cane, my vulva spraying golden rain on my feet and theirs.

Everything had gone according to plan. Elle, Daryl and dear James had used me as I wanted to be used: caned by one while fellating or hand-stroking another, while the third entered my cunt, with fist or cock. Yet as dawn glimmered over the lake, *I* was the one who complained, when my exhausted tormentors wanted to stop! (Subs are *always* happy to complain.) My web was woven, and I hadn't told a single lie. I had mentioned Don, without saying he'd thrashed or even seen me. I masturbated in front of the mirror as soon as I got home at dawn, even though my pussy was still sore from my fucks. Moaning, with my index finger fully inside my anus and my fingers caressing my welts, I wondered if I'd mentioned Don because I subconsciously *wanted him* to thrash me . . . and more. I say, according to plan, because anal sex was *not* part of the events of Friday night, as recounted above. Slowly but surely, to the brink, *and beyond* – those are the watchwords of submissive ecstasy. Butt-fucked I would be, in my own time, when I really, truly dreaded it. Would the pain of anal penetration by Donkey Don become pleasure, after a really severe bare-ass caning? Only one way to find out.

6

Damaged Meat

It wasn't too difficult to hook up with Don again. Plattsburgh is a small place. He hadn't changed, and had the same cockiness, in every sense of the word. He treated my accidentally-on-purpose running into him as exactly what it was, deliberately running into him, then pretending it was coincidence. Men need that ego food. He still walked with a kind of genital swagger, and it would be idle to claim I wasn't as thrilled as ever, particularly as I now *wanted* the pain of his penetration, and in my anus. Yet, with the thrill was a kind of foreboding: there always is, when you contemplate an act of submission, even if you've endured it many times. I think I masturbate so much, to stop myself shivering, not just at the pain I crave, but *because* the monster in me craves it.

Don was a high-school dropout, of course, as part of his macho image, though I knew for a fact that his father was an accountant. The way he figured, if you dropped out of high school around May, then you got the pick of all the good jobs before the graduate hordes hit the streets in June – great jobs like gas jockey, burger flipper and so on. By now, he'd moved up in the *beau monde* of Plattsburgh, and was really proud he had gotten a job as a gravedigger at the cemetery, so that he could make jokes about bones and stiffs and suchlike. I

71

always used to wonder what attracted me to Don, apart from his dick, or maybe the smell of pizza, but understood now – it was because he presented no mental challenge. That was why my mom and dad smiled when I mentioned him, and never said a word against him, though mom did wrinkle her nose when I came home from baby-sitting, and losing my virginity, and joked that I smelled like pepperoni, at which I had the grace to blush.

It was a few weeks after the episode by the lake. I'd had no dates with James since then, despite a few perfunctory phone calls. I sensed he preferred to forget the night when we had all been so rampant or was afraid I would snitch or go to the crisis centre, or something. As if! I played with myself, and used up a lot of zucchini, as even Elle pleaded tiredness due to her summer job at the mall, and Cher Baxter, my other best friend, was up to one of her madcap let's-run-away-to-Hawaii romances with some jock. So I spent time hanging out at the mall, one of the few places to hang, without seeing Elle until one day, sure enough, Don showed.

There were quite a few people I recognised, so there was no point in being coy or subtle. I gave Don a big 'Hell-oo!' and led him to the food hall to buy me a whole lot of ice cream, in an ice-cream parlour called Devilz-D-Lite. It was a pretty hot day – the mall a/c dated from World War I – and I wore only a braless halter top and a short pleated cheerleader's skirt, on loan from Cher (her real name was Cerise), without panties or shoes. Don, deprived of his black leather jacket, though still camouflaged, as on the rainiest day, in wraparound sunshades, wore a glowing red pair of boxing shorts and a string T-shirt, to best display his chest and abdominal hair over the various bulges acquired by weight training at the Elm St gym. Yawn. Men never understand that women don't care about muscles and stuff. As long as their clothes hang neatly, it's cock that interests us, and all the power that cock implies. Yet I had a certain respect for Don, in his dogged attempt to revert to blue-collar. He worked out, while James 'kept in shape'. I told James, if he ever went *jogging* – yuk! – he could forget me.

Devilz-D-Lite was what passed for swank in that particular mall. The idea was that eating high-calorie ice cream was a sinful passion – 'lite' was a sop to diet nuts – so the whole décor was black, and all the ice cream served was dark in colour – chocolate, black cherry, blueberry, no plain vanilla. The serving-girls were dressed in really corny costumes, in some kind of thin black latex, like imps, or little devils, with tails, and masks, high stilettos and mesh black stockings. It was expensive, as sin is supposed to be, in New England. There were a lot of single middle-aged guys in there, rediscovering their passion for dark ice cream. When we sat down at one of the booths, with chairs and tables far apart, and uncomfortable on purpose, so you wouldn't linger, Don had the decency to ogle my pantiless crotch, and promptly add a hard-on to his various bulges. I let Cher's skirt ride up, and parted my thighs so he got a good peek at my silky-growing mons and nicely glistening pussy lips, which distracted him somewhat, for when we had been going together, I was in my normal jungly state down there.

Small towns are small towns, so I wasn't really surprised when our waitress turned out to be Cher herself, on her summer job. She was a sunny brunette, ripely swelling, with a passion for collecting sports stars. I squealed in girly rapture and told her how sinful she looked in her black rubber leotard thing, and so on, while she winked at my – *her* – skirt, and, having taken our order, told me I could keep it as long as I liked, as her current jock – Hawaiian idyll still at pre-budget stage – didn't approve too much of her wearing clothes. I crossed my legs. Had Cher seen my bare beaver? Come to think of it, was a growing-back pubic mound technically a beaver at all? Summer in New England sets all kinds of puzzles. My beaver, or otherwise, was scarcely an opening topic for conversation, so I said as brightly as I could:

'This the graveyard shift, then, Don?'

He squirmed a bit and mumbled something. I followed up with a stare at his really juicy erection, and said, 'See you're taking your work home.'

He looked up from my honeypot, his eyes probably expressing puzzlement under his sunshades. I nodded at the bulge in his shorts.

'I mean, is that a *stiff* in your pants, or are you just glad to see me, after the *boneyard* . . .?'

OK, it's corny, but I was a teenager in upstate New York, for heaven's sake. Don gave me the kind of grin commonly termed lop-sided, turning it into a leer when he caught on I was genuinely interested in his bulge, and shifted, so that I had a better view.

'You still do things to me, babe,' he growled, trying to sound husky.

I put my bare right foot on his shin, and began to crawl up his leg.

'Oh, yeah?' I said. 'Then why did you dump me, lover?'

What he *wanted* to say was, 'You dumped *me*,' but, being Italian, shrugged, and said it was just one of those things, like every girl in Plattsburgh was clamouring for his meat. My toes reached his shorts, and kept on going, until I had my toes and sole clamped on his erection. It was an easy manoeuvre, but unavoidably public. I didn't care – I'd be out of Plattsburgh soon. I slurped black cherry ice cream while my foot began a steady massage of his stiff cock. He swallowed and began to flare his nostrils and gasp a bit, when my toes started to massage his swollen glans, and specifically, his piss-slit. We made a little small talk, to the general effect that our relationship could just as easily take off again, if he could find a window in his social calendar, but now I got my left foot up, and under his shorts, until I had him sandwiched, with my left foot on his naked penis. I hooked his glans between my big and second toes, and began to jerk him off. Few men can resist a toe-job, by the way. It turns them to toothpaste.

'College, eh?' he stammered.

'NYU,' I said, '*probably*. I have other options.'

That would have given him excuse for his 'native New Yorker' lecture, telling people they wouldn't stand the pace of the big city, which he knew all about, having been born and raised there – meaning he had spent a few months as a baby in an apartment on West 10,000,000th St or somewhere, before Pop made a whole bag of money in textiles and started a factory up here in lakeland, where the labour was non-union moms and teenagers. Don used to hint that he had mob ancestry, as if every Italian was in the *cosa nostra*, but his dad's good fortune was one of those 'only in America' things. The US has an enormous jail population, and to celebrate, or hope for, some con's release, people tie yellow ribbons to trees and car fenders and stuff. Being an accountant, Don's dad saw a market niche, so he started up a business making nothing *but* yellow ribbons – plain cotton or linen, or silk, imported from communist China. So, to walk tall in your trailer park, you just *have to* fly a 'Funicello yellow'. It's true.

I didn't get the New York lecture, as my toe-job was taking effect, and his face was red, with his mouth gaping. His cock was trembling, with that shivery, super-hardness that lets a girl know the sperm's coming. I debated whether to leave him gasping, or do the thing there and then, and I figured that homely New England wisdom is always best, in this case, 'Don't start what you won't finish.' Plus which, my own pussy was spurting come all over Cher's pleated cheerleader's skirt, and I had to resist the urge to get my fingers on my clit and bring myself off – but that would have been excess spectacle. As it was, I wondered what sort of detergent I'd need to get the stains out. I tightened my toes around his glans, with my right foot pushing on his button-hole from outside his shorts, and he made a little whimpering noise, and suddenly erupted all over my bare toes. He panted, and gasped, trying to turn the sounds into a macho growl, but I had him in a toe lock, and I milked his cock of every last drop of cream. My whole left foot was bathed in hot spunk, and there was a huge damp stain on the crotch of his shorts. Slowly, I withdrew both my feet as he started to grin in that grateful manner men have, and without letting my left foot touch the floor, I did one of my yoga things, which was to raise it over my breasts so that my toes were pressing my chin. With my eyes fixed on his, I licked all his cream from my toes.

'Do we have a date, Romeo?' I said.

'Sure,' he gasped, looking relieved to be seated, so he couldn't topple over.

'Pick me up at eight, tomorrow night,' I said, scooping the last of my ice cream and avoiding an aggressive washcloth that was wiping our table.

I looked up, and saw that it was piloted by Elle, wearing one of those impish uniforms, with her rubber tail waggling furiously behind her long, mesh-stockinged black legs. She had an eye mask, and whiskers, and a one-piece black latex swimsuit, cut low at her breasts and high at the waist, with her hair piled high in a spike. I opened my mouth to greet her, when she snapped:

'Looks as if he's *already* picked something up.'

Don shrugged, shuffling his thighs.

'Oh!' I cried. 'You guys know each other.'

Don shrugged again, and so did I. So, they were getting it on – big deal! A couple of months, and I was out of there.

'*I* know *Don*, if that's what you mean, Trudi. But I wouldn't dream of spoiling your date.'

'That's super-royal of you, Elle,' I said.

'I'll let Don do *that,*' she said, 'so you be on your best behaviour tomorrow night, Don, and maybe Trudi won't hurt you – *again.*' She swished away, with her rubber tail whirling like a cheerleader's baton.

Obviously, I wondered about Elle's bitchy remark and her triumphant/scornful sneer as she waltzed away. I didn't call her, though, but waited for Don with more than normal curiosity. Had our drift-apart really hurt him? Unflattering to his male ego, flattering to my female one. However, he seemed as sporty as usual when he picked me up in his truck – not a proper truck but one of those machomobiles which is just a car that thinks it has a big dick. I was wearing my little black dress, but with full underthings – scalloped black bra, panties, girdle and garter straps, fishnet stockings, and *shoes,* fantastically high stiletto heels, in mirror-black. I let him kiss me a bit, and fended off his gropes, standard procedure before the dating ritual, as we both knew we'd get it on later. We had a meal and saw a movie, took in a couple of clubs, and later we ended up back in his truck. Now that it was under streetlight, I saw a pile of canvas in the back of the truck that I hadn't noticed in the darkness before, and Don said it was nothing but a couple of bodies, and would I like to take a look. I ignored that. I was too horny, past the joke stage of our date. Don had changed tactics, and kept his hands off me all evening, on the principle of 'let her beg for it', and by the time it came to the crunch, I *was* ready to beg for it. Not just his cock, but also – the first thing I noticed, apart from his bulge – his studded leather belt on my bare ass. We sat in his truck and he kissed me, brutally. My hand went to his zipper. He was beautifully hard for me.

'Not here,' I said. 'I know somewhere private, a cove on the lake. We can fuck all night long, under the stars . . .'

While he drove us to the cove, I had his cock out of his pants and was tonguing his big swollen glans, lightly enough to make him moan but not hard enough to bring him off. When we parked and got down on the sand, he was the one in a hurry, though the brute didn't have to beg. He didn't even turn the engine off, but ordered me to drop my dress and panties, then my bra, but didn't take his own clothes off. Slowly, he removed his T-shirt, and then the belt of his jeans, which he coiled around his fist. His cock bulged through the jeans. I stood with the headlights shining on my body, nude but for stockings, girdle and garter straps, with him in his jeans. I could feel my breasts quiver, and the nipples stiffen, in cold and fear, and the sand gritting the mesh of my stockinged feet.

'Turn around,' he hissed. 'I want to see what he did to you.'

'Who?' I said.

'*Turn around and show me your butt!*'

I obeyed, trembling.

'Move forward. I want to look at you up close.'

I inched ahead, until my fesses shone in the head-lights. I knew the welts of my thrashing from James and Daryl hadn't faded, as I inspected them, and kept them raw with my hairbrush, every time I masturbated. I felt now that a spanked, blotchy derrière was part of me, or, at least, a fashion accessory. My masturbation was every day, sometimes twice, and always using an anal stimulant; it was only then, shivering nude by the lake, with my slit gushing come, that I realised how deeply I longed for Don's giant cock to bugger me. The trickles of come from my cunt, down my inner thighs, and even wetting my mesh stockings, sparkled like diamonds in the truck's headlights.

'You *are* a slut! Your ass has been whipped! You think I don't know what goes on?' he spat, uncoiling his belt. 'Why should I waste time on damaged meat? You and that fucking *James* . . .'

'That's over, Don! I squealed. 'Anyway, even if it weren't, what the hell business is it of *yours?* I could ask

78

why my friend *Elle* took such an owner's interest in you at the mall!'

'Elle doesn't own me, bitch!' he cried. 'Leave her out of this!'

His bulge was massive. I wanted those jeans off, and that cock oiled with my own come, pounding my anal passage.

'You mean she's *in* it. How long have *you* two . . .?'

'You're disgusting, you know that? I should whip you!'

'Ohh . . .' I whimpered. 'Oh, Don . . .'

An electric current coursed up my spine, and my cunt simply gushed with hot wetness. The bulge of his cock cast a huge shadow.

'Why?' I said, pleading. 'I deserve a beating, for being butt naked, waiting for a fuck, while you inspect the damaged meat . . .? OK, I *have* been whipped, and I *do* deserve it. Why not get your pants off? Nobody's around, you can do what you like with me, Don. Fuck me in the ass, make me go down on you, yes, even use that belt to *spank me!'*

'You *are* some filthy bitch! Wash your mouth!'

But he was unfastening his jeans, stepping out of them – no undershorts, just that monstrous cock towering close to my lips. I crouched below him, flicking out my tongue to connect with his glans; he grunted as I began to play with my juicing pussy, masturbating with wide, probing strokes to my throbbing clit, and letting him see the gash juice sliming my palms and sparkling in the light.

'Why does spanking and ass-fucking upset you?' I whispered, pressing his glans with my lips, and caressing the pisshole with my tongue tip. 'Haven't you whopped a girl's ass before? Or butt-fucked her?'

'Sure!' he sneered, his cock trembling as I swooped to take his glans right to the back of the throat, with my lips on his ball-sac and the balls cupped in my palm, squeezing the orbs lightly. 'Uh . . .! Don't stop . . . *bitch!'*

I parted my lips, to speak, with the back of my tongue still nuzzlng his piss-slit. Speaking when giving head makes your words resonate through the cock, and the flesh vibrates.

'*Whip my bare ass, then,*' I mumbled, through his cock-meat. '*I don't mind. Then you can butt-fuck me . . .*'

Suddenly, he jerked round, peering into the darkness at the back of his truck. His movement was at the hips, not strong enough to take my head with him, but enough to draw the cock halfway out of my mouth, and I had a glimpse of his bare ass. It was covered in weals: big, ugly dark weals, as though he'd been whipped. He nodded, and turned back, but realised what I'd seen. My mouth was off his cock now and I leered up at him.

'So *that's* why you never took your pants off to fuck me,' I whispered. 'All that time! Who was it? Surely not *Elle . . .*'

He slapped me, viciously, on my face, then again on my bare breasts. It hurt.

'You fucking bitch,' he muttered numbly. 'If you breathe a *word* . . . I'll do what your stinking slut's mouth told me to do. Butt-fuck you and whale that bare ass of yours.'

'Don,' I said, still crouching, and getting my tongue on his balls, 'the offer still stands. If you want my silence, you'll have to do those things to me . . . *now!* Whip me, and do me in the ass. James has never been there, he's not man enough . . . *no one has.* That's why I wanted *you.*'

My heart thumped, and my pussy was a torrent of come, yet I was deadly scared. He pushed my hair so that his cock plunged into my throat. I couldn't talk; I heard him groan, breathing harshly, over the thrumming of the truck's engine. Behind him, something stirred, at the truck. Two figures sloughed off the canvas covering and jumped to the ground. Both had tails. One reached into the truck and turned on the windshield wipers, while the other advanced, holding a set of booster cables. It was Elle, still clad in her ditsy she-devil's uniform from the ice-cream parlour. Moments later, she was joined by Cher Baxter.

'You're wrong in one thing, Trudi,' said Elle. 'James is *way* man enough for a butt-fuck.'

'*Mm!*' I squealed, with Cher's fingers joining Don's in clamping my face to his cock. As my heart chilled and I moaned again, a hot stream of piss jetted from my helpless, gaping cunt; something was very wrong.

'What you'll find out,' Cher said, 'is, if *Donnie's* man enough to make you scream, with his donkey dork up your butthole, little Miss Cheerleader.'

She twirled her cheerleader's baton, looped on a string around her left thumb, in a perfect circle.

'Hey, don't call me Donnie,' he protested. 'I don't know this ass-fuck stuff. You told me – *Ow!*'

Elle slapped his face and grasped his balls, squeezing.

Vap!

'*Ow!*'

Cher whipped Don's bare ass with the booster cables.

'Just obey orders, *slave*,' Elle hissed. 'What are a slave's instructions?'

'To . . . to obey a lady at all times,' Don sobbed.

'This *bitch* has asked you to whip her, and fuck her in the ass,' said Elle. '*Do it,* before she pisses herself again.'

I screamed, in that starry black sky, but only the stars and the silent lake were there to hear me. We were on a shore where there were a lot of sand-vines crawling between low, rocky outcrops, sand-vines being a tough creeping weed that grows a lot in New England. Elle grabbed my hair, twisting it around her fist, and dragged me, kicking and flailing, across the sand-vines to a low rock. I couldn't resist, as the pain in my hair was so terrible, and my agony was worse when she dragged my torso across the rock with my bare tits scraping its gnarled surface. She pulled my head low and knotted my hair to a hanging tree branch, while I felt Cher grasp one then the other of my ankles, and lash it tightly in the sand-vines, tough as whipcord, and rendering me helpless, with my legs wide apart, showing my whole pussy and anal region, and my buttocks perched on the gritty rock face. Elle, meanwhile, got each of my wrists lashed to a creeper of sand-vine beside the rock on which I was now a prisoner. I suppose I yelled, 'Please, no!' and suchlike – I do remember that my mouth drooled uncontrollably, and that my pussy slipped and slithered on the rock, for I was juicing with heavy come. My captors saw it, and laughed, as I heard Don's belt whistle through the air.

Vap!

'Ahh!'

I do remember that first scream, as the heavy studs struck my naked fesses. It was searing agony that pulsed through my whole body, making me shudder, and my gorge rise. The belt slammed my cunt against the rock, and scraped my bare nipples, with excruciating pain, against the surface on which they were squashed.

'Oh, God, Don . . .' I heard myself wail.

Vap!

'Ahh!'

'You *begged* for it, *bitch!*' spat Cher Baxter, my so-called friend. 'You're one of *them* . . . a fucking submissive!'

Vap! Vap! Vap! My torture went on as though there would never be an end. My bare ass danced and squirmed as the leather seared me like a white-hot lance, over and over. The only sounds, over the truck's thrumming and my own gasps, were sharp snaps, as if tree branches were being broken. There are a lot of birch trees in that particular cove, and I looked up to see both my girlfriends, in their rubber costumes that now seemed dreadfully sinister, breaking off long wands of birch wood.

Vap! Vap! Vap!
'*AHH!*'

Don delivered three strokes vertically, right up my cunt, anus and perineum, and I wriggled frantically, splattering the rock and the sand beneath my writhing pubis, with a terrible jet of piss.

'Oh, God, please,' I whimpered. 'OK, I asked for it . . . but tell me how many strokes!'

'Just 50,' said Elle, continuing to break off birch branches. 'You've taken more than half already. There's a good stream of come from your dirty little whore's cunt, so don't pretend you don't enjoy it.'

Vap! Vap! Vap! I was speechless, except for a gasping, gurgling retch in my throat, partly in horror that she was right. The more my bare ass squirmed, the hotter the flames of my stripes, the more and more I juiced, and the harder my clitty throbbed, mashed against the sandy rock. I could feel my belly begin to flutter, and my spine tingle, in the approach of orgasm; the knowledge that 50 lashes with the strap was only the *beginning* of my punishment made me hornier and hornier. I had reached, surprisingly fast, my submissive's plateau, where no pain is quite enough . . .

Vap!

'*Ahh! Ahh! Ohh!*' I sobbed, writhing and slamming my cunt and titties on the rock, as though to punish myself for playing their game. 'You fucking bitches1'

'That's the 50,' said Elle, wrapping and knotting a vine around her sheaf of birch rods.

A hand – Cher's, I guess – plunged into my exposed cunt and pummelled inside my pouch, until it withdrew, slopped with my come, to anoint my gaping wide anus bud.

'*Ahh!*'

My scream was genuine horror, for my asshole was now brutally impaled, not by Don's cock, but by a hard wooden tube – the cheerleader's baton I had so willingly relinquished to Cher Baxter. The pain was indescribable, and I screamed and screamed as she forced the wood into my clenched butthole; then, the same, awesome magic worked, as it had when I played with myself. Halfway down my hole, the sphincter just surrendered, relaxing, so that Cher's baton slipped right to my anal root and she began to bugger me fiercely.

'Stop ... stop ...!' I begged, but my screams had turned to whimpers, for my anal walls were clutching the penetrating tool, squeezing it into my sucking anus.

'Warming your butthole, bitch, for Don's meat. That's bigger than the baton,' Cher hissed, as she rammed the wood again and again, wrenching my anal elastic, although the baton slid easily in and out of my hole, as it was so copiously lubricated with my own come and ass grease.

She buggered me with over a hundred strokes, before the hot wood, slimed by my own asshole, suddenly withdrew, leaving my sphincter still sucking at air. I whimpered, then sighed, sobbing, as the wood was replaced by the real hot flesh of Don's cock. There was no resistance; I gasped at his size that slid into me, filling me easily and threatening to burst my whole belly as he butt-fucked me with incredibly hard thrusts, his heavy body straddling me and pinning me to the rock. Behind him, I heard the vap! of the leather, as one of the girls lashed his own bare ass, and he jerked at its impact.

'Tool her till you spurt, slave!' rasped Elle's voice.

'Yes, Mistress,' Don whimpered.

Vap! Vap! Vap! Each lash of the strap on his own bare jerked his giant cock against my anal root, and I groaned, sobbing and whimpering in the knowledge that when he spurted, I would orgasm. He buggered me for ages, it seemed – in fact, I think, about five minutes, as his own bare butt was whipped by my sweet-as-candy girlfriend Elle. At last, he groaned, and his spunk filled my asshole, and I shook, as orgasm flooded my entire body – cunt, tits, belly, everywhere. I almost fainted with the intensity of my come, and was too dazed to register the details of my next torture. They unfastened me, but with my burning fesses and my body still hot and fluttering from my come, I could offer no resistance, as I was placed belly down on the hood of the truck. Each of my ankles was roped to one of the swishing windshield wipers, and my teats squashed against the hot metal, with my wrists roped to the front fenders. My nipples were each clamped in a booster cable, held by Cher, who fastened the other ends to my gash flaps, closing my cunt tight. The clamps on booster cables are designed to hold the electric cords firmly to a battery terminal, so I invite you to consider the agony of having them clamped to the naked nipples and beaver. I began to scream again. My legs parted and closed helplessly, like a metronome, as Elle and Cher lifted their birch sheaves. Piss and come sprayed from my squashed cunt, the liquid hissing on the hot truck hood, which seared my teats and thighs and cunt as I tried in vain to rise, but could not, restrained by my nipple and beaver clamps.

Crack! Crack! The two birches slapped my raw bare buttocks, one immediately after the other, and my tits and belly thumped the truck, as my body shuddered and I screamed to the bottom of my lungs.

'Ahh! Ahh!'

I don't know if you, the reader, have ever suffered a bare-bottom birching. If you have then you'll know that no words can do it justice. The whip, the cane or the strap have their own special agonies, but the birch, flogging of the naked fesses with over a dozen vicious wands, is beauty and horror supreme. The birch crackles on a girl's bare ass, its dry swishing a symphony of pain. It doesn't smart sharply like a cane, or jolt, with an ugly welt, like a whip; it sneaks up on you, that harmless rustling scarcely a tickle, until, a split second later, as the birch twigs withdraw lovingly and slowly across your naked bottom, the full awesome majesty of their agony hits you, flushing the entire buttock expanse with pain, as though the rods have explored your every crevice. A girl *takes* a caning, but she is *exposed* to a birching. There is no submissive thrill like it. I took 50 lashes with the birch – 25 from each girl, that is – and I orgasmed twice during my birching, sobbing helplessly in a delirium of shame, pain and unspeakable wanting. With my thighs opening and closing to the rhythm of the windshield wipers, they flogged me on the full pubis, lashing my perineum, clamped gash and anus, from behind. They flogged me on the thighs, and the tops of my buttocks, until my stockings, girdle and straps were shredded. When the birches had ceased to flail my naked ass, I sobbed for more.

Instead, I was let loose, and thrown on the sand. The truck revved, and my torturers drove off, with Elle's parting instructions a whisper over the ripple of the lake: I should walk back to town, and find each item of my clothing hanging from tree branches, at random, along the way. There was nothing for it but to obey; first, I stumbled to the lake to cool my stinging body, and when I was immersed up to my neck, I looked up at the starry sky, and masturbated, bringing myself off almost at the first touch of my swollen clit. I began the long walk back to Plattsburgh, ducking out of sight when headlights neared, or else into thorn bushes or briar patches to retrieve my garments. I smiled through my tears, as, piece by piece, I dressed, on my way home, though without putting on my shoes. I walked barefoot, holding them by their ankle straps, between my teeth. I willed myself to recall my humiliation, and mused on James's treachery with Elle, for who knew what unspeakable pleasures. Maybe she was *his* submissive . . . My pussy moistened as I walked. I had had everything I wanted from my New England home town.

7

Full-Hair Beaver

I never let a man fuck me unless he whips me first, and pretty much the same applies to women, although only a select few are permitted to dildo-fuck me, whether in ass or pussy. But that's today. Before going further, I should explain my attitude to lesbian scenes. I don't call myself lesbian, or even bisexual, and I distrust females who do. What two naked women can make each other feel is sensuous and expert, and is not to be insulted by insipid classifying, like 'dyke' or something, as if we are only puppets, and can't do what we please. But I don't mind if a master calls me a dirty lesbian slut, because shame and insult are part of a satisfying punishment, and words can sting like canes. It's a cliché that a woman best knows how to please another woman in the gentle art of mutual masturbation – which is what lesbian sex comes down to, and none the less pleasant for it – and it's true. That's what same-sex scenes do for me – it is like having a second self to masturbate with, or to whip my bare ass or tits in a way that is so painfully *knowing*. To make 'dyke' into a lifestyle, and think a plastic or rubber toy in your holes is better than hard cock, and the pungent sweet stink of *maleness*, is simply banal, and missing several points at once.

After that scene with Don, Elle and Cher, it took two weeks for my bottom welts and cord marks on my wrists and ankles to fade, and even then, not completely. An expert could tell I'd been flogged raw. During that time, I masturbated constantly, feeling the welts solidified to a lovely hard crust on my ass, which smarted as I walked, before gradually flaking off. The fall semester was approaching, and I also contemplated my choice of college. As I had told Don, I had options. There was a trust fund, in my name, from great-grandmother Fahr, who had invested wisely in real estate in the old days in New England. Not all the Fahrs were from Plattsburgh, and, technically speaking, I owned parts of New Hampshire, Vermont, even Yonkers, and – I blush – Paterson, New Jersey. The monies were mine to dispose of, in graduated release, the older I became, and although I couldn't just go out and buy myself an executive jet or anything, I was especially free to shop around when it came to education. It was a very New England thing, that is, righteous, and even in my attitude to spanking, I find my puritan roots asserting themselves. I mean, I must be tied or whipped *this* way, the proper one, as laid down in The Good Book, as I call my mindset of flagellant instructions. My trust fund was structured so that I could never be poor, but never frivolous either. I couldn't just call up my trustees, an ancient law firm in Manhattan, and beg the price of a six-pack, but I could use it as collateral to buy yet more real estate, or education. At periods in my life, monies are disbursed as a reward for my not needing them! The general idea is that the fund should continue to grow, and fund my own great-grandchildren, and theirs too. My dad hinted that if I was really, truly in need of cash, I could get it, but I'd have to go and see the trustees in a dress and shoes, and talk like Abraham Lincoln or somebody.

The Fahrs had always been a New England family. Even my parents, who came from the 1890s, insisted that hard winters were worth it, for the beautiful fall foliage, and the purity of life in New England. They told horror stories of time spent in sleazy Florida and flaky, craze-crazed California, whence they had gratefully come home to settle, by the placid old New England virtues of Lake Champlain. So, the furthest they imagined me going was New York, or maybe Vassar, not too far away in Poughkeepsie. I couldn't quite make Vassar, or Columbia, so settled for NYU, which isn't bad, really, except that NYU girls are supposed to be 'easy'. I still had no plans for a career, other than a hardening knowledge that my physical needs came first – my *submissive* needs. If marriage came into the picture, it would be one of convenience – mine – to a hard-ass brute, rich, naturally, who would treat me like a plaything, and whip me like a dog, so that I could rule the roost with my bruises . . .

Otherwise, I envisioned an academic career, in the field of anthropology, where I would be free to conduct my own research, and roam. The two didn't seem contradictory, and I knew 'anthropology' would sound good and intrepid to my crusty old trust fund. Basically, at that stage, I was content to drift, but so many more fantasies kept adding themselves to my original ones, that I knew, sometime, I would *have* to make them come true: anally gang-fucked, by hairy, brutal males, then whipped, and roped hand and foot to some dusty western railroad track, or, paradoxically, an exotic queen, obliging my epicene male slaves to gang-fuck me, in between peeling my lunchtime grapes, as I tongued hard, massive young cocks, slavering over erection after erection, and swallowed their spunk, or made them come between my tits and rub the cream all over me, while others whipped my naked trussed buttocks. I imagined sucking the rock-hard cocks of my tireless ephebes to orgasm, then making them spurt into a golden bathtub, so that I could soak in hot spunk. Just the normal American housewife's dream. That's the basis of America, our right to dream, and even before I left Plattsburgh, I presaged something my English friend Juniper later told me. She was caning me on the bare at the time, in prison.

'You Americans lack culture,' she said. I was too busy squirming under her cane to argue, and I had her boot in my mouth. 'Meaning a general knowledge culture, which Europeans acquire instinctively. We English would be embarrassed to forget the capital of Portugal, but an American may be a world expert on dinosaurs, or Chinese porcelain, and not even know where Portugal is – and furthermore, not give a hoot. America is a country of enthusiasms and specialties, and success means finding your specialty, and pursuing it. It could be space travel, or collecting stuffed toys, or, in *your* case, miss . . .'

Her cane again sliced my naked buttocks, and I writhed, my gorge heaving; her question, which was no question really, required no answer. Later, I'll get to Juniper; suffice to say, I knew as a teen that *my* American specialty was flagellance, corporal punishment, and – however great my shame, my juicing cunt gave me away whenever I mouthed the word – *submission.*

After a semester at NYU, not a world architectural glory, I knew I wanted something different. New York City is fine, and enthrals out-of-towners, but to a New Englander it just seems like a chunk of proper New England gone awry, with all the noise, dirt and desperate people. I had to wear *shoes* all the time! That's what mainly decided me to look elsewhere, which the terms of my trust fund permitted. Of course, there was a deeper reason, too, which was my submissive sex drive, as I now thought of it. Naturally, I made myself available for males who seemed suitable, but there were so few genuine dominants around. In Manhattan, everything is an act. If TV and magazines decree body piercing, or hair dye, or astrology, or weepy-crawly sensitive men, or hunky macho men, then that's what people go for, and 'advice centres' spring up, to take their money and teach them the act. There is a spanking scene, but it seemed to be mostly for sweaty married guys – from Yonkers, or Paterson, NJ – with contact ads in those magazines where the ink comes off on your fingers, and it's generally accepted that the females who place, or answer ads, are hookers.

Or there were swingers' palaces, with Roman names, and hot tubs, supposedly for liberated couples, but the same applied there, too: another act. In New York everyone is always looking over their shoulder, wondering if they should be somewhere else, or being seen with someone else. 'Uptight' was a word from my parents' day, and it seemed to fit. My looks counted against me! Guys were scared to be seen with a blonde centrefold, who looked like a 'trophy date'. And their constant diddling with internet gizmos, as if some deal might slip through their fingers, due to a moment's inattention! A sub wants *all* a man's attention, or at least her bottom does. The honest sting of real leather or rubber is what matters to *this* old-fashioned New England puritan, not the modern loser world of beeps and clicks and screens.

I did have a few good dates, and adequate fucks, but the guys were a wash, in the end. They got so icky and sentimental – relationship, relationship! When I smacked my bare bottom, and said that before considering the R word, I needed sterner treatment from a male who wasn't afraid to give an insolent bitch what she deserved, they backed off. In Manhattan, a sub is part of a sinister package, of dope, crime, blackmail and everything. My corn-fed blue eyes and perfect bod just had to be entrapment by junkies, or the mob, or the cops. The media hadn't made *real* bondage and spanking cool . . . it was OK to *look* like a bondage queen, and half of NYU did, but it was only sham.

91

Context, too, is important. A sub scene has to be unhurried, and preferably in deceptively tranquil surroundings – though even a dungeon can be tranquil – in contrast to the high intensity of spanking. Accommodation in New York is cramped, and generally shitty, and there's not much room for the imagination to flower. I had a one-room apartment, without a/c, downtown on Varick St, and everyone said I was lucky to get it. Juniper later told me that the British don't like to live in apartments at all, but in suburbs, which are not the sort of uniform A-frames or tract homes or American gothic you get in the US, which make moving to the the 'burbs kind of a surrender. Where Juniper is from, somewhere near London, everyone decorates their home to look individual, and lots of spanking (with plenty of etceteras) goes on in tranquil suburban villas. Manhattan is anything but tranquil. There's little temptation to be caned or bound, with police sirens wailing all over, and junkies battering each other for real – I thought a lot about Montreal, and how calm everything up in Canada was, even for a big city. Spanking needs a leisurely mindset.

So, in buzzy New York City, this wholesome New England girl was left to do a whole lot of masturbating, thinking of good old Donkey Don's cock up my asshole, and his belt on my bare, with my wicked naked birching from Elle, under the pure starlight of Lake Champlain. I reckoned I shouldn't need to go to a foreign country – the US itself must surely have plenty of starry Lake Champlains, even if they weren't lakes, or very starry, and plenty of men with big dicks and belts, who knew how to fashion a birch for my bare ass. Manhattan doesn't have any birch trees, even in Central Park, and if it did, and you took some, it would probably be some kind of fantastic federal crime, and they'd send you up for 25 years.

There was one good scene, however – I may call it an *affair* – and that led to other scenes, so my time in that crummy apartment on Varick Street wasn't wasted at all, and I did score good credits at NYU, in my eclectic mix of anthropology, English literature, and French (a whim – I wanted to scare Marc, Helena and Yvette, if I ever saw them again). I met a guy who *wasn't* uptight. It helped, I guess, that he lived in a big, ultra-cool apartment up in the East 80s, just off 3rd Ave. He was an art dealer, which didn't impress me. I know something of art, and can keep my distance, just as I can with music. Photos lie; music lies. Pictures are too easy: I knew that from Marc. They were just his form of power, and money. People in history who saw visions were blessed, but if they heard voices, they were burnt. I listen to my voices.

I met Peter Murchy – another German! – at some party for artsy people over on West End Avenue. The occasion for the gathering was that they had discovered a store that sold lobsters with only one claw for some low price – it was a Puerto Rican place, maybe they have lobster fights or something – so our host had to go out and buy up a million lobsters with only one claw, and throw a party to celebrate, with the usual crowd of party-chasers, lesbian photographers, unshown painters, 'becoming' novelists and other types you get on the upper west side. Peter seemed to be meditating on his lobster claw, dipped in some goo, but he singled me out, without hearing a word I'd said. That is, he waved the goo across my bare breast, as if I were an example in some argument, without touching me or my little black dress with the shoelace traps, knotted in a bow. The visual, you see: corn-fed centrefold, with a dress that would fall off in a flick, barefoot, braless and pantieless, in the midst of Manhattan outrageous. I stared him out, and he raised his eyebrows, offering me the lobster claw, dripping goo. I smiled back, and opened my mouth, flicking my tongue across my teeth. He smiled, and put the lobster claw in my mouth. I crunched, sucked, and spat shell. Some of the goo – I think it was guacamole – dripped down the cleft of my tits, and I scooped it, before it could ruin my dress, giving everyone a fine jiggle show. I let my breasts and hardening nipples quiver, as I sucked the dip from my fingers.

I guess *I* must have seemed the outrageous one, either devastatingly natural or a harbinger of trends to come – post-ultra-modern kitsch, or something. I sensed power in the man, though he was smaller than me, but wiry, and I had been masturbating so much, I needed a fuck – an imaginative one. An art dealer might do. Having assumed that I wasn't from New York City, he offered a stroll down to Riverside Park, not far, to see Grant's tomb by moonlight, and I accepted. I mentioned I was from Plattsburgh.

'And a barefoot,' he said. 'How apt,' as though barefoots had something special to do with Plattsburgh.

'How did you know?'

I had stashed my slingbacks in the vestibule.

'The way you walk. Do not put your shoes on. Knot the straps, and wear them as a collar. You will not come to harm, walking barefoot with me.'

I obeyed, trembling slightly at the ease with which I obeyed, and we left the apartment building. I was still trembling when we reached the stone likeness of the great man. We were alone in the ribbon of parkland; the Hudson river gleamed idly to our west.

'General Ulysses S Grant,' said Peter. 'Saviour of the union, from the confederate hordes. I am fond of the old rascal – a slave-owner himself, he saved the nation from slavery. Perhaps they didn't teach that in high school.'

I agreed that they didn't.

'So many people, so many contradictions!' Peter sighed. 'Ulysses was not just a slave-owner, but a cruel one, too. He whipped his slaves harshly, for the slightest misdemeanour.'

'Females, too?' I asked.

'Females, especially,' he replied.

I reached out, and caressed the stone figure.

'Do you think he whipped women naked?' I asked, feeling the seep of come at my pussy, beginning to moisten my inner thighs. I avoided his eyes: we both *knew*.

'I imagine so.'

'It makes me shiver. It's so strange,' I said, with my come oozing faster – it would not be long before a tell-tale trickle on my thigh would shine in the moonlight.

'Shiver in fear?' he said, mildly. 'Or curiosity?'

His eyes darted briefly to the hem of my dress, then back to my own; the perfect gentleman, he could not have failed to see the hot seep of my come halfway down my exposed bare thigh.

'Both,' I replied, and looked at him full in the eyes, then turned to the statue and placed both my hands on it, with my feet on tiptoe, and my butt raised a teensy bit, as though ready to be spanked then and there.

Peter did not touch me. I looked round.

'Both,' I spat.

With the hot flow of come trickling on both my thighs, and dripping on to my bare ankles, I followed him to a yellow cab, already lowering my head in shame at what I knew I must endure – that which I craved. I slid across the yucky vinyl back seat of the taxi, my path lubricated by my pussy's oil. Before I settled, Peter had whipped out a handkerchief and placed it under my juicing cunt.

'Cotton,' he said. 'More absorbent than silk,' then gave the driver his address, ordering him to go through the park.

He took my hand, and gently raised the hem of my dress the fraction required to expose my soaking big bush to the moonbeams. I shivered, but sat ramrod still as he grasped my knuckles, pushed my thumb inside my pussy, and began to masturbate me. At no point did his skin touch mine, except on my fist, to guide my thumb. I moaned softly; he reamed my cunt, pressed my clitty, making me jump; then repeated the process, several times, until my cunt kerchief was soaking wet. As we left the park, and emerged on to 5th, he took my thumb and poked it in my mouth, then closed my lips around it. I tasted my salty slit-juice. He did not issue a command, but I stayed sucking my thumb as we passed the super of his apartment building, who nodded respectfully, and all the way up in the elevator, until we got to his apartment. He nodded, and I removed my thumb.

'Sucking your thumb, like a little girl,' he observed, his tone neutral. 'Rather rude – if you were a little girl, I should punish you. But, as you are a *big* girl . . .'

He opened the door to the balcony, and motioned me outside, standing close beside me. I looked down. It was a long way to the street, where the traffic crawled like strings of sparkling diamonds. I gasped, but didn't cry, as I felt his forefinger lift my dress, then fully penetrate my cunt. He probed, until his fingernail was pressing my womb-neck, and I moaned softly as the juice flowed in a hot wet torrent from my cunt. I altered my stance so that my thighs and buttocks were parted, and felt his finger slide from my slit, and begin to tease the wrinkle of my anus pucker. His fingernail sliced my ass bud, which hurt, and I drew breath sharply. Lubricated by my cunt juice, his finger penetrated my anal shaft easily, pausing halfway, then, in a second ruthless thrust, hitting the root of my rectum, and seeming to fill my asshole with that stubby muscular finger. He began to ream my butthole very swiftly, which had me gasping, and my cunt juicing all the more. My hand crept to my pubis, where my full-hair beaver was soaking with sweat and come, for I couldn't resist the urge to masturbate – but he clicked his tongue, which I accepted as an order not to move.

I was giddy with pleasure and fear; the traffic below was a wet, dazzling blur; Peter finger-fucked my anus, drawing his finger right out to the nail, before ramming it fully inside me again. I was gasping; I felt faint and dizzy with pleasure, knowing I was in this man's power. The sensation of being ass-fucked with full withdrawal on each stroke is like no other. Then, he paused, to ream my anus pucker again, and permit the entry of his index finger, squeezing it into my butthole beside the first. The nails scraped most painfully at my anal elastic, but I parted my buttocks further, and he got both fingers up against my ass-root, and began to claw and pinch me; I moaned, my pussy a torrent, and my clit throbbing madly, aching for the single touch that would bring me off. He resumed a rapid finger-fucking of my anus with both his fingers in tandem, and I almost came, fainting with pleasure. The pain of those two fingers ravaging my tender anus was truly dreadful, and I couldn't help whimpering. My nipples were rocks under my dress, and as I gasped, he slapped each one hard.

'Silence, bitch,' he whispered.

Then he slapped each cheek of my face, and his hands grasped my buttock-meat, kneading and pinching my bare fesses, quite hard and quite painfully.

'Uhh . . .' I moaned.

'Am I hurting you?' he whispered.

'You know you are.'

'Do you wish the pain to stop?'

'No. You bastard.'

His fingers jabbed viciously at my anus root.

'*Mm! No . . .*'

'You *are* a big girl, and a long way from Plattsburgh. The pain will get worse before it gets better. But you know that. You have been caned before . . . perhaps birched.'

His hand was still kneading my bare buttocks, fingernails tracing the welts of my flogging. He pressed his groin to my buttocks, and I felt the swelling of his cock. It was monstrous, far bigger than two, or any number of fingers he could finger-fuck my ass with.

Crack! I jumped, as his palm spanked my exposed left fesse. I clenched my buttocks, trapping his fingers in my anus and holding my breath, expecting another spank, but none came. I breathed out, slowly – then squealed, as his other hand plunged four fingers into the maw of my cunt, and he lifted me, perching me on his fingers in anus and pouch, his wrists hard against my pubic bone. I wriggled, with my whole weight taken on his impaling fingers, and my cunt showering his wrists with come, as he carried me into the apartment. The whole hem of my dress was soaked in my come, and all crinkled up.

'You know what you want, Plattsburgh girl,' he said.

'Yes,' I whimpered. *'Yes . . .'*

I did enjoy the view, only his apartment was one of these art dealery places where you were terrified to sit down, or use anything. He dealt in pop art of the 1960s: that K-Mart coffee mug was actually a pop art original, worth $50,000, that Sears cushion was a new post-post-realism sculpture, worth $100,000. You get the idea. There was even a coffee table, in pure shiny white, which I supposed was PVC plastic, and was a life-size nude sculpture of a muscly girl crouching on all fours, big ass and big, pink-nippled dugs hanging under her, with her head lowered, and blonde mane covering her face, so that you would put your book, or coffee cup or whatever, on her shoulders, ass or spinal nubbin. She had a shaggy full-hair beaver, though her body was otherwise hairless. There were eight stripes fanned across her butt, in the shape of a buterfly's wings: four stripes on each cheek, radiating out from the crack of her ass. They were pinkish dark, and very realistically molded in the shiny plastic, to look like cane welts, or being a thumbnail's depth, ploughed furrows, and I wondered at the ghoulish imagination of the sculptor –

more likely, in New York, sculptress. There was nothing on the table: I supposed Peter didn't want the shiny PVC to get scratched. There was a string around her neck, I mean, the table's neck, with a price tag attached: $150,000. It turned out the only things not for sale in his apartment were his hot tub and his bed. I was afraid to squeeze a tube of toothpaste, for fear it was a genuine Picasso. The setting above the Manhattan traffic was as romantic as Manhattan could be, and I wondered how many Plattsburgh girls had ever been fucked in a live art gallery. My wonderment was premature, for fucking was, literally, the last thing Peter had on his list.

He said that we must have a drink, and invited me to sit. I felt faintly ridiculous, though giddy with pleasure, my thighs wriggling as he held me by cunt and ass, in two muscular arms. The armchairs in the salon were all bright pastel shades, and I was afraid they were living sculptures or something, but he dropped me between the armrests of an upright black rosewood throne, carved in intricate abstract design, and seemingly out of place. He withdrew his fingers from my wet holes, with a loud plopping sound, and invited me to make myself comfortable. I was perched with my beaver on an armrest of the chair, whose seat was covered by a cloth, rapidly moistening as my come dripped on it. Peter clicked his tongue in disapproval, and removed the cloth: I gasped, for the seat of the throne contained two prongs, carved from the wood of the seat itself: one was in the shape of a monstrously big cock, the other the same, scarcely any smaller. They were intended as dildo and butt-plug.

I sank, with my thighs sliding on their film of come, and felt the shafts graze my cunt and ass bud. I held myself above them, on the armrests, but I hesitated too long, for Peter grasped both my erect nipples and pulled my breasts down, very sharply, tugging the rest of my body by the pinched nipples. I cried out as the twin prongs entered me. The pain was terrible, for the surface of the wood, though polished, had not been sanded smooth: they were like those prophylactic rubber ticklers, except that the tickling part was solid gnarled wood. My whole weight was on those massive dildos, and both penetrated me to the full, with my wet dress falling over my beaver, and my bare thighs firmly pressed on the seat, so that, for all the world, I was just a society girl trained to sit with her back straight.

Except that it was hard to sit straight, with those huge ticklers inside my holes. The vulval penetrator had a whorl, just by the clitoris, which I learned was accidental, but, I thought, by leaning forward, I could use it as a clit-massager. I tried to do so, discreetly, and jerked when the stub of wood touched my clit and an electric shock of pleasure jolted my spine. I knew that one more touch would make me come, as I longed to. I was soaking wet.

'Sit still,' Peter ordered.

He grasped the hem of my dress, and, very delicately, drew it up, so that my breasts and belly were exposed, along with my cunt forest. Gently, he unfastened the shoestring shoulder straps, and the dress was now a shapeless pile of cloth, draped on my teats. He lifted it over my head, shook it, folded it carefully, and opened the door to the bedroom. There, he opened his closet, and hung my dress on a wooden hanger. I had to twist to look into the bedroom: it seemed an ordinary bedroom, if more than normally luxurious, with blue sheets and drapes, black rosewood furniture, like my throne of impalement, and a thick blue woollen carpet. He returned to the back of my throne, and I gasped, as two thick rubber flaps a foot in width sprang across my belly. Each flap had eyelets and cords, which Peter used to bind me expertly in a corset that clung way too tight for comfort, squeezing my belly horribly, so that the skin around the corset rim was wrinkled in concertina folds, and forcing my tits up, to shiver like melons above my rubber restraint. Similar, smaller restraints clamped my ankles to each leg of the throne, spreading my beaver wide, to show pink amidst my wet blonde thatch, which I could feel dripping come, its fronds tickling the thigh-skin below my cunt lips. My wrists were placed in cuffs on the tip of the throne's armrests, but, to my surprise, the cuffs remained unlocked, and my arms were free. That was part of the game: I could reach down and unfasten my straps, if I wanted, or dared. Peter lounged in one of his million-dollar pop-art armchairs, pressed his fingertips together, and looked at me.

'You are privileged to sit in the penitential seat of the nunnery of Santa Rosa Dolorosa, in Vera Cruz, Mexico,' he said. 'It was for errant novices who had been caught enjoying carnal pleasure, usually meaning masturbation. The girl had to sit as you sit, for a day and a night – the so-called prongs of sin smeared with chilli paste, or else with honey, and a cargo of live ants wadded in her slit and rectum. If a girl pissed herself, as you may very well do, Trudi, you'll note that the seat is slightly concave, so the evacuation may run into the chamber beneath. An uncontrolled girl was obliged to consume whatever evacuations were in her chamber, before her release.'

I shuddered.

'Scared?' he said.

'Yes. What happens next?'

'You'll see. I expect you will take champagne,' he said.

'Yes, please,' I gasped, my corset almost unbearably tight.

Peter snapped his fingers. At a bound, the coffee table – the nude crouching girl – sprang into life. She rose to her feet, breasts quivering, and without facial expression, her naked, gel-slimed body padded into the kitchen. The cane-stripes on her buttocks quivered as she passed me.

101

8

Plaything

I suppose I must call my relationship with Peter Murchy an 'affair', although those words seem too dignified for our sessions, or one prolonged session, interrupted and resumed, of flagellant pleasure. 'Curiosity' might be better: mine was certainly satisfied, and my appetite whetted for more, at the hands of Peter, a true master, who in due course showed his mastership by dropping me, just when I had become addicted to him. Back to that first, nervous evening, though, which set the pattern for the rest, each taking me further into shame, pain and submission. No, it wasn't a curiosity – he had done it to countless other girls – rather, a programme.

The white-skinned, gel-smeared nude girl brought me a glass of champagne, which I held awkwardly as the arms of my throne were too narrow to hold it. Peter asked me to excuse him, went into the bedroom, and re-emerged wearing a black silk robe, tight-fitting, in place of his baggy pants and loose shirt. It was just an ordinary bedroom, not a dungeon or anything, except that the king-size bed had no pillow. I saw that his compact body was very muscled, and his chest billowing with steel-grey curls. He had crimson leather moroccan slippers, with curled copper toecaps. I sipped my champagne, while the nude girl brought a glass for Peter, then resumed her position before me, as a table.

Peter sipped, then placed his glass at the base of her spine, and stood. He opened a desk drawer and took out two implements: one, a thin cane, about two and a half feet long, light brown and shiny, the other, a simple ping-pong bat, covered in green rubber.

'Ottilie is a table,' he said. 'Use her as such, or she shall be disappointed.'

I placed my glass at the cleft of her shoulder blades, trying not to squirm both in pleasure at the exquisite pain of the plugs in my cunt and anus, and in the unspeakable shame of my spread thighs, exposing my juicing pussy. Tucking the cane under his arm, Peter took stance over Ottilie's bared buttocks, raised the ping-pong bat, and began a brisk paddling of the girl's croup. Tap! Tap! Tap! The slaps were measured, not harsh, but shifting, to cover the whole area of Ottilie's naked buttocks, which pinked and suffused to a deep, mottled blush.

'Any spanking must begin with a warm-up, to relax the gluteal nerves, Trudi,' he said, 'in preparation for the proper punishment to follow. I expect you know.'

After paddling Ottilie about 60 or 70 slaps, Peter laid down the bat and raised the cane to his arm's length, The cane flashed, whistled, and Ottilie's fesses quivered, no more than an eye's blink. Yet the top welt on her left bare buttock now glowed a deep, ridged crimson where Peter had lashed her with perfect precision. Neither wine glass had even trembled, and the only sound Ottilie made was a little gasp, that could have been pleasure, or agony, but scarcely surprise. I writhed on the prongs impaling me, as my cunt seeped heavy come. Peter delivered a second stroke, precisely in the next weal, and so on, until, in the space of two minutes, Ottilie's naked buttocks had taken eight savage stripes with the cane. She voiced no cry, and I am not sure she even blinked her eyes. The trembling of her caned bare fesses seemed to come from some nervous mechanism within her buttocks, out of her control. I was anything but controlled: the sight of that sumptuous nude body, caned so severely, and taking it so passively, made me desperate to be touched on my clit, and to orgasm. My desire grew, furiously, and my come flowed faster, in the knowledge that Peter was showing me what was in store for me.

'Ottilie is a good piece,' he said, removing the wine glasses from Ottilie's marbled flesh, after the eight strokes were complete. 'She drooled a little at first, but has learned to control herself. At first, she took eight strokes three times a week, then four times, and now, twice a day. When her croup has taken sufficient strokes, and her value accrued accordingly, she shall fetch a good price at auction. $150,000 is already too low, of course. She has taken 90 cane-strokes since then, five days ago, so a realistic estimate should now be $240,000. One must gauge these things precisely. At $1,000 a stroke, a greedy dealer might cane his piece up to the million or over – forgetting that at auction, the piece must repeat all her caning history in one set, without crying, screaming or breaking down. Another eight strokes – ten, to round the numbers – and Ottilie will fetch a quarter million dollars at next auction, after proving herself by a caning of 250 strokes.'

'250 cane strokes, *on the bare?*' I stammered, my heart thumping, and a chill in the pit of my stomach. *'No . . .!'*

Suddenly, I lost control; a jet of piss surged from my piss flaps, and gurgled, as the liquid washed my bush, cunt and thighs, before draining into the bowels of the throne. Peter smiled, and lifted the cane, pressing the hot wood to my nipples.

'Only with this oak rod,' he said, 'not a hickory, or full rattan. A good piece can take up to a thousand, with long-term training. The auction strokes need not be with full vigour, provided they are regular and constant. As long as she reaches her tariff in silence, she may squeal as much as she likes afterwards.'

'You . . . you talk of a living girl as a *piece?*' I gasped.
'In the trade, we call works of art "pieces". What greater work of art, than the body of a girl?' said Peter.

'That's *sick!* You're not going to make *me* into some *piece* in your sicko fucking auction!' I shrilled, realising at once how foolish I sounded, impaled on twin dildos, with my belly in a rib-crushing corset, my tits squashed up like tomatoes, nipples erect, and my pussy spread pink and wet, flowing with hot come, for anyone to inspect.

Peter laughed.

'A girl from *Plattsburgh?*' he said, mildly amused. 'Could *you* obey orders like submissive Ottilie, remaining immobile, as my table, until my uncertain return, and further instructions? I think not. You may be useful as a plaything . . . My plaything from Plattsburgh. Most apt.'

Only much later did it occur to me that Ottilie might have assumed her role as table only when she heard us approaching the apartment; but that would mean she had still been following instructions, to await Peter's catch for the night. By that time, I was indeed his plaything, and preferred to think of nude Ottilie, alone and still in that darkened apartment, awaiting her – *and* my – master.

'Let me see,' he said, as Ottilie crouched motionless, her caned bottom glowing. 'What parts are you most fond of, Trudi? What do you look at, when you masturbate in front of the looking glass? Don't deny you do, a girl as ripe as yourself. Is it those tits, or those lustrous plummy nipples? The delicious labyrinth of your cunt folds, or that obscenely lush forest, quite smothering your wet beaver? Your legs . . . Your magnificent big butt . . . I suppose we must experiment with them all, over time.'

'I'm not some dumb animal!' I said, though the delicious pain in my pierced rectum and cunt raised my voice to a shrill. 'Let me go!'

He shrugged.

'Let yourself go. Your hands aren't tied. I'll order Ottilie to fetch your dress, and shoes, and open the door for you, if you wish.'

I began to sob.

'You *know* I don't . . . Oh, *please,* do what you must do with me.'

Peter clapped his hands, and the girl sprang to her feet, still expressionless, and not a hair of her lacquered mane astray. She vanished into the kitchen.

'You have eaten lobster denuded of claw,' he said, 'at that ridiculous gathering. Now, I shall show you to a Maine lobster – *homardus americanus* – properly equipped with *two* claws, and who, moreover, is still alive, as other girls have found, to their painful satisfaction.'

I wailed, and fought hard not to piss myself again, as Ottlie appeared at the kitchen door, holding a giant, greenish-black lobster, its claws straining against their rubber bands.

'Don't worry,' said Peter, 'Ottilie has filed down the inside claws – *somewhat.*'

Ottilie approached, expertly holding the creature by its front claw-legs, while unravelling the rubber bands from the claws, which began to snap furiously, inches from my bare breasts. Ottilie lifted the lobster until the cold, slimy claws brushed my nipples. She moved the beast nearer, her face expressionless, and I screamed as agony seared my clamped nipples. She pressed the kicking lobster to my helpless breasts, then withdrew, to resume her squatting position. I tried to raise my arms, to tear the monster from my naked flesh, but Peter had quietly locked my handcuffs. The lobster's claws fastened each of my nipples in a grip like white-hot pincers, and my screams and sobs, and straining at my bonds, were uncontrolled, save by the insistent and agonising pressure of the prongs, cramming my butt and cunt.

'*Oh!* How *could* you?' I sobbed at Ottilie.

She did not reply, but kept her submissive crouch, looking nowhere, and without expression. At no point had her face showed emotion, not a smile of amusement, or even contempt. Like her, I was just a piece.

'Peter, *please!*' I gasped. 'I can't bear it!'

Shockwaves of agony filled my breasts and my spine. I writhed and squirmed and sobbed, driving the massive dildos further and more painfully into my bottom holes, as the claws of the lobster pinched my nipples to pale pouches of skin. Peter approached and put his hand between my legs.

'You are juicing well, plaything,' he murmured.

'Oh, God! Cane me on the bare, like Ottilie – give me 250! Just get this thing off me! Get it over! Please . . . *Ah!*'

Peter touched my clitoris.

'Oh! Oh!'

He began to rub my throbbing, swollen clit, as the lobster claws chewed my nipples, sending jagged mixed waves of pleasure and agony coursing through me.

'Ahh . . . don't stop . . . .ahh . . . YES!' I heard myself shriek.

My cunt was juicing frantically, my anus and pouch writhed on their dildos, and as Peter pinched my clitty hard, I scarcely noticed that my bladder was emptying again, flooding my thighs with hot, acrid piss, so strong was the orgasm that convulsed my belly.

'Oh . . . oh . . .' I sobbed, as Ottilie sprung into life again and removed the lobster claws from my bruised nipples.

Peter snapped open my handcuffs, loosened my ankle ropes and began to unlace my corset. I slumped on the throne, gasping, until he gently lifted me from the prongs that impaled my holes. They came loose with a gurgling, sucking sound, then a loud plop.

'I guess you're going to cane me now,' I wailed, 'and make me drink my own piss,'

Peter yawned.

'Next time,' he said. 'I'm tired, right now.'

'*Next* time? You certainly make assumptions!'

'Ottilie will give you your caning pants,' he continued, as if I hadn't spoken. 'You will wear them, and nothing else, under a raincoat, when you arrive at precisely 11 p.m. on this day next week. No make-up. Hat and umbrella are optional, depending on weather conditions. You shall travel barefoot all the way – taking a cab, of course.'

'Now, wait a minute –!'

Ottilie handed me my dress and shoes, as well as a package, containing soft material.

'Goodnight, plaything. You can let yourself out, I trust. Ottilie – pillow, please!'

Ottilie entered the bedroom and lay down on the bed, on her back, with her legs wide apart, showing her pink cunt-meat. Peter ignored me completely and followed her in, shedding his black robe. Nude, he lay on top of Ottilie, his massive erection jutting from his forest of pubic curls. Ottilie's hand moved unerringly, to seize the huge cock, just at the corona of the glans, and guide it into her slit, pressing Peter's butt, until his tool was right inside her cunt. Like me, Ottilie was a head taller than Peter, and, as he straddled her, his head came just to her ripe, massive teats. With his cock in her cunt, he buried his face in her breasts, and in moments, I heard both of them breathing heavily, unmistakably asleep. I dressed, dimmed the lights, and tiptoed out, holding my package of 'caning pants' (?), fearful of upsetting a coffee mug or other priceless artwork.

Only in the creaky old elevator did I expel my pent-up frustration in a hiss of rage. The bastard! Who did he think he was? What kind of pompous asshole said *weather conditions,* not just 'weather'? And not even giving me the thrashing I'd *dreaded . . .!* My fingers crept to my raw, bruised nipples, and my hand to my dripping cunt. My anus hurt terribly. The bastard! I was expecting to be shamed and caned, and to whimper for mercy! I thought of my naked buttocks quivering and red, darkening to purple, under that thin, whippy cane, while Ottilie held me down, leering at my agony, and fingering her clit. Then, the new agony, as that massive glans nuzzled my ass bud, and the cock-shaft penetrated me, plunged to my root, and fucked my asshole to bursting. How *dare* he! The *bastard!* Yet he had the nerve to put that mammoth cock right inside that *bitch's* cunt, and not even fuck her, but go to sleep, with his cock stiff inside the hairy slut's beaver! It was a slow elevator, and there was time for me to masturbate my soaking cunt to piss-wet, gasping orgasm before I reached the lobby.

Crack!

'You are three minutes late,' said Peter, and his palm crossed my face with a stinging slap as he closed his apartment door behind us.

'What? How dare you –'

Crack!

He slapped me again, harder. Tears sprang to my eyes, and I almost let go of the raincoat that I was clutching high, to cover my breasts.

'You are here to obey, plaything, not to ask questions. You have obeyed your instructions so far, as regards your attire, and caning pants – don't spoil my mellow mood.'

Caning pants, indeed! I had never felt so ridiculous, hunched in the back seat of the cab. Outer coats were cut low that year, so to hide my nudity I was obliged to hold the top over my breasts, which only drew attention to said nudity: that, and the fact that I wore only those ridiculous caning pants, like pyjamas or hareem pantaloons – *and* I was barefoot! – made me look like someone escaped from a mental institution. The rain was streaming, and despite my maroon beret and umbrella, my mane was plastered to my head, with water cascading beneath the dark blue Burberry.

The caning pants were grim prison-grey, as if to mock the sumptuous fabric, but the colours didn't clash *too* much. I had never heard of caning pants before, and, when I opened the package, thought, What funny pyjamas! But it was only pants, no top. They were of superb sheen cotton, like a dream nightie, with a bowstring at the back of the waist, and no pockets: baggy and shapeless, but ending in a pretty little lacy frill that clung just below the knee. They reminded me of baseball knickerbockers, only what made them caning pants was that the buttocks were uncovered. From the front, after I'd ogled the mirror some, I had to admit they looked really daring and coquettish, though, technically, quite modest, with the crotch bagged loose at the pubic bulge to focus attention on that region unseen. A turn round revealed my bottom entirely bare. Below the bowstring was just naked buttock, extending several inches across my haunches, and with the scooped aperture baring my thighs six inches below my underfesses. In chic circles, that would have been a knockout, and ultra-coquettish as fetish teasewear, especially as the garment was of such fine cloth, and could not, obviously, be worn with even a thong underneath. A single pull on the bowstring would send the pants cascading to the floor, thus fully exposing the wearer's naked pussy and buttocks. For Peter's purposes, though, it was a utilitarian garment.

For a whole week, I had sworn I wouldn't ever come here again – I wouldn't play his stupid games – I hardly *knew* the man, and didn't even know him *at all*, in the biblical sense, I mean, we hadn't fucked. Nor had he offered me the chance to bring him to orgasm, with my lips, or even my hand, That, too, is a way of knowing a man, as you lick the frenulum of his glans – that little fragile clover-cleft of flesh, so sensitive a touch will make any man a girl's prisoner – and listen to his cries when his spunk comes. Yet, here I was, cold and wet and frightened, slapped for being three minutes late, by a man I didn't know, whose manner indicated *he* knew all he needed, or cared, about the plaything from Plattsburgh. It wasn't as if I'd no other options – I'd met a fellow student, Kevin, a lovely muscleman from California, but a lamb in chaotic Manhattan. He smiled the sunny West Coast smile, but seemed a little taken aback anywhere that didn't resemble a beach, and wasn't sure how to approach women who had all their clothes on. He had bought me coffee twice, and I was waiting for him to gather the nerve to date me . . .

'A hot bath is drawn,' Peter snapped, 'although it has been cooling for three minutes. Fold your caning pants carefully, bathe for exactly five minutes, and put them on again when you rejoin me. Before you enter your bath, you will fill a specimen jar with your piss. It is sitting on a ledge, just inside the bathroom door, and you will replace the filled jar there. During your bath, you will masturbate to orgasm. Do not close the bathroom door.'

I took off my Burberry, leaving my breasts to swing naked.

'Anything else?' I said. 'By the way, where is the famous Ottilie?'

Smack! Smack!

'Oh . . .!'

He rewarded me with slaps to each of my bare teats.

'No questions, Trudi,' he said. 'After your bath, you will rejoin me, crawling on all fours. The thermostat is adjusted to maintain the equilibrium of your body heat, so you should feel no discomfort as you cool, after your bath.'

I opened my mouth, gaping – the *nerve* of the man, the sheer, odious *efficiency!* – but the scent and warmth of the bathroom drew me. At least I was allowed to *walk* in. The specimen jar was the first thing I saw; it was one of those clear glass kidney-shaped things, only with a little spigot at the bulbous end, like a wine decanter or something. Frankly, I was longing to go, so I just dropped my caning pants to my ankles, squatted over the jar, and pissed a good long stream of yellow fluid into it, until it was well over half full. My jet of piss was so strong, I didn't splatter my caning pants at all, which had been a worry. Peter seemed to have guessed my need, for right from the moment I had hailed the cab downtown, I was bursting to piss. I did as I was told, and replaced the stinky jar behind my bathtub. Well, I thought, wrinkling my nose as I slipped into the foaming bubble bath, after making sure my pants were folded as ordered, at least he remembers my *name*.

There was a clock beside the bath; I let the delicious suds soothe me, checking that my nipples weren't too bruised from his vicious tit-spanks, then relaxed, soaping every inch and crevice of my body, then closed my eyes. I conjured up one of my New England village fantasies, about being roped naked to the public whipping-post and flogged for sinfulness by the very blacksmith whose huge tool had made me sin, by lifting my virginal petticoats, parting my virginal thighs and taking the throbbing hard male-meat into my virginal cunt. I rubbed my stiffened clitty, feeling the oily rush of my come, silky and smooth against the soapy lather, the two consistencies mingling but not fusing. My fingers penetrated my cunt, then my butthole ... while my thumb pressed my clitty harder and harder, in circular, reaming motions, replicated by the movement of my index inside my anus. As I approached climax, the face of the blacksmith cleared, and Kevin, nude and erect, came into focus. I masturbated at the thought of him caning my bare ass, then at the huge West Coast cock that might await me under his pants, but that image too

112

faded, to be replaced by a body muscled and compact, and it was Peter himself I saw whipping my bare buttocks, and, eventually, entering not my cunt but my *anus*, with the giant cock I knew for a fact existed. I widened my anal aperture to let the mixture of suds and my own come float in, and my finger was silky against the anal elastic as my cunt gushed come, my clitty throbbed, tingling with electricity, and my belly heaved. I threshed the water, whimpering as I orgasmed.

I looked at the clock, and saw I had half a minute to go. I closed my eyes again, for just a few seconds more . . . to find that the ten minutes had passed, by a quarter of a minute. I hurried to towel myself, in a big pink fluffy towel from a scented pile – as any masterful male knows, nothing can delight a girl like the instant, melting glow of a fluffy towel – and, swiftly donning my caning pants, did not reconsider Peter's outrageous instruction. I noticed my piss jar had disappeared, but, without pause for thought, I rejoined him, crawling on all fours, still flushed from my diddle and the intensity of my orgasm. I blushed as I looked up at him – which he observed, smiling – but I had the sense to say nothing, until addressed.

'Our first game tonight will be the truth game,' he said. 'You have already incurred a caning for your lateness of arrival and in leaving your bathtub late.'

I shivered.

'What must I do?' I heard myself mumble, then cry *'Oh!'* as the cane bit me on the bare left fesse.

'I ask the questions,' said Peter, 'and give the orders. Nod your head twice, if you agree.'

I nodded my head, once – paused – then nodded a second time.

'You will take position bent over this footstool, Trudi, with your buttocks presented high and spread,' Peter commanded me. 'If I am displeased with your answer to any question, your bare buttocks shall be caned, but you shall take the punishment *in silence*. First – describe your masturbation fantasy in the bathtub. I assume you carried out my instructions and masturbated to orgasm?'

I nodded, twice.

'Good. Art has no room for bad faith. Go on.'

I bent over the little circular wooden stool, whose rim bit my belly, leaving my titties dangling at one end and my ass dutifully spread and reared at the other. I placed my knees apart and balanced on my fists, feeling my pussy moisten as I felt his eyes on my spread buttocks and cleft. I began to recount my fantasy of being flogged naked at the town whipping-post, haltingly at first, but with growing confidence, until – *vip!* – my bare buttocks jumped at a vicious cut from his cane.

'Ah!' I cried.

Vip! A second stroke sliced my bare, in the same weal. It smarted hideously, like a branding iron on my naked flesh, and I gasped, sobbing.

'It's the truth, I swear!' I blurted.

'Silence, girl. You seem to be under the misapprehension that punishment follows untruth. Life is, as they say, a bitch, Trudi, and so is punishment. Continue, leaving out no detail of your fantasy, or your masturbatory acts.'

That was one thing I learned about submission: the normal rules of cause and effect don't apply. A girl has her bottom caned, not necessarily for any crime, but because it is there to be caned. I obeyed my master, describing over-luridly my maidenly cries and blushes before I parted my thighs in that fantasy stable; the giant swollen tool of the blacksmith, as he penetrated my virgin cunny, the pain of my defloration; the worse, horribly worse, pain and shame of being stripped naked, roped to the post with coarse, scratching hemp, and flogged back and bottom by the man who had seduced me.

114

I say over-luridly, because, perhaps, some small part of me wanted to satisfy Peter's curiosity, and save my bare fesses from the dreadful slicing tap of his pert little cane. If so, it didn't work. I saw that my flagellant story, and that of my accompanying masturbation, with all the facts of my ass-reaming and clit-rubbing, had the effect of raising his cock. I punctuated my narrative with gasps, and frantic clenching and wriggling of my naked, reddening buttocks, as Peter's cane sliced me on the bare more and more frequently – *vip! vip! vip!* – a dry sound, like cracking walnuts. That was what the larger part of my intelligence wanted: to stimulate the sadist, so that he would reward my exposed ass with weals.

'The flogging takes place in public?' Peter murmured.

'Yes – all adult men and women are eager to witness my shame.'

Vip! Vip! Vip! I gasped, careful to stifle a scream at three stingers, right in my cleft, the tip of the cane brushing my wet cunt-hair.

'And your deflowering, in the stable: no witness there?'

'Why, no . . .'

Vip! Vip! Vip!

'Oh . . .'

Squirming, and panting hoarsely, I could not restrain a cry when the cane sliced right into the soft flesh of my open vulva, gushing come – the pain of a caned wet cunt is maddening. He seemed to ignore my broken rule.

'No faithful betrothed, to witness your degradation, and cheer the loudest, as your paramour flogs you?'

'Wait . . . wait a minute,' I groaned, tears blurring my vision. 'Yes, that's right! I forgot . . . My betrothed is there, watching as the brute fucks me, *with my consent*.'

'Really . . . Yet, he does nothing?'

Vip! Vip! Vip!

'Ah! He can't . . . You see, the blacksmith has tied him up, and forced him to watch, as he fucks me. And

115

. . . I laugh at him, as he reddens in shame, watching my cunt juice under fucking by another man's cock.'

Vip! Vip Vip! His stroke quickened, and my ass felt like a huge glowing coal, yet the come quickened in my gash as my belly began to tremble and flutter in the sweet, tingly rush that leads to orgasm. It was the new knowledge of my power I had, even exposed and whopped, to turn my master on. Fantasy feeding on fantasy . . .

'It is he who denounces you to the parish, I suppose?'

The cane-strokes were assuming an even rhythm now, with short pauses between each whop. I had lost count at 30, but had long since reached my plateau, where my coruscated flaming buttocks desired that and even harsher caning to satisfy and stimulate my itch: the delicious peak only a submissive girl knows, where punishment and reward are the same.

'Of course . . . but I cannot stop seeing the black-smith, even though he whips me so hard. No, *because* he whips hard! I want his tool, you see, and he has made me crave a naked whipping, too . . .'

Peter's cock was a massive bulge in his pants.

'Crave whipping? Only that . . .?'

Vip! Vip! Vip! My ass was a flaming mass of seared bare flesh, and between my cheeks, my pussy was a faucet of come, drooling in a pool on Peter's carpet.

'One thing leads to another . . . The blacksmith starts to fuck me in the anus! My first buggery is such hideous pain' – (I was able to graphically describe my own buggery, by Don) – 'but I soon find I crave that, too – especially as my brute of a lover *forces* my fiancé to watch! He owes him money, you see! How he blushes, seeing that giant tool not just in my cunt, but fucking my squirming raw anus, poking me right to his balls, and spurting the cream so hard it drips over my anal pucker and into my bush.'

Vip!

'Mm . . .'
Vip!
'Mm . . .'
Vip!
'Mm . . .!'
The clench and squirm of my seared nates assumed the rhythm of Peter's cane, as my fantasy transformed my New England blacksmith into West Coast hunk, Kevin. I knew my ass must be deep crimson by now, and the pain was intense, almost – yet, deliciously, never *quite* – unbearable, with the rod striking again and again in deepening welts. Peter was expert: he neglected not an inch of my bare, from the upper buttocks and haunches, where the skin is tenderest and bruises most colourfully, to the underfesses and top inner thighs, where harder strokes are required. Yet, enslaved and groaning in my whopped agony, I was subtly assuming control.

'I think of Kevin's huge cock, just fucking me and fucking me, doggy style, as he spanks my bare ass, making me come and come and come, drenching his balls with my cunt juice, until he's so horny, he whips out his tool and plunges it right up my ass, penetrating me without any resistance, my butthole is so greasy and clinging and hot for his cock to ram my ass root so *hard* . . .'

Vip! Vip! Vip!

'That is no fantasy, Trudi,' whispered Peter. 'You *have* been butt-fucked, if not by this western *cowboy.*'

'. . . and his come, so thick and hot and creamy, just filling my butt, and squirting out my pucker on to my quivering thighs, soaking my bush, stinking of his cock and my anus . . . and the feel of that hot cream right in my anal walls just drives my clitty wild, and my cunt is pouring with come as I diddle myself, and I orgasm, masturbating as he spurts into me . . .'

Vip! Vip! Vip! Vip! Vip! Vip! Six slices took me directly on my squirming anal pucker and cleft, and the

117

pain was so dreadful, I screamed and convulsed in orgasm at once. My ass felt on fire, and the come spurting from my pussy was like bubbling lava.

'*Oh! Oh!* Ah . . . yes . . .' I sobbed, gasping, as my cunt gushed come. '*Yes . . .!*'

'Go on with the fantasy,' said Peter.

'Uhh . . . I can't. It ends there. That's when I came,' I lied.

I didn't want to give him too much power – to know that I'd actually come masturbating at the thought of *his* cock fucking my ass.

'Would you like me to bugger you, Trudi?' he said.

'You know I would . . . *Master*,' I panted, and it was the truth – I'd wanted my story to goad him into action.

He smiled thinly and opened the closet. Inside was a nude female, trussed entirely in white ropes, which left only her nipples and pubic region fully uncovered. Her mouth was open, the lips and teeth forced wide by a metal brank, like a surgical speculum used to hold the vulva open, and which seemed to be made of a bent wire coat-hanger – a nice thrifty touch, I thought, unless it was another million-dollar piece of conceptual art. Her throat bobbed in a constant swallow, for, hanging in a tilted wine basket above her lips, my piss jar dripped yellow fluid on to her tongue through the opened spigot.

Her arms and legs were bound fast together, and she leaned backwards on the wall of the empty closet, her body's weight taken by a single thin chain, taut from the ceiling, whose end knotted in her abundant cunt fleece, which was almost pulled from its roots. Two thicker chains, bolted to each wall of the closet, ended in bulky nipple clamps, and stretched her titties into wide flaps on either side of her, tightening when her loins jerked up, to ease the pain on her wrenched pube fleece. Her feet dangled helplessly, inches from the carpet, and the wrenched slit of her vulva glistened with come and piss, which soaked the intricate knottings around her buttocks and thighs. Peter put a finger into her slit, and took it out wet with her come, pressed it to his lips, and licked it.

'Your story has so excited Ottilie,' he said, 'that, in fairness, she must have prior claim. It was a test, you see. If her cunt remained dry during your story and the sounds of your caning, she might be unbound. Sadly for her, she has failed, and must be punished for giving way to her brute female instincts. You may leave, Trudi, if you wish, or stay, and witness Ottilie's humiliance.'

Ottilie's face was wet with tears, as she shook her head frantically from side to side, her eyes beaming pure hatred at me. Drops of my piss spattered her face and tits as her head jerked. I looked up from my caning stool and saw the flaming crimson of my own caned buttocks. That small part of my brain yelled, *No! Don't go too far too fast! What would mom say . . .?*

I felt a surge of guilt: I hadn't called mom in ages, but wasn't it mom who had beamed so, after my father took her upstairs for a spanking? Wasn't it mom who always insisted that good manners, and consideration for others, were the highest morality?

'I . . . I couldn't be so rude as to leave, Master,' I said.

9

Voyeurs

The ropes that bit and bruised so cruelly on Ottilie's nude body were pure white silk. It was frightening, but fascinating, how her whole pubic skin, and her bush, were pulled into a kind of pyramid by her fleece chain. Frightening, because it must have been terrifyingly painful, but fascinating, because . . . all fascination is imagining yourself instead. Naturally, I wondered what her punishment was to be for allowing the sounds of my caning and my fantasy confession, to excite her. I couldn't blame her for exulting in the tap-tap-tap of Peter's cane on my bare, as I guess it wasn't fun to have to drink another girl's piss. I assumed she knew it was mine, and got satisfaction from my own pain. Maybe, I sensed with a shiver, my fantasies were her own reality.

Peter ordered me to rise from my caning position, and I did so, gingerly rubbing my welted buttocks through the open caning pants, which were soaked with my come, and translucent where the voile clung to my thighs and pubis. My weals were very painful to the touch, yet I continued to caress myself, digging my fingernails into the rutted welts which criss-crossed my bare bottom, and which were hardening like corrugated board. Ottilie stared at me with malevolence, sensing, I supposed, a rival for the giant bulge at Peter's groin. Would it be *my* cunt he chose to enter and not spunk in

120

. . .? Mischievously, I jiggled my bare tits at Ottilie's roped ones. As I leaned forward, I got a close-up view of her distended vulva, and saw that the space between her inner and outer labia was curiously wealed with marks, like tiny whipmarks, radiating out from her cunt in a pretty pattern – as though she had been caned by elves, with tiny little elfin wands, which was of course impossible. Peter noticed my interest.

'Ottilie has been a candle girl,' he said, 'while working in the *wild west*. Now, to her punishment.'

I was curious what a candle girl could be, but also curious that Peter's sneers about the west went a little further than the New Yorker's normal disdain for anything beyond 10th Avenue. Not that I knew for sure Peter *was* a New Yorker, or even an American, come to that – his voice was one of those fruity cosmopolitan ones you hear in old movies from the 1930s. My thoughts wandered to Kevin. *He* was from the golden, whole-wheat-toasted west, and looked it, and I inspected Ottilie's porcelain white New York body with a slight glow of pride at my own nudist's suntan, however faint, and of course with my bottom skin marred by the dark bruises of Peter's caning. I mean, Ottilie was strongly muscled – as I was to find out – and in rude health, yet her skin was *really* white. It wasn't a New Yorker's sunless pallor, which is just an absence of colour, but a white that *was* pure colour, glowing, like fine antique marble. You could see her veins and arteries, as though her skin was very thin, like a body-builder's, and the vessels pulsed with vigour. She wasn't albino – her eyes were hazel, hair glossy black, and her nipples, as far as I could see under their clamps, a deep pink – it's just that she was so . . . so *perfectly* white, like a sculpture.

The drops of my piss, spattering her tits, shone vivid yellow on that pure skin – one more reason for her to resent me, I guessed. She'd heard my confessed fantasy, too, about Kevin – could it be, by some staggering chance, that she knew Kevin, and had a thing for him? It wasn't unbelievable – I knew that Kevin liked to hang around museums, and here we were in an art dealer's apartment, so it wasn't far-fetched that Ottilie and Kevin were an item, or wannabe item, on her side. The more I thought, the more real it seemed – part of Peter's insidious scenario. Kevin seemed so innocent in New York, where every male's glance, especially at a body like mine, is like a big neon drool. Kevin was laidback – his easy charm suggested he had so much tan, jiggling, firm-bunned California pussy, he was glad of a rest to attend to matters cultural. Plus, he was always the gentleman, with an old-world courtesy that seemed more and more *western:* not the LA car chases, and explosions, and cops shouting 'motherfucker' that you get in garbage movies, but the sure, masculine serenity that allowed him to rise when I entered, bow slightly, open doors for me. Open a door for half the females in New York and they'd run screaming to the women's crisis centre. I blushed inwardly, understanding that he was a *challenge* – I wanted to see him in his habitat, flexing his pecs, or whatever it is musclemen do, on beaches in California, then whipping me cruelly with a sheaf of bark strips from redwood trees, sliced thin. I suppose if he'd been from Alabama, his courtesy would have seemed old southern, and I'd have longed to be whipped with kudzu vine wrapped in magnolia blossoms. After my few seconds' musing, he was even more of a challenge, now that I sensed a rival in Ottilie. She was a real sub bitch whose surly body language *demanded* whipping, but surely Kevin hadn't – would never . . . ?

My imagination had gone far enough for me not to demur, when Peter said that Ottilie was to be caned on the bare buttocks as part of her punishment, and that I was to administer the discipline while he watched. He released her from her suspension, simply by snapping her nipple clamps open, then, with his Swiss army knife, slicing a tuft of her pubic forest so that the chain sprang loose and her body dropped, with a neat hole where the cut hair had been, like the cone of a volcano. The flagon of my piss was nearly empty, and the spigot continued to drip over Ottilie's body, still completely helpless in her roped bondage. She was tied like a mummy, with only her tits, ass and cunt left bare, and I had to drag her, clutching her hair and pulling her wet titties – clawing her nipples to be precise – to the caning stool, still wet with my own come; then prop her on it, ass upwards. Her buttocks were tightly closed, so there could be no cleft strokes, but her bare globes were shiny wet with her come and sweat, and my piss, and I knew a bare-bottom caning on wet buns would hurt her all the more – there's a scientific explanation for that, I think. My duty suited me fine, in my new jealous-bitch mode. I was *sure* Kevin was fucking Ottilie – *sure* of it – and maybe she'd even drawn him into a little mild spanking. That pure white ass would get the whipping of its pure white life!

Peter handed me the cane. I didn't ask why Ottilie deserved punishment – Peter's explanation, according to the rules and structure of a submissive scene, was more than satisfactory – nor why I was to act and he to watch. He had warned me not to ask questions, and a well-trained sub knows not to. In fact, a really good sub says nothing, but can speak volumes with a pout, or squirm, if not beaten with enough manly vigour. I reasoned that my own role, though technically dominant, was really submissive, as I was offering my body in shame, the object of Peter's voyeuristic fetishism. I was right, but not quite right enough, as it happens.

I took stance beside Ottilie's trembling bare buttocks, with my legs crooked at the knees, and spread quite wide, to lower me for close work with the short cane. I felt the scooped hollow of my caning pants stretch, thus exposing my own bare bottom. Peter began to slice open some of Ottilie's knots, explaining as he did so that Ottilie was the *finest ropist in the west* – that sneer again – and had attended to all but the final part of her own bondage. The names of the knots slipped past me – cat's paw, sheepshank, surgeon's half hitch, and so on – but Peter explained that to add spice to her punishment, he would untie one of Ottilie's hands and leave her to free herself from the rest of her bondage, while I caned her. The faster she worked, the shorter her caning, so he advised me to lay my strokes fast and severely. I needed no urging.

Vip! I brought the cane down hard across those juicy white buttocks, leaving a most satisfactory little pink weal, right across her butt-meat. Her globes shivered, but didn't clench; she was intent on her fingering of knots in her breast area. Freeing her upper body would give her the leverage to swing round and loosen the ties on her legs. She worked fast, so I began to cane her bare ass hard and in earnest. Vip! Vip! Vip! Vip! Vip! Vip! My strokes were coming on the half-second – I was pleased to draw hoarse breath from her, and see those proud white buttocks pink severely, then start to twitch and clench, in anticipation of my cane-strokes. I felt come seeping from my cunt as her tender white buttock-flesh writhed, shivering and naked under my cane. Vip! Vip! Vip! Vip! Vip! I didn't let up, but the only sound from Ottilie, apart from her increasingly hoarse, rasping pants, was a muttered 'fucking bitch!' Peter, behind me, clicked his tongue, and said that as punishment for her 'little lapse', Ottilie would have to describe to *me* her expertise in degradation, and how she came by it, otherwise her flogging would begin over. Vip! Vip! Vip! Vip! Vip! I sliced her hard, with five fast stingers right on top ass, just below the spinal nubbin, where the skin is thinnest and the cane most painful.

'Uhh . . .' Ottilie moaned,

Vip! Vip! Vip! Vip! Vip! Vip! I followed those with three whops to each haunch, the side meat now starting to blossom luridly, as haunches always do. A hand – Peter's – clamped my juicing cunt and began to masturbate me. He would pause, to stroke my whole anal and vulval cleft, wiping my copious come over my perineum and anus pucker, and that made my come gush faster. A caner, I submitted to the grossest of pawings, from a master's hand unseen. Vip! Vip! Vip! Three strokes to underfesse . . .

'Ahh!'

That shriek was from *me*. I felt Peter's hands clutch my hips, and with one smooth, brutal thrust, his cock impaled my anus, sliding up my come-greased ass tube like a piston, and monstrously filling my rectum. I gasped in pain and dread, mixed with shameful delight, as he started to ram my asshole with pitilessly hard thrusts. I sensed that he was in total control, and was going to butt-fuck me senseless, until I myself gave way and orgasmed, but without giving me the satisfaction of his cream's spurting at my anal root. As I was buggered, I continued the caning to Ottilie's now crimson derrière, timing my strokes to the rhythm of my buggery – two cane-strokes to each plunge of Peter's huge hard cock in my anus shaft. Peter purred that Ottilie would now please tell us how she had become addicted to filthiness. Ottilie started to speak, whimpering at my caning, which quickened in time with Peter's penetration of my anal elastic.

'I never meant this to happen,' she sobbed, her crimson bare buttocks squirming fiercely under my cane, though no less than my own croup, with my hole impaled by Peter's sword. 'I did it for money, at first, to pay off my debts . . . I'd do the dirtiest things, and then I understood that I liked the shame and the pain, because, being in debt, I *was* dirty. They were so subtle.

My training was mild, pleasant even. My breaker-in was a gentle young stud, who intrduced me to – to all the things I'd have to do, but at my own pace. Anal and oral sex, toe jobs, hand jobs, everything, including taking basic bare-ass spanking. Putting things into myself – at first, just Hershey bars and fun stuff like that, but weirder and weirder, like, bending over backwards on my fingers and toes, with burning candles in my ass and pussy, to be trained to assist at poker games and such, where the room's only lighting was from candle girls. You had to let it sputter down until it burnt out in your pussy juice or ass grease, without making a sound, though it truly hurt. Then the drips of hot wax around your cunt, that hurt all the time, too, but you couldn't moan or anything, on pain of a titty-whipping. They would make a really big dildo of frozen KY jelly that I had to masturbate with until it melted. I learned to masturbate to orgasm – *real* orgasm – while people watched. Then the stable mistress introduced me to the crop, then the whip, then the cane. My pain threshold grew, but I wasn't getting paid during training, so I was eager to start working with customers – soonest started, soonest over.'

What – Ottilie was some kind of *whore?* Vip! Vip! Vip! *'Ahh! Please . . . no!'*

Peter clicked his tongue, whether in approval or disapproval of her plea, I couldn't tell. I was finding it hard controlling my own breathing, and my urge to groan, as that huge cock thudded with merciless power against the root of my anus. Peter's cock was rock-hard, seeming scarcely human, though fleshy hot: as if he buggered me with a heated crowbar. A man's stiff cock speaks to a girl, begging to release the spunk from his balls into her wet, warm place; Peter's didn't. It was, literally, a tool. My body was lathered in sweat, and my caning pants saturated with come gushing from my swollen slit, so that drops fell from the voile on to

Peter's carpet. My belly trembled, and I knew I'd come soon – delight at Ottilie's reddened fesses and the gorgeous pain of my own buggery added up to too much pleasure not to orgasm.

Vip! Vip! Vip!

'*Ahh*! Oh, please, not so *hard . . .*'

'Good, good,' said Peter, his breath only mildly excited as he pounded in my butthole. '*Harder*, Trudi.'

I obliged, slicing the weals of that bare, now plum-coloured flesh as hard as I could; despite her sobs and whimpers, Ottilie was making progress at unscrambling her knots of bondage.

'It wasn't so bad being a maidservant,' she whined, 'and you got used to the harness and leash and stuff. Even the pony races weren't too bad, though girls always got more of the whip than was needed to make them run. It was the *private and particular* sessions that I dreaded, and then came to crave. The men treated me like an animal. They tied me up, and whipped me – fucked me, of course, but also made me take it in the ass, then lick their cocks clean. Twosomes, threesomes – I always had the most painful or dirtiest of it. Like, I'd have to suck a guy's cock, while another guy buggered my asshole, and another fucked my cunt, and all of that while the stable mistress whipped me. It never stopped! Five or six sessions in one day, sometimes, until I hadn't an inch of skin left unwhipped, and my pussy and asshole were on fire.

'Often, I'd have to pull a train – ten or more cocks, one after the other, in either hole, or both, and spanked or whipped before and after. There were worms, chilli peppers, even live crawfish, put up my holes while I was whipped, and the guys placed bets on how long I could last without crying. The horror is, *I came not to mind.* Then there was the bondage – at first, the rope mistress tied me, but later, she showed me how to do the knots, and I was able to present myself to the customers

127

already halfway bound, which they liked. I was their fantasy figure, see, it was as though I never spent a moment unbound, and all they had to do was tighten me up, as I really wanted. Soon, it *was* what I really wanted! No gag or cunt clamp or nipple vice too tight, no brank or ankle hobble too heavy. If I was alone in my pen, I began to miss it. It was like, if my ass wasn't smarting from a whip or cane, or my tits and cunt left unclamped, no one really cared for me. I was nothing but a female animal, to be harnessed and whipped and used, and spied on. All girls like attention, and I came to crave the attention of filthy perverted voyeurs as the highest honour. I wanted them to drool at my whipped bare tits and ass, and even my caned pussy, and bet how many shot glasses I could fill with come, rubbing my clit as I sucked their dicks. I *wanted* to fill a whole row of shot glasses with come! That was their cruellest trick – crushing me, until I *longed* to be crushed, then rejecting me. I'd earned my ticket out, and I ... I begged the stable mistress to let me stay! But they kicked me out of there, said I was *old meat ...! At 21!* I came back to New York, paid my debts, and – began to seek out *the scene,* the creepy perverts I'd always detested so!'

My mind whirled, and I realised I had been masturbating, right from the start of Ottilie's confession, rubbing my clitty hard as Peter's huge cock pounded my anus, and still managing to land stroke after cane-stroke on the quivering jellies of Ottilie's bare croup. I was not long to orgasm – but what was this 'stable'? Some weird whorehouse, where girls were kept in pens, and brutalised beyond belief? Yet one which they joined willingly, and, once broken in, didn't want to leave? And where?

'You haven't told us of your specialty, Ottilie,' Peter said. 'That for which your alabaster skin so admirably suits you ... *the slab job.*'

Vip! Vip! Vip!

'Ahh!' Ottilie screamed, and those were my last cane-strokes, for Ottilie's knots were loose, her legs apart, and I'd landed three stingers right on her shiny, juicing cunt, which poured come all down the rope-burned skin of her thighs.

I saw her anus bud, and like her inner labia, it was ringed with the elfin weals of a candle girl. There was a plop, as Peter suddenly withdrew his cock from my anus, leaving me gasping on the brink of orgasm. I was going to continue masturbating – just a few more twitches to my clit would have brought me off, at that stage – but Ottilie at once turned on me, with vicious claws to my nipples, and began to pull my hair. I felt an agonising thump as her knee connected with my throbbing stiff clitty. I lashed out in response, punching her on the tits, face and belly, then drew back, to kick her full-leg in the cunt. She howled, and went down, and soon I was squatting on her tits, with her hair wound round and round my wrist, pulling it by her roots. I began to slap her face, pausing to reach behind me and punch her belly or cunt, which was gushing thick oily come as she squirmed, her titties pinned helpless beneath the soaked crotch of my caning pants.

'You fucking bitch!' she squealed.

'Whore!' I hissed in return.

'A contest, shall we say,' Peter murmured. 'The winner to be awarded slave's duties for tonight . . .'

I really wanted to hurt her – even though I'd caned her bare ass purple, that didn't really seem like actually hurting her. So I continued to slap, gouge and punch. I was furious that she'd deprived me of Peter's cock – I wanted that monster in my ass again, or in my cunt, even if he didn't spunk, just so I could masturbate myself to repeated orgasm. *I* wanted to be the pillow that night! My punishment of the *bitch* (!) was made easier if I twirled my pelvis so that my cunt slopped on her bare titties – slopped, I mean, because I was gushing so much come. As I slapped, her erect nipple was rubbing my own throbbing clitty, like a little dildo or a zucchini or something, and the thrill was maddening. Every punch or slap, and I'd feel electricity jolt my belly and spine, as that nipple tweaked my clit, and my cunt was just a *lake* of come, and suddenly I just *shrieked,* for I exploded with the most massive orgasm I'd had for ages. I turned, gasping in triumph, to see Peter, holding my beret and raincoat, ready for me.

'What –?' I began, looking from his suavely smiling face to Ottilie's, grinning fiercely.

'It seems that Ottilie is the *victrix ludorum*,' Peter said, 'so *you* may go home, plaything, and await my call.'

I won't go into how speechless and indignant I was in that creaky old elevator, nor how the super raised an eye at my come-soaked pants as I went through the lobby, with droplets of come still trickling on my bare feet. I could give lessons in being speechless and indignant in elevators in New York City.

Of course the call came, and of course I answered it, ever curious as to what new punishment, new shame, but the same frustration, Peter had in store. He used me for a tool, refusing to surrender me his spunk. But the shame was real, the whippings were real, and I craved them. Each role I had to play whetted my curiosity for the next one. There were other girls besides Ottilie, and other men, too, who fucked me while Peter watched. Peter was a voyeur – yes, one of the perverted voyeuristic creeps that Ottilie had known she would find plenty of in her home town Manhattan. Her tale of being broken in at the mysterious stable was replicated by my own sessions with Peter. All I could gather about Ottilie's place of shame was, it was west of New Jersey – to my relief – and west of the Rockies, too. But there was a lot of empty territory west of the Rockies besides California, where such an establishment might well exist. My off-on courtship with Kevin seemed teasing, on his part. Did he seriously want to get into my panties, as I assumed men did, or was he playing some kind of game of his own? I freely confessed to Peter, as he caned me, that my fantasies of Kevin's muscular attentions hadn't gotten very far towards reality. Some of the scenes I played with Peter, though, became my own new reality.

Total housemaid was one, and, I admit it whetted my appetite for more. That's what Peter called his scenarios – 'whettings' – and, later, I understood why. I had to dress in ridiculously skimpy uniforms, frilly things and lurid fishnet stockings and pointy heels I could hardly walk in, with crotchless panties and peekaboo bras, real Frederick's of Hollywood stuff. I had to obey the silliest orders, like, fetch him a dry martini, then return to fetch the olive, then again, to fetch a second olive, again, for a pretzel, back, with a less salty pretzel, and so on, holding everything between my teeth, and, for each alleged mistake, receiving a short whopping on my raised bare ass, with the panties so gauzy as to offer zero protection to my bare. That was when Peter was in mellow mood. Sometimes, I was just tied up in ropes, full-body, as Ottilie had been, and wrapped around a pole, or a chair, to await caning, while he dined. He would make me take a bath, then dip my head in the water until my lungs were bursting, while he sliced my naked soapy buttocks with ten cuts from his cane, very fast. After a too-brief pause for breath, down went my head again, and I took another set, until the bathroom was awash with suds spilled by my threshing bare bottom.

Otherwise, a total housemaid stayed nude, hands tied behind her back, and ankles in a heavy wooden hobble bar. For most serving tasks, I had to crawl, and do everything with my teeth, each action accompanied by the vip! vip! vip! of that dreadful little cane, until my bare ass flamed. For cleaning tasks, I wasn't released – I had to clean the whole bathroom with my tongue, and wipe everything dry with my pubic bush. When my hands were unbound, I had to masturbate myself to orgasm, while Peter watched, before sending me home. He always asked about Kevin, and I told him the truth, that we were getting to know each other. Actually, I didn't have the *nerve* to hit on Kevin, and say straight up that if he wanted to fuck or spank me, he could – fearing an exquisitely mannered rejection. A girl sub has her pride.

After one such session, I was grimy and lathered in sweat, but Peter wouldn't let me shower. I had to don a frilly French maid's outfit to serve a small dinner for Peter and his guests, a thirtysomething couple slightly younger than him. The difference was, I had full girdle, garter straps and nylon stockings, but no panties at all, and my skirt was a ballerina's tutu that ascended rather than descended from my hips, revealing my entire naked cunt and ass. My pubic bush was peppered with little pink sequins, on stick pins. Neither Peter nor his guests paid me the slightest attention, save to give orders, and note whenever I made the smallest error in pouring wine, or other service, while wrinking their noses at my body stink. Peter had cooked the dinner himself, and it seemed there were a hundred courses. They threw scraps on the carpet, and as they were guzzling their after-dinner liqueurs, I was ordered to crouch and eat up all the scraps of food. Each took turns at caning my buttocks as I tried to eat, until I'd taken over 50 stingers on the bare.

That dinner was deemed a success, and Peter made my service a fixture at his soirées. His guests were always couples, younger than himself, and vaguely connected with the art world. They would dress conservatively, and with impeccable taste, while my own outfits, or lack of, were sluttish, with ripped stockings,

132

torn bra and the like. After sneers about lowlifes, they would make me masturbate for them, taking turns to cane my bare, never less than 50 strokes. At one dinner, I *was* the dinner, at least, the table setting. I lay nude on my back, wrists and ankles roped to each table leg. On my nude body, Peter balanced metal chafing dishes, heated by candles, with soups, meats, fish, hot rolls and everything. There was only a tin plate between my bare skin and the burning candles, so tears misted my eyes as I lay gasping and straining to keep absolutely still. In addition, Peter had stuffed my cunt brimful with foie gras, to which the guests helped themselves with their fingers, the object being to excite me so that my seeping come would flavour the foie gras. Whether I quivered and spilled soup or not, I always got a bare-ass caning. Peter was one hell of a foodie.

Once, Peter had as his guests Clarence and Janine, the owners of a new gallery, *'fétiche'* (small case) somewhere midtown. I gathered that it was terribly chic and *exclusive*, as if the name wasn't enough. There was to be an opening exhibition the next week, and Peter was invited. For that dinner, I was roped to the table belly face down, with the chafing dishes balanced on my ass back and thighs, and when the table was cleared, I wasn't unbound, but Peter asked me if I agreed to be dessert. I said yes. I knew it meant a whipping – which, eventually I got – but not before Clarence had buggered me, in full view of Peter and his wife: she had her skirt up to her hips, and was masturbating her cunt, while bending down, with pigeon-like jabs of her head, to fellate Peter, as her husband tooled my rectum. He had the grace to grease my asshole with my come, but I still shrieked and squirmed as he drove his cock straight to my ass root, no teasing or testing, just instant buggery – but I was roped so tightly that the table scarcely shifted. Clarence complimented Peter on the quality of his slave's asshole, nice and tight and elastic, but satisfactorily broken in. That was the first time I heard the word slave, referring to me, and it made me feel all giddy and tingly, and my pussy slopped with juice at the thought of being a man's *slave*. My come flooded the damask table linen, and when I felt Clarence spurt his spunk in my anus, I rubbed my clitty on the lacy pattern and shrieked in climax. I took 50 lashes with a three-thonged leather whip on my back, and 50 with a cane on my bare ass, as reward. I wept at the pain.

As a further reward, Peter arranged a dinner for two, in his own apartment, for me and Kevin! I was to explain that Peter was out all night, and I had borrowed his maid, and his home. Peter insisted that fine wines and candlelight would ensure my seduction of Kevin, with the veiled threat of a terrible whipping if I failed to deliver the show, which Peter would be watching from the closet. I felt a bit guilty about fooling Kevin in that way, but reasoned that what he didn't know wouldn't hurt him, so I went through with it. Peter even bought me a new dress, a silk dinner dress with only one strap, and covering not too much of me: also, new shoes, stilettos, of course, and stockings and garter straps. He forbade me to wear panties. With Peter comfortably seated in his closet, I installed myself in one of his chairs that wasn't an actual artwork, with the the maid-cum-cook busy in the kitchen. It was Ottilie!

She wore a starchy but very decorous 19th-century-style uniform, and called me 'ma'am', just like a real English maid, without a hint of our previous meeting. Ottilie was a splendid role-player. Kevin arrived, and, keeping complete silence, she served a fabulous meal, Californian-style – salads with funny names, Belgian this, and Swiss that, raw fish and so on. We made small talk – Kevin said his work was in animal welfare, at some kind of dude ranch, which made him seem even more of a West Coast good guy – but with both of us wearing the *fuck me* look. When Ottilie had cleared everything, and seen us to the couch with coffee and liqueurs, she took her leave, and . . . we did it. He was so gentle and kind, even though he ripped my dress off me a little too hard and the strap broke, and he promised to buy me *two* new dresses. I fellated him, and we fucked three times on the couch, once in my ass. His cock was even more fabulous than our gourmet meal – I mean, it felt bigger than Donkey Don's, bigger than Peter's, bigger than anyone's had a right to be, as I lay, squirming and impaled, with that monster shooting glorious pints of hot cream up my cunt or anus. Though we were nude, at one point he asked me to put my dress back on, which was ruined anyhow, and he ripped a hole in the crotch and fucked me through the hole in my dress, which was just a sopping rag of my come. He said it turned him on that I wasn't wearing panties, but out west, split-crotch ones were popular. It gave a guy a thrill to be fucking a girl with her clothes on, and it thrilled me too.

'By the way,' he said, as he was butt-fucking me, 'right now, I'm technically Nevadan, not Californian.'

'Same difference,' I gasped, although Nevada sounded so much more empty and menacing and exciting.

'You easterners,' he laughed, pounding my butthole.

In between fucks, I sucked him off, making him moan, as I tongued his frenulum at the apex of the glans, and bringing him to rigidity almost at once. He had such power – his balls were beautifully big, which accounted for all the spunk I drained from them. I like a man with big balls, as well as properly hung. I suggested a spanking, and he pretended to think I was joking. When I assured him it turned me on, he gave me a master's spanking, in silence, with over 100 slaps, until my bare ass was seared crimson. I bet him I could take a strapping with his leather belt, on top of the spanking. Like our fucks, my belting was accomplished in almost professional silence. I can't deny, knowing a voyeur was observing me made my cunt really wet. We parted with kisses, and Kevin told me to compliment Peter on his maid.

'For a New Yorker, Ottilie was certainly quick to learn western cooking,' he said.

Moments later, Peter emerged from his closet, and purred that my performance had been so *satisfactory* that he proposed to accept the invitation of Clarence and Janine to bring one of his slaves to their gallery opening. He ordered me to report promptly, and I agreed, though miffed that even after my performance, and with an obvious hard-on, he didn't ask me to spend the night. I should have *known* – just as I had my raincoat on, *Ottilie – bitch!* – let herself in once again at the front door, smirking at me as she proceeded to the bedroom, stripping off her clothes as she went. On my way down in my friend the elevator, I consoled myself that the one slave Peter was bringing to the gallery was *me*, not Ottilie. Then, I thought, how did Kevin know Ottilie was a New Yorker? How did he know she was called Ottilie?

10

Slutmaster

I was jolted awake by a hand at my crotch. I clutched it – the hand was Kevin's, so I clutched it some more.

'Easy,' he said, smiling. 'We're just coming in to land, and I was making sure your safety belt was fastened.'

It was, under his tuxedo jacket, which had covered me while I dozed, the whole five hours from the little backwater airfield several miles west of the George Washington Bridge. I was nude beneath his jacket, a curious attire roomy enough not to outrage the public, had there been any at 3 a.m., Eastern Standard Time. I remembered my shudder that the airfield might actually have been Paterson, New Jersey. I rubbed my eyes, and looked down from the porthole of the executive jet, on Pacific Time dawn streaking pink over yellowish-white desert. I shifted, my butt still smarting from the drubbing Kevin had given me at our scene in Peter's apartment, days before, and wondered if the pink sunstreaks over the desert qualified as a poetic evocation of my own naked backside. It was only days after Kevin's beating me on the bare that I realised what a master he was.

My welts took time to ripen and harden, but when they did . . .! My whole ass tingled like a big throbbing clitty. That may sound gross, unlike his belting and spanking, which were *so* subtle. By the way, I'm assuming that the reader is at least familiar with spanking by hand, and possibly caning, on the bare, thus with the subtleties thereof. If not, there should be no alarm at the large number of spanks or strokes a seasoned bottom can take, and how frequently fresh weals can be applied over ones still throbbing and stiff. Like a master chef, a good chastiser knows how to season the bottom under his command. Girls can take a thousand or more cane-strokes in a single session, spread over three or more hours – that's 'pace caning', not punishment drill – and I'm living proof. But I must backtrack, to explain how I came to be on Kevin's private jet, about to land in Nevada.

Before we parted, I'd agreed to meet Kevin again, at my own apartment on Varick Street – which was a reminder to me to pay the rent – the day after the reception at the *fétiche* gallery. I hadn't told him about that, as I imagined the pervery I would find there, hopefully with myself in the middle of it, and, while Kevin had beaten me effectively – still too early for my bottom to know just how effectively – I didn't want him to get the idea, just yet, that I was a 99 per cent committed pervert. Where was that final, elusive one per cent? Though I only sensed it at the time, that was why I agreed so readily to go to Nevada with him – to complete myself. How I regretted my decision, and so soon, and for so long, and so bitterly! Yet when I reached the magical 100 per cent, all was worth it.

I arrived punctually at Peter's to find him in his tuxedo, ready for the reception. I wore my voile caning pants, as instructed, otherwise nude, with nothing underneath, and nothing on top, save my trusty Burberry and beret. Peter opened my raincoat and fastened jewelled silver clamps to my nipples, covering them just enough for modesty, and held on a silver chain about four feet long. That was my leash. Then he applied red lipstick around the clamps so it looked as though my real nipples were on view.

He pulled the bowstring of my caning pants and they fell to my ankles. With three double-edged adhesive strips, he applied a huge triangle of black fur – a *vison*, or pubic wig – to my real, blonde bush, making my pubic forest twice as large as it actually is, which is way large, as I've told. I was instructed to pull up and refasten my caning pants, and I obeyed. A chauffeured limo awaited us downstairs, and this time I was bereft of my raincoat though permitted to keep my beret at a jaunty angle. My caning pants were sparkling and freshly laundered, of course, and the sheer voile fabric clung to my swaying haunches, outlining the ridges of Kevin's beltmarks, with the welts, visible on my fully-bared portion, glowing a sullen crimson. My jet-black *vison* was clearly visible through the dark gauzy voile of my caning pants' crotch, its hairs so thick, in fact, that the false bush stood out in relief. Peter led me by my nipple leash through the lobby, where the super's eyebrows had long since ceased to somersault, and into the back of the limo. The driver was Ottilie, wearing a brown uniform shirt, unbuttoned to show her khaki bra, with skirt and stockings and a thick leather belt, like a policewoman's.

That stole my thunder somewhat, but I lightened up when she deposited us at the gallery, somewhere in the 40s, I think. It had an awning overhanging the sidewalk, and a line of tough guys in black leather, shielding us from the photographers and street people swarming around. Peter got out, opened my door, and tugged my nipple chains gently. I followed him, as regally as my breast leash and bare feet would allow, through the open doors of *fétiche*, where my arrival was greeted in the vestibule, with applause, by a throng of men and women. The light was very dim, but all seemed dressed in normal evening wear, like Peter. There were minor celebrities I recognised from TV or magazines. I was the only pervert on parade. I blushed . . . I was furious! But

I showed no expression, and gradually my anger turned to an icy sort of joy, that is the joy of true submission. A *slave* has no *right* to be furious. I curtsied to the throng, as far as my nipple leash would allow. The leather-padded door to the inner gallery was unlocked, and the crowd made way for Peter, leading me by my breasts.

The gallery was smaller than I expected, and smelled fishy. I mean, it really smelled fishy. I stifled a yelp, as something sharp bit my bare toes, looked down, and saw the floor was a carpet of oyster shells. Behind me, there was a steady crunching noise, as the other guests entered.

I advanced carefully, grimacing in pain as the crustacean shells hurt my soles, but careful not to cry. The room was lit by candles, and the walls were covered in paintings. In its centre, a huge canvas sailcloth covered some kind of hung installation, suspended on ropes from the ceiling, obviously the *pièce de résistance*. Beside it, a second set of ropes dangled empty.

I gaped at the source of the candlelight, for every candle was stuck in the upstretched cunt of a nude girl, bent backwards in crab position, supporting herself on one arm only, and her body shining with gel. Each girl held a basket, wired around her waist, and holding several oyster shells beneath her cunt, into which her come dripped as she masturbated with her free hand. In the dim light, I saw that every picture was of *me!* They were *obscene* ... really obscene, showing me fellating cocks, ass jerking under buggery from some enormous tool, and caned or whipped on the bare. Had I really done those things, or been observed doing them? Numbly, I guessed I had. There was fervent applause, which I gathered was directed at me, or rather, my slave masters, Clarence and Janine, as the authors of this humiliating trick. They were not the only authors; from the shadows stepped Marc Robichault, whose exhibition it was. Now I recognised the scene in Montreal, the mischievous bodies of Yvette and Helena, my pain and shame in Marc's studio by the river. Yet his imagination surpassed reality: some of those things I could *never* have done! Or *could* I? I shuddered. Yes, I could. I *wanted* to. Marc murmured to me that he hoped he had read my dream correctly. He had, the bastard.

As the last guest entered and Clarence locked the door behind us, Janine pulled the cover off the centrepiece, the hung installation. *It was me!* I peered, as far as my nipple clamps permitted, and saw that it was a nude female, made up as my lookalike, blonde hair, tan body and all. She hung with her bodyweight taken by her knotted hair, wrenched to its roots, by her fingers, individually coiled in wire, and fastened to the end of a ceiling rope, and by a massive silver butt-plug, also held by a separate ceiling rope. Her thighs were spread, showing her pink, dripping cunt, the wet pouch-meat fully exposed. Her thighs were bent backwards with her toes touching her buttocks and her ankles knotted to her wrists over her crimson croup. Tiny silver bells hung from nipple clamps, which bit the nipple tips to white. Her shoulders bore recent whip marks, and her bare buttocks were livid with stripes of fresh caning. She jerked her head, stared at me, and winked, jingling her nipple bells. It was Helena. Peter gestured towards the ropes hanging empty.

'For you, slave,' he purred. 'It is a twin installation . . .'

Now I saw that the evening frocks I had vaguely noticed were not frocks at all but artful body paint. The females were nude, painted with dresses, complete in every detail, apart from their spike-heeled shoes, which were real. At a signal from Marc, each woman bent to pick up a pair of oyster shells from the floor and began to masturbate her clitty with one, holding the second bivalve's crust beneath her juicing cunt until it was sufficiently filled with come, to offer her master. While the females masturbated anew, the males slurped come from the shell, careful not to spill any on their real tuxedos. Marc gave the bound body of his wife a push, and she began to swing, the ropes at her butt-plug and hair straining. It must have hurt her awfully.

'The theme of Marc Robichault's exhibition,' said Clarence, 'is "Slavery in Motion". Our friend Peter Murchy has been kind enough to contribute his own slave, a *Miss Trudi,* all the way from *Plattsburgh, NY.*'

Everybody cheered, as if I was a freak on some dumb TV game show. Janine made her way through the crowd – her dress, too, was body paint – selecting oyster shells from the baskets of the masturbating candle girls, and offering them to the guests. Peter drank; I was glad that as a mere slave, I didn't get one.

'When you are ready, my dear Trudi,' he murmured, through a drool of girls' come on his lips, tweaking my nipple chain quite hard and pointing at the set of ropes meant for my own body.

Janine pulled the bowstring of my caning pants and they fell to my ankles. I had to step out of them to walk, and they were whisked away, leaving me nude. I gaped at Helena's trussed and swaying body, her ass red with stripes from the cane, which Marc was even now fetching down from a wooden rack on the wall, beside a painting of me, nude, hogtied and caned on bare, sucking Marc's cock, and with a snake, stuffed or live – I wasn't sure – in my anus. I was sure *that* had never happened! Maybe it was going to. Part of me wanted it to.

'*When* you are ready, *slave,*' Peter snapped. 'The photographers will be here soon, and just think, Trudi, my plaything from Plattsburgh will be a celebrity in the big city! You'll have your 15 minutes of fame!'

'I . . . I'm not sure I *am* ready,' I heard myself stammer.

That was the other part of me speaking. There was a hiss from the crowd; crowds can turn nasty. Marc swished his cane, with an awesome whistling, before it cracked on Helena's bare buttocks, just above her toes. My tethered lookalike body jerked, frantically, and she gasped in pain.

'Come on, slave,' hissed Peter. 'Don't let's make you suffer more than you need. *Some* pain, for *lots* of fame!"

At that, the *one* part of me vanquished the other. That is, my New England puritanism surged. I knew what Peter was about – the pop art, 15 minutes of fame, all that tacky 1960s shit – I didn't *want* to be a 15-minute Manhattan celebrity for creeps in Jersey, reading tabloid trash. I wanted to be *real*. I gasped, as a jet of cold liquid squirted my bare ass; it was KY jelly. That squirt was followed by another, and another. Peter had my nipple leash tightly coiled, immobilising me, as body-painted females pawed and clawed at me, rubbing the greasy gel into my skin, and beckoning me towards the ropes, where Marc stood grinning, ready to bind and hang me beside his wife. I pissed myself, a long, frightened yellow stream that steamed and hissed over the naked females. Some of them opened their mouths to drink my pee; one lifted a brimming oyster shell to my own lips, and tried to make me drink my own fluid. I felt fingers stuck into my cunt, and they went in easily, to come out oily.

'She's juicing!' cried a woman.

I *was* wet; it added to my shame, and my fear. Wet beaver means a girl *wants it*, no matter what! My head spun; I didn't see the tall tuxedo emerge from the shadows, until he had scooped me in his arms.

'Lady says she isn't ready to party,' said a familiar western burr.

'*Kevin!*' I gasped. 'What –?'

'Time to get you out of here,' he said, smiling to the guests, who all drew back. 'How'd you like a vacation from all these here *New Yorkers*? My jet's due to take off for Nevada in a couple hours. Things are *real,* out west . . .'

He unclamped my nipples and hoisted me over his shoulder, like a calf for roping. I felt his raw male power and my pussy moistened.

'Yes . . .' I moaned. *'Yes!'*

Kevin took off his tux jacket and covered me in it, as we climbed into the waiting limo, just like the one which had brought me. I was beyond surprise that the driver of our limo was, once again, Ottilie. And then Kevin assured me the rent on my Varick St apartment was taken care of. And that he had known Peter, Clarence and Janine for some time, via Ottilie herself, who drove in stony silence.

'We like to keep an eye on the scene back east,' he drawled, as we sped through the New Jersey night, towards the airfield. 'In fact, we own Peter's building! We funded the gallery, too. That's why I could lift you out of there, girl. Peter is kind of strange. His wife treated him badly, and fucked around a lot. It got so she treated him like a slave, and fucked other guys in their own home, with him having to watch, you know? But the more she treated him like dirt, the more he wanted her, so he turned addiction into virtue. He became a voyeur, went out and found studs for him to watch, as they fucked his own wife's brains out. She left him anyhow, and he was heartbroken, and still wants revenge, kind of. His wife was a big blonde girl, very like you, Trudi.'

'Then you knew our scene was a set-up!' I blurted.

'I *guessed*,' he said. 'Peter hoped I'd really hurt you.'

'But you didn't,' I said. 'I liked what you did.'

'I know,' he said. 'It is entirely up to you if you choose to . . . to go further.'

My spine tingled, and I felt my pussy start to moisten.

'So "we" are rich', I said. 'Who *is* "we"? This dude ranch of yours?'

He laughed.

'It's a little more than a dude ranch,' he replied. 'It's called the "First Amendment" – cute, huh? But serious. We just call it the stable, mostly, although, as a girl stable, it's more luxurious than most. It's partly a casino. You could say rich – don't forget, only in Nevada is gambling legal, statewide, and Americans spend more on gambling each year than on all other entertainment together. The name comes from our belief in the constitution, American values, and the American way. *Freedom,* Trudi.'

'The first amendment means freedom of expression,' I said, vaguely. 'I mean, politics, X-rated movies –'

He patted my thigh. I didn't mind.

'You forget the most important part of the first amendment,' he said, like some old-time preacher. 'Congress shall pass no law abridging the freedom of speech, or *the right of the people peaceably to assemble.* At the stable, we are a peaceable assembly.'

'And for what purpose?' I asked, shivering, and my clitty and spine tingling, as I could well guess.

'Entirely legal purposes,' Kevin said. 'Don't ask more questions until we get there, and if you don't feel comfortable with us, here is a first-class air ticket back to New York, from McCarran International.'

He handed me an envelope: inside was, indeed, a first-class ticket, in my name, from Vegas to NYC. We had arrived at Kevin's, or the First Amendment's own airplane, and he helped me out of the limo on to the steps. Ottilie saluted. Something struck my mind as we boarded.

'Gambling is legal in Nevada,' I said.

'As everyone knows.'

'So is prostitution.'

'That, too,' said Kevin, smiling at me. 'Want to go home to Varick St?'

'Nope,' I said, in what I thought was a western drawl. The airplane door clicked shut.

* * *

It was colder than I'd imagined in Nevada. Kevin said the desert was cool in the winter, but in early spring temperatures were scorching. The sky was always bright and cloudless, though, and the First Amendment – the stable – had the advantage of being right on a hot spring, so the earth was warm at any time of year. We landed at an airstrip, with minimum facilities, just a hangar, some kind of dark-glass lounge, and several executive jets parked beside the marked runway, that was no different from the hard desert around it. A 4WD, parked in front of the lounge, drove to meet us, and Kevin ushered me inside as soon as we were down the staircase. The vehicle had black glass so that you couldn't see in; as I sat in the back seat, with pink fluorescent lighting glowing beneath its soft black leather, I realised that I couldn't see out, either. Kevin took my hand.

'I'll have to explain just a few things,' he said, 'because you won't need to see me much, except in my official capacity, and I don't think *you* need much breaking in.'

'Now, wait a minute –' I began, as the limo crunched off across the desert, but Kevin put a finger to my lips.

'That's *if* you decide to stay with us, as a stable girl,' he said. 'The first two weeks are hard, but you don't even have to try them. The car will take you to Vegas, for a flight home. If you do sign up, I think you won't have any trouble being promoted, to croupier, or pleasure girl.'

'I *would* like you to explain,' I said, nervously accepting the impeccable *caffe latte* which had appeared from a machine in the back of the front seat.

I'll paraphrase Kevin's explanation, which fooled me into signing. It wasn't untrue, it just left out the basic reality, which was that I was signing up for serfdom, as a bonded servant, called 'slave' for the tastes of the stable's clientele, and, in reality, little better than one.

146

He was quite right to trick me, of course: submissive girls can be unreasonable creatures, and must be obliged to obey. The stable, grandly called the 'First Amendment', was a pleasure palace built around the hot springs I mentioned. This being Nevada, it was a resort hotel, gambling casino *and* brothel, catering for the most grotesque, or exquisite tastes – *sexual* tastes. The executive jets I'd seen parked at the airstrip were from all over the world, and belonged to men so rich that gambling with mere money no longer thrilled them. They gambled, instead, with girls' bodies. Of course, Kevin didn't tell me that exactly. He was more concerned I should understand *why* girls freely signed up for duty in the first place, and freely remained in service: money. The white desert haze that had greeted me on my descent from the plane couldn't have been more different from the rolling green hills of New England, but it was still America. I was quick to understand.

'We are the richest country in the world, in theory,' he said, 'and the US government holds in reserve one troy ounce of gold for every American – but it's purely symbolic. The Swiss, for example, hold 11 ounces of gold for every citizen. We get a lot of Swiss customers here. Wealth is an illusion, built not on gold, or production, and the pioneer virtues that made this country great, but on credit. Americans are rich because we spend money we don't have on things we don't need. It oils the machine. You've seen the TV ads from finance houses that can "solve all your credit card problems" – you owe big, and they take the deeds to your house and your car and such, and instead of having to dodge 20 banks, you only have to pay off one guy in dark glasses. Some people get stupid, and cheat, and then there is more than one guy in dark glasses, who can get angry with her. So a girl who likes shopping too much has a problem there. Then she remembers that she has one ever-renewable asset – her body. It isn't every girl that the stable can help – only girls who are, or can learn to be, totally submissive. Male staff at the stable spend time in the field as recruiters. A debtor girl may indenture herself as a bondservant, until she has earned enough at "beauty duty" in the stable to pay off her debt, which we have already settled for her, usually discounted at 50 per cent. She is free to leave the stable any time, with the risk that her creditors may consider the discount no longer applies, and want the rest of their money.'

I interrupted to say I assumed 'beauty duty' was sexual in nature, and involved spanking and the like.

'I wouldn't fool you,' Kevin said, fooling me, with his big cowboy beam, 'but no girl is obliged to do anything she doesn't want to. Only thing, if a girl is un-cooperative, her beauty duty takes a whole lot longer. That rarely happens – most girls compete to stack up those extra credits, to be in the slave mart or on the roulette wheel or poker table. Guys pay big, and expect obedience in return. For example, if a client buys you in the slave mart, he can gamble you away at cards to a new owner, or else bet how many strokes of a cane your bare ass can take . . .'

'*What?*' I cried, yet the familiar tingling thrilled my belly, and my pussy moistened.

'There's a lot of variety in gambling,' said Kevin. 'These are the highest of high rollers, guys who'll bet $1 million on which fly lands on a window first. The money isn't important, it's the thrill of play. Our guys like to play with girls, as sex toys, and play to the max . . .'

I wasn't sure I liked the idea of being a fly on a window, but the idea of being a sex toy was exciting. Suddenly, he rammed his hand into my cunt flaps. I cried out, but he withdrew his fingers and licked them, beaming at me again, as I wrapped his tuxedo round my naked body.

'Seems the idea turns you on, Trudi,' he said. 'Haven't you ever fantasised about being a high-class hooker, or an enslaved princess, auctioned in some oriental slave mart, amid the perfumes and spices?'

His fingers brushed my cunt again, and I gasped as he touched my clitoris.

'Yes, I have,' I murmured, feeling my cunt seep.

'The stable, strictly speaking, means only the accommodations where the girls reside, under the supervision of the stable mistress,' Kevin said. 'There is the games mistress, the ring mistress, the whip mistress, and more, all of which you'll meet during basic training. We call the whole place the stable for convenience. In fact, it is very large, and contains several gaming halls and theatres, adapted to various fantasy role-playing scenarios. There are no motor vehicles inside the stable, and all locomotion is on foot, or by old-fashioned western buggy, pulled by girls instead of horses, all polished up in bridles and harnesses. You're strong, Trudi, and might excel as a buggy girl. A versatile girl might find herself a buggy girl in the morning, a poker girl in the afternoon, and a harem girl at night. The important thing, every girl's progress is updated daily on computer – how many services she's *agreed* to perform, how many whip-strokes taken, how many buggies pulled, how many bare-breasted boxing matches she's won, and so on. It all adds up to dollars on her account.'

A printer whirred beside the coffee machine and a document slid out over my thighs.

'That's a standard contract,' Kevin said. 'Read it, and sign it, if you like. We're almost at the stable.'

His hands were at my pussy again, and I could not resist. I touched him between the legs and felt his massive bone.

'Aren't you going to do me, Kevin?' I whispered. 'I'm juicing for it.'

'OK,' he said, thumbing my clit until I was giddy with desire and felt the need for orgasm surge in my belly.

Casually, Kevin slipped out of his pants and flipped me over on my belly. The contract fluttered to the floor.

I felt his fingers at my come-soaked gash, then at my anal bud, oiling it. He penetrated my asshole brutally, without preamble, making me cry out in pain as he began to fuck.

'Oh . . . oh . . .' I heard myself gasp.

He slid a pen between my fingers.

'Sign the contract. It's only a formality,' he said, buggering me fiercely. 'For the voters' list, and your social security record.'

'It's just that . . . I don't have any credit card debts,' I gasped, writhing under him, as the fullness in my buggered asshole made my cunt pour with come.

'I know. That's why you were such an agreeable challenge. But don't let the other whores know. They'll either hate you or leech off you.'

'*Whores?* Wait –'

Brutally, Kevin turned me over, and slid his cock from my anus into my cunt, with a suctive noise. His cunt-fucking was as hard as his buggery; I squirmed and sobbed as the massive tool seemed about to split me in two, ramming the neck of my womb like a jackhammer. My gash was a Niagara of come. I was trying not to orgasm, to prolong the brutal pleasure of his ramming.

'Figure of speech,' Kevin said, his voice seeming distant. 'All a question of trust, in this business. You do trust me, Trudi, like a good *submissive?*'

My fingers scrawled a signature, somewhere on the contract, splattered and moist with spray from my juicing cunt. Kevin withdrew from my pouch and forced my head down between his thighs, with his glans at my lips.

'Now suck, bitch, and suck good,' he hissed. 'Swallow my wad, you fucking slut.'

His cock was slimed with my own come and ass grease. His fingers balled inside my pouch, and he began to fist-fuck my cunt, as I went down on him, gagging, as his massive cock thrust right to the back of my throat. I squeezed the shaft and tongued his corona and pisshole until I heard him grunt. One hand was pressing my hair down while the other fist-fucked me.

'You'll do OK, cunt,' he growled, with a heavy chuckle. Yeah, you'll do ...'

I licked hard at the base of his glans while the pisshole slammed my throat and his fist slopped, punching my vulva in my lake of come. I felt his cock tremble, in the onset of orgasm, and my own belly and clit flutter with it. I ignored the part of me that said something was wrong, that I shouldn't trust the man ... When a glorious hot cock is about to spunk in her throat, and her cunt is swimming, and she knows her bare ass is going to be owned and beaten by male brutes, a sub girl doesn't want reason. His first creamy droplets came, then his cock began to jerk spasmodically, as his hand pressed tighter on my mane, and he wrenched my clitty between finger and thumb. I shrieked as my vulva exploded with the lava of my own come, while I almost choked on the huge jet of hot spunk he disgorged into my throat. It kept on coming, spurt after spurt of hot sperm, all of which I swallowed, obeying his command, although it came so fast that some of the spunk overspilled on my face, and his tux, which already glistened with drops of my come. As the last spurts of his spend ebbed, he snatched the tux from me, with a snarl.

'Look at this, you sloppy bitch! Needs cleaning!'

The 4WD pulled to a halt and he opened the door, pushing me out, completely nude. I sat up, my head whirling, and tried to focus on the massive stoneworks I saw before me, until Kevin emerged, dressed, from the car, and pulled me by my wrist.

'I'll lead you through the maze,' he said, somewhat more gently, 'and then you're in the care of the stable mistress. That's the beauty of the First Amendment – the law can search us any time, but you can't land a helicopter in here – they have to get through the maze first.'

'What are you, Kevin?' I sobbed, bitterly. 'The chief seducer?'

He slapped my bare breasts.

'Listen to what's said!' he snapped. 'We all recruit, in the field. Here, my title is instructor – I *break whores in*! But you're *already* fit for the slave mart, you filthy fucking sub. If you want to know, they call me the slutmaster.'

11

Bondsmaiden

I wolfed down the coffee, bacon and eggs, and hotcakes with my favourite maple syrup, as I looked out the window of my new fabulously luxurious apartment. The elevator had taken us right to the top of one of several similar towers, each built to resemble some famous building, like the Chrysler building, or the Kremlin, or something out of ancient Rome, and I recognised a French château – all kind of tacky, Vegas-style, but cute. I figured that stable girls got to live in their own penthouses, just like the high-class hookers we were! Way in the distance was a racetrack with little figures, nude girls it seemed, under whip, and pulling racing carts. So far, it was as Kevin had said. It couldn't be that bad at all. I had visions of being summoned on the phone from my apartment to present myself in costume for whipping and degradation in slave mart, dungeon, or whatever, knowing that pampered luxury eventually awaited my return – just as I had known, that night of torture on the beach, with Cher and Elle, that comforting Plattsburgh wasn't far away.

In the distance was the bleached desert to the horizon; in close, was a maze of turrets and cupolas and domes, crammed together, as though I were encased in some medieval Italian city. It was kind of as I imagined Vegas, only more tasteful and compact. My brief glimpse of the stable complex, from the outside, had made me think of a *ziggurat* from ancient Ur: after we had passed the uniformed guards at the high security hedge, prettily decorated in topiary nude females, we reached a fortress, or temple, the walls tapering upwards as if to form a pyramid, but stopping halfway. Kevin placed his handprint on to one slab of rock, and the wall slid noiselessly open to admit us. The only thing Kevin said to me was that I would be taken to my quarters. The entry maze had given me a foretaste of the stable entire: impossible to negotiate, alone, the warren of passageways, circling and doubling back on themselves. Kevin deftly led me, nude and shivering, on a hempen halter, until we came to a vestibule like a hotel lobby, with a lady waiting to take my leash from Kevin. I assumed her to be the stable mistress. She took hold of my rope and dismissed him, after his greeting 'Hi, Miss Verri! Nuther live one!' The lady introduced herself curtly as Miss Veronika Kuhl, and ordered me to address her as 'Miss', with just a moue of distaste at my filthy state, before we whooshed up to the top floor in the elevator. The floors were not numbered. She did not let go of my halter until we were inside the apartment door, one of only two on that top floor.

That ride with Kevin in the 4WD must have all been a bad dream ... although, I could still taste his spunk in my throat, even after a long, scented and utterly blissful shower. I was wrapped in a gorgeous pink fluffy bathrobe, under the eye of Miss Kuhl – hey, another German girl! – with long, straw-coloured mane impeccably coiffed, and dressed in a crisp executive suit of black linen and white blouse, rather low-cut so that her push-up bra showed quite a lot of cleavage, and with the skirt short, so that when she crossed her white-stockinged legs I could see a shiny sliver of white panty, as well as stocking tops and straps. Her shoes – sharp, shiny stilettos – were white, too. She scrutinised the screen of the laptop computer sat on her thighs, through little rimless eyeglasses, perched on the upturned tip of her pert nose, and hanging round her nape on a gold chain. The maid who had served my breakfast waited docilely at the hot food cart, her hands folded demurely in front of the starched white apron covering her pubis and which was her only clothing, apart from pink mesh stockings and stilettos with garter straps and girdle to match and, bizarrely, white fluffy ankle socks over her stockinged feet.

Her bare breasts had big cherry-pink nipples, as if to match her wispy raiment, and the breasts stood very high and swelling, as though they had silicone implants, but I could see they wobbled and quivered as she breathed, so they were real. Furthermore, her nipples were pierced, and she wore a gold chain studded through the tiplet of each nipple bud, the chain being looped taut around the back of her neck, so that the natural pertness of her breasts had an added twist, of nipples permanently perked up, like big pink acorns. Every movement of her neck or head made her nipples and breasts tremble, so I could see her titties were real. She was a brunette, with her hair plaited in two braids, with pink ribbons, like a pre-teen, but she had a lithe, muscled toughness under her curves, making her easily my own age, as, indeed, was Miss Kuhl. One a maid and one a mistress – I already had a good idea of what it took to get promoted here, and ached for a look at the prim Miss Veronika Kuhl's bare backside. I could see it was very large and ripe, but not, I assured myself, equal to my own (!), and that her titties would spring out pretty big from her restraining bra, under which they couldn't help bulging, like gourds. Her legs were long, too, like mine.

'Well, Miss Fahr,' she said, looking up from the laptop screen, 'it seems you are quite an unusual bondsmaiden.'

That jolted me, just as I was slathering another hotcake with butter and syrup; the bare-breasted maid had already replenished my plate once and I still had room for more. Her words reminded me that I had signed something, in the throes of sex, that I had bound myself over, as – what was it? – an indentured servant. 'Bondsmaiden' sounded nicer, but meant the same thing: a virtual slave. But if this five-star room was to be my quarters, then the job had its upside, I reasoned. I peeked at the serving maid who faced me, although I was able to get a few tantalising glimpses of her bare ass: there were weals etched there, I was sure, as well as thicker stripes across her bare back. Her weals seemed faded; I imagined that she had won her spurs, as it were, and been promoted to maidservant. That made me moisten in my pussy, for I knew I should have to go through such an ordeal: by close scrutiny, I saw that her otherwise flawless bare teats were marked in tiny welts fanning out from her nipples. The thought of breast-caning made me juice more, and I felt my face flush.

'You may remove your robe, Miss Fahr, if you are too hot,' said Miss Kuhl, pleasantly. 'As Kevin has undoubtedly explained, in his way, you shall have occasion to spend ample time in the nude, here at the First Amendment. It is clear that you come to us not altogether unprepared.'

The far wall, facing my king-size bed, flashed with a huge image: it was a giant telescreen, and the image was of my own naked body, writhing under Kevin, with my legs wrapped round his back, as he fucked me in Peter's New York apartment. I gasped; Miss Kuhl smiled thinly. Image followed image: Kevin's buggering and whipping me, my buggery and caning by Peter, my fight with Ottilie . . .

'Yes, Miss Fahr, we know something of you: as for what happened to you in *Plattsburgh* – she pronounced it as though it was a German name – we may only guess,

156

and hope it inspired you. Obviously, it must! You have already discovered your *submissiveness,* and are unladen with money worries – a righteous example of *American virtue.'*

She curled her lip slightly as she said 'submissiveness', and pronounced the 'v' as 'f'. She also curled her lip as she said 'American virtue'.

'Kevin, though somewhat crude, is an effective tool,' she said, 'and judicious in his choice of candidates. Your lack of debt means you are here by enthusiasm rather than obligation. Before I explain further the workings of the stable, perhaps you might share the experiences that enabled you to join us so readily. I invite you to speak freely, Miss Fahr.'

The nude maid teetered on her pink stilettos and filled my plate with steaming hotcakes, fresh butter and syrup. I tried not to speak with my mouth full as I gave her the account of Plattsburgh, as already detailed above. As I spoke, she tapped at the keyboard of her laptop, murmuring 'mm' and 'so' from time to time. Once, she said, 'A barefoot! Fascinating!' The images of my whopped ass and fucked cunt or anus kept playing on the screen, as I ate, which was rather unnerving. When I had finished my tale, she snapped her laptop shut, and the image vanished. She placed the computer on the coffee table, took off her eyeglasses, folded them and slipped them into her bra, in the cleft of her breasts. Miss Kuhl smiled, her big mouthful of white teeth like a baby barracuda's.

'We Germans do so like to eat, Miss Fahr.'

I blushed! It was true. Was that a proposal of friendship?

'Sometimes, we are not picky what we eat. Your friends up north – Elle, Cher and Helena – seem eclectic girls, while our own Ottilie remains one of our most *provocative* outside agents. Are *you* eclectic, Miss Fahr?'

I lowered my head, blushing again, and my pussy unmistakably wet. Where was this going?'

'I guess I am,' I murmured in reply.

'Then you should profit from your term here, as well as financially. The First Amendment – I will call it the stable, as we all do – is a charitable endowment, devoted to the arts of pleasure and good taste. It totally differs from Las Vegas or Reno, while offering greater choice to the pleasure-seeking male customer – sometimes, female.'

She gestured outside, to the maze of rooftops.

'The stable contains chambers for every conceivable variant of sex pleasure,' she said. 'As a stable girl, you have a chance unique in the US, to profit from, and enjoy your body. Your first two weeks should pass easily, as you are already familiar with the devices of corporal punishment and bondage. After that, you shall find your own fantasies fulfilled, along with those of your various masters. A bondsmaiden's paramount rule is total obedience at all times. Take your robe off, please.'

I paused, in the middle of a forkful of hotcake.

'I'm sorry?'

Vip!

Still smiling, Miss Kuhl took her eyeglasses from her tit cleft and whipped my cheek with the golden chain.

'*Ah!*' I cried, dropping my food and clutching my face.

Vip! The chain lashed the upper portion of my naked breast. Sobbing at the twin smarts, and with trembling fingers, I let my bathrobe fall and exposed my nude body.

'What is your favourite colour, *Trudi?*' Miss Kuhl asked me.

'Red,' I said, automatically.

Vip! The little chain lashed me full on my bare nipples.

'*Uhh . . .!*' I yelped, as much in surprise as in pain, although that golden chain packed a smart on bare titties.

The sudden brutality took the edge off my excitement and told me to be wary. Miss Kuhl raised an eyebrow, expecting something.

'Uh . . . red, *Miss*,' I said, wincing at the pain in my nipples.

'How interesting. Most girls would have chosen a shade of blue.'

'I was thinking of the maple trees in fall, back home –'

'Are you sure?'

I bit my lip, swallowed, and blushed, for now I wasn't sure at all. Miss Kuhl pressed her point.

'Do you like being spanked on the bare, Trudi?'

'I can hardly deny the video evidence, Miss.'

'Let me rephrase. Do you truly *like* being punished with whipping?'

'No, Miss! I hate it! How can anyone like being hurt so awfully? I like the *idea* of it. The shame . . . the surrender.'

'You are submissive,' she snapped; it wasn't a question.

I hung my head.

'Yes, Miss,' I whispered.

'Therefore, you enjoy being whipped and humiliated.'

'It isn't a question of enjoyment, Miss. It is my nature. It is like going barefoot. I don't enjoy it as such . . .'

'But you would not feel right, if deprived.'

'That's it. Submission *works for* me, somehow.'

Miss Kuhl lifted her black linen mini-skirt to reveal silken white panties, matching her blouse. The panties weren't more than a thong, covering what seemed a completely shaven pubis. Her girdle and garter straps were white, too. She put a finger under the thong and slid her panties down her thighs. I saw that the gusset was quite stained at the anus.

'Kneel, and eat me, Miss Fahr,' she commanded.

There was no point in pretending surprise or ignorance, for I knew what she meant. She prised open the lips of her shaven pussy, and showed me deep shiny pink. She was already juicing – as was I. Her cunt was superb; the hillock delicately moulded in the shape of an upturned fruit bowl, atop perfect elongated whorls of inner and outer labia, and the clitty standing stiffly to attention. It seemed designed with military precision – even the seep of come I observed trickling at the bottom of her *labia minora* was drill-straight. I didn't need any encouragement: I wanted to eat that superb cunt, as a work of art. She began to finger her clitty, in precise, one-second taps.

'Hurry, girl,' she murmured. 'I cannot abide delay in my mid-morning come. Normally, a slave like Darla, here, would do me, but she has other duties just now.'

I looked round at the teat-pierced maid, and she didn't seem to have any other duties, but I rose, then crouched before Miss Kuhl's parted thighs, and plunged my face between the lips of her gash, getting my tongue directly to her clitty, and beginning a wide, up-and-down slurping, using the flat of my tongue to cover the vulval lips, perineum and clitoris itself. Miss Kuhl grunted, and shifted her bottom, and after five or six sweeps, her cunt was flowing with quite copious come, that tasted good and salty – which was just as well, for her next command was that I should drink every drop of it.

'. . . since you seem so piggishly fond of eating,' she added with a sneer. 'Now, you will raise buttocks and spread wide, so that Darla may attend to *you*. It made me sick to my stomach, watching you guzzle your food, like the *slut pig* that you are. Darla *knows* what *pigs* deserve.'

I gulped, almost choking, as I swallowed down a particularly strong gush of fluid from her cunt, for I understood – as if it could have been otherwise – what

Darla's 'other duties' were. I was to get my first whopping at the stable. I was trembling, but still intent on my duty of tonguing Miss Kuhl's cunt. I obeyed, raising and spreading my buttocks in the correct position, and shuddering in the knowledge that my own bush, vulva and ass bud were fully exposed to a malicious vertical cane-stroke. I felt juice trickle down my gash flaps to my inner thighs, as I dreaded, yet craved, a vicious slap of the cane, right inside my cunt lips or on my throbbing clitty. If, that is, it *was* to be a cane – I'd no idea how they did things out west. Were there birch trees in Nevada? Were there *any* trees?

Darla opened a big rosewood cabinet, the size of a bookcase, and I jerked my head up to look. I only got a glimpse, for Miss Kuhl slapped my cheek, very hard, and hissed that though I was a dirty little slut and submissive, I had plenty to learn about total obedience. I returned to my task, wishing I was free to masturbate my own throbbing clit, which was sorely in need of a tickle, to bring me to the orgasm my cunt craved. My juice was gushing even more freely, after my brief glimpse of the cabinet's contents. There were displayed, neatly labelled, as in a museum, examples of every type of correctional instrument: hickory switches, elmwood canes, horsewhips and bullwhips, even several bushy birches.

'Darla shall cane you on the bare, with a hickory switch, until you bring me to satisfactory climax,' said Miss Kuhl, with scarcely a tremor in her voice, even though I was licking and chewing her clitty as hard as I could. 'It may interest you to know that each instrument in my correction cabinet has a sound, American provenance. The switch that Darla shall use on your bare ass, for example, was used to chastise fractious whores and other female *recalcitrants* in one of the 100 brothels of Virginia City, in the silver-mining days of the Comstock lode. Particularly recalcitrant – that is,

161

unwilling, or sulky – girls were "whupped round the houses", the cane handed over to the proprietor of each saloon. The record number of strokes with this instrument was 746, taken in the space of an afternoon by one Maybelle Berry, who was whipped naked around the city, then tarred and feathered, and locked in the cage, as they called the female detention centre, for a week, until her weals healed. Of course, her beauty made it desirable for her to go back to work, and every silver-miner in Virginia City wanted to fuck "Whupped Maybelle" from the rear, so as to feast his eyes on her wealed bottom. So, her recalcitrance was profitable in the long run. However, we do not want *you* to prove recalcitrant, and it is my stable mistress's job to dissuade you . . .'

Vip!

'*Mm . . .*' I moaned, jerking, as the four-foot cane whistled then streaked across my bare buttocks with a kiss of fire; my teeth fastened on a wet, chewy segment of Miss Kuhl's *labia minora*, making her grunt, whether in pleasure or discomfort, I couldn't tell.

Vip! I was stroked again. Darla was a strong girl, and I felt my buttocks clench involuntarily at the smarting pain, and anticipation of the whop, which, I figured, would come on the second . . . Vip! It did. My bare ass squirmed as I tried to ride the searing pain of the hard, springy wood on my naked skin. I tongued Miss Kuhl's streaming cunt quite frantically, thinking that she must climax soon, her juice was so strong and copious – then, my whopping would finish. Yet, as always, despite my gorge's rising at the agony of just three bare-ass cane-strokes, I wanted to endure, until I broke through, on to that glorious plateau of pain and butt-squirming shame, where I wouldn't want my beating to end, ever . . .

Vip! Vip! Vip! Wow! She caned hard, this Darla. There was muscle in those arms! Darla seemed a

162

trailer-park kind of name – what was she, some southern girl who'd gotten into trouble with stolen credit cards or something? I began to wonder about the type of girl I'd be meeting. They couldn't *all* be nice respectable housewives with too much enthusiasm for the mall, happily coupled with a harmless penchant for bare-ass spanking. Vip! It was all I could do not to open my mouth and scream – instead, I deep-kissed Miss Kuhl's cunt and swallowed half a cup of her come. Vip! Vip! Vip! Three searing cuts took me crossways, in quick succession. My eyes were blurred with ears as my scalded bare bottom writhed; I knew that Darla sensed my (unforgiveable!) snobbery, and was punishing me for it. She really *wanted* to hurt me – a fantastic turn-on. Vip! Vip! Vip! My face and trembling bare titties were soaked in Miss Kuhl's come . . . *she too* wanted me hurt, just like Cher and Elle . . .! My own cunt juiced hard at the thought of both these vengeful females, awaiting their chance to slice my (to them) virgin bottom.

My eyes blurred as I wept, tears streaming down my face and mingling in the salty pond of the woman's come, gushing at my lips. I smelled Darla's acrid sweat and heard the jangle of her nipple chain as her breasts bounced at each cane-stroke. How much better, when a *master* got hold of me! Vip! Vip! Vip! Darla was striping my bottom *all over*. I felt my belly tingle. I was reaching my plateau, sure that my ass and haunches – Darla knew how to bring tears, with a haunch stroke – would bear the coruscated dark welts of this caning for a good long time. Vip! Vip! Vip! My belly and spine were tingling, as I thrust my buttocks wider, and higher, my furrow wide open, begging for it . . . *there!* Vip! Vip! Vip! God, how it hurt! My teeth clenched and my ass seemed scalded by spears of red-hot steel! Darla lashed my perineum, gash flaps and anal pucker with three stingers that had me melting in a lava of pain; I bit hard on Miss Kuhl's cunt lips, and she grunted, come

163

pouring from her squeezed slit, and pressed my head to her pouch. I could feel her belly tense and quiver, and sensed I was going to bring her off pretty soon.

Vip! Vip! Vip! I didn't mind now – the hot golden pain was part of my bare fesses, throbbing in tune with my stiff clitty and gushing cunt. Nor did I mind when Miss Kuhl wrenched my mane to the panties stretched between her thighs, and told me to lick her stained gusset clean, where her asshole and cunt had soiled. She breathed hard as I transferred my tongue and licked the garment until it seemed clean under my saliva, which I didn't dare spit out, despite the acrid taste. Miss Kuhl was giving herself a pause, not wanting to come too soon and thus terminate my whopping. Vip! Vip! Vip! Those hickory strokes kept lashing my bare backside as I licked her soiled panties and trembled and wriggled, until I thought my fesses would float away as two moons of pure naked pain.

Through tear-blurred eyes, I saw that Miss Kuhl had her fingers to her swollen red clitty and was masturbating hard as I licked her panties. Then another wrench of my hair pushed my face once more between her thighs, the trembling flesh squishy and bathed in her come, and I got her clitty between my teeth and bit hard. My own come was flowing fast, and I felt that just a few more strokes with the hickory would bring me off; I tried to slap my thighs together, in the general intensity of my ass's wriggling, thus touching my clitty. It worked, and I felt jolt after jolt of pleasure course up my spine, as my come-wet thighs banged together after each of Darla's cane-strokes.

'*Ahh . . .*' Miss Kuhl yelped, then growled, faster and faster, pressing my head against her cunt; her juice flowed so, it was hard work to gulp it all down.

Vip! A single stroke seared my anus bud, cunt lips and swollen clitty, and I exploded; my belly spasmed, and come flowed from me like a spurt of hot oily piss.

I cried out as a fantastic orgasm shook my entire body. Behind me, I heard a raucous cry:

'Yeah! *Uh! Yeah* ...'

I looked about me, now that my caning had ceased, to see Darla's tits bouncing, as her belly trembled, and her quivering thigh muscles glistened with come, pouring from her cunt, where her fingers danced under her apron: throughout my caning, Darla had been masturbating. I was so astonished at the sight of her massive pubic forest soaked in sweat and come, and the soiled apron fluttering over the big fleshy cunt flaps, that I didn't observe Miss Kuhl rising; with an expert fluid motion, she wrenched my hair to the roots, making me scream, and forcing me on to my tits and belly, while her shoe pinioned my neck to the carpet. With equal speed, Darla had a coarse hempen rope looped around my wrists, forcing them behind my back, above the crack of my ass. Before I could speak, the rope looped between my teeth and over my tongue, then down across my ass-cleft and around my knees, leaving only my calves and feet free to kick in feeble protest. Darla placed a fluffy sock on the small of my back, and stood on me. She was heavy.

'Enjoy your exercise, Darla?' Miss Kuhl said. 'I expect it is fun to be on the giving side.'

'Yes, Miss. Thank you, Miss,' the girl replied, in a strong southern accent. 'I liked whupping *her,* because her ass seemed so big and wholesome, like she hadn't been rightly tarred before. A rich yankee, you said. Huh!'

'Indeed. But you won't remember any of Miss Fahr's details, will you? As far as the sluts are concerned, she is hopeless, debt-ridden trash, like the rest of you.'

'As you say, Miss.'

'Otherwise, your normal daily corrections could be increased, and become *exceedingly* painful.'

I felt Darla's body shudder.

'You remember the last time I *birched* you, on your bare bottom?'

Darla shuddered again.

'Yes, I do, Miss. I couldn't sit comfortable for a while.'

'You wouldn't like another naked birching.'

'No, Miss! Regular whopping hurts fine. I'll keep quiet.'

'Then you may hogtie our new arrival,' Miss Kuhl said, addressing me. 'Darla is a useful slut, whom I keep as one of my own personal slaves. She has been with us over a year. Hogtie Miss Fahr more tightly than usual, Darla, for I fear she may, after all, prove a little *recalcitrant.*'

Darla laughed, a velvety chuckle.

'Them recalcs, huh?' she said, as she began to unwind the rope coil and add to my knots. 'Hate the bitches. Dungeon's too *good* for them, *I* say. Girl can't take her whacks, shouldn't mess things up for the rest of us.'

I was helpless to ask exactly how a recalc was defined, and how I could avoid becoming one, and, anyway, I figured that *whatever* I did, Miss Kuhl would find me recalcitrant. To the horrible smarting pain of my bare-ass flogging was now added rope burn, as Darla stitched me in a cross-weave of heavy knots, bruising and restraining my breasts and vulva especially, and leaving no inch of my naked skin unbitten by the harsh rope – just like Ottilie, hogtied in Peter's closet, in New York. She muttered, as she worked, like a homily:

'Cat's paw . . . clove hitch . . . sheet bend . . . bow-line . . .'

The knots grew tighter and tighter, their constricting web making me gasp, as my belly was squashed, my ribcage and titties crushed, and my thighs bent and squeezed across one another, leaving my bare feet flapping backwards. The rope secured my mane, forcing my head back, and causing unbearable strain on my bound breasts.

'I got to thank you, Miss,' Darla said. 'Trussing a yankee's no harder than trussing a pig, and a sight more fun.'

'Darla has an agricultural background,' said Miss Kuhl. 'Missouri, I believe.'

'Right, Miss. On the farm – well, not a farm, proper – a girl gets used to naked whupping real early, not like these eastern city people. Washburn, Missouri, is no place for soft asses. Hill folk strap a girl by the belly, tits down, on a table, just six foot long and three foot across, more like a board, really, with just a leather strap across her back, so she's pinned. She can wriggle and screech all she wants, but that switch keeps landing on bare ass, with all the folks laughing, and betting how much she can take. I got whupped *so much!* All I'd *done* was boost a TV, or maybe a car, or maybe one of them plastic cards. Didn't seem fair at the time, but I got to like being whupped bare-ass, gave me a tingly warm kind of feeling, and my pussy got wet, so they'd make a game out of beating me till I was slipping and sliding in my own pussy juice. Polished the table nice and shiny, too, they said, for the cunt oil seeped in good, gave the wood body. The table would tilt up, so they could climb on to me, and . . . *you* know. Bone me in the ass, that's what. Cornholing, we call it. I got married when I was 16, because I thought things would be better, but they weren't. My Bobby used to string me to the back of his pickup and whip my bare ass with a tire iron, with his friends watching, and drinking and all, and sometimes Bobby would let them whup me too, or even cornhole me, while I was still crying from my beating, and with my ass all purple. He watch the weather on TV, waiting for a storm, and he'd tie me to the lightning rod and whup me bare-ass naked while the rain soaked me, and it hurts so bad on wet skin! Sometimes I got strapped round a tar barrel, with my head pushed underneath, and got the hickory switch on the bare ass, getting up for air only when my thighs fair slapped the barrel and my butt really *shook*. About 100 cuts, maybe 200, I lost count after a while, but I took it and never tried to run away, for I knew I'd been bad, even if not *so* bad. I kind of liked it, and knew I had to be punished for *liking* being punished, *and* liking the cocks spunking in my cornhole, too. Took 13 cocks in my cornhole, one after the other, one time, and a whupping on top. By then, I knew I liked the whip, and figured I could find more high-class action elsewhere. So I boosted some wheels, an '07 Buick, I think, and got to Utah, then to Nevada. Law don't bother looking so far, but those banks and credit people never do give up, specially as they weren't my cards in the first place. Used to get a bed and food at truck stops, if I let the truckers give me the strap on my bare, while I sucked them off. That was *nothing,* after Missouri, but I felt I could be more classy, so I heard about the stable, and here I am. You think *I've* whupped you hard? Just wait till the *men* get to you, missy. Those titties . . . gotta be 44s, C cup, at least. Oh, *yeah . . .*'

She pinched my nipples hard, between fingernails, and I squealed. How could this lowlife *bitch* come from the same United States of America as *me*? (See the attitude I've had whipped out of me?) I tried to interrupt, and tell her I was just as rural as herself, but the rope gagging my mouth made it difficult to form the words, so all I could do was groan, and shake my head, which earned me an agonising kick from Miss Kuhl's stiletto point, right in my cunt flaps, and needling my clit – just before Darla attended to my whole vulva, stuffing coiled rope inside my cunt, until my pouch was bursting, and sliding a fourfold width to my deep anus, then finishing her knot, so as to encompass my clitoris in a web of tickling hairy rope.

'Don't reckon her asshole's had much tool, despite what we saw on your screen, Miss,' Darla said. 'I mean not real Missouri cornholing, like every girl gets, when her stud approves her. I reckon that asshole is *truly* fillable.'

'Filled it shall most certainly be,' purred Miss Kuhl. 'I shall enjoy watching our yankee friend squirm.'

Darla stepped back, pulling up her fluffy socks and smoothing her apron, both wet with her own come, and apparently satisfied with her bound creation. I was in agony: unable to move a muscle, or even to ease the pain of my fearfully tight bonds. My entire body was encased in rope. All I could do was flap my bare feet.

'Ah, yes,' said Miss Kuhl. 'Our barefoot. The number three boots, please, Darla.'

There was an awful clanking sound, and I moaned and whimpered as I felt Darla lock my feet into horrible cold slabs of metal, heavy as lead. Darla hoisted me to my feet, and held me by the armpits, until I found I could just about stand, my feet entombed in grotesque surgical boots, with heels and soles at least a foot off the ground, and twisting my feet horribly. Not only was I expected to stand, but walk as well! Prodding me with the hickory switch, Darla directed me towards the door of the apartment. She opened it; I hobbled, staggering and with pain wracking my bound legs, past the elevator to a stairwell.

'The slutmaster may have misled you into thinking that this apartment was to be your lodging,' Miss Kuhl said, 'for you can see, of course, that it is my own. Bound sluts must travel by the stairs, I'm afraid, until they complete their basic training. *If* they complete it.'

With Darla preceding me and poking me in the cunt if I failed to move, I edged on to the first step, and by swivelling my body, got myself down on to the second. I felt like some grotesque monster toy.

'Where am I going ... *Miss?*' I managed to blurt, through my rope gag.

'To the dungeon,' said Miss Kuhl.

12

The Dungeon

'Get in there, you fuckin' yankee whore!' Darla snarled.

What she actually said was 'gitten thar', like something you hear in movies. I mean, didn't they teach these people English, in Washburn, Missouri? I thought that later. She pushed me in the small of the back and sent me staggering into darkness and the stench of bodies, before slamming the door shut behind me. I was delirious with pain, and stumbled forward, unable to prevent myself collapsing. My fall was broken by straw, which covered the stone floor. The dungeon was lit by tallow candles, giving off a foul and smoky odour. I lay on my back, gasping and sobbing, my eyes too blurred by tears and misery to focus on my surroundings. My flogged ass hurt terribly, and my ropes bit me. I knew my skin would bear the rope burns for a long time, and suspected it would be quite a while, too, before my buttocks were fresh for new caning. I shifted my neck: it was all I could do, for my bondage was so expert as to hold me otherwise helpless. My heart thudded in fear, as I knew I was easy prey for some new savage Darla to whip me as I lay. I moaned as I felt my bladder weaken, and my thigh ropes were hot and wet with a strong flow of my piss. I lay in the pool of my own fluid and as soon as I could stifle my sobs, I shifted on to my side, and looked around.

I distinguished shapes in the darkness – nude female bodies, squatting, crouching or laying flat out, none in full bondage, but all in a curious restraint. Beside each girl was a polished wooden stave pegged into the floor, the girth of an exceptionally thick cock, but three or four feet in height. The staves widened at the top, in the shape of a glans penis, but that part was out of proportion to the shaft, being longer and thicker than the glans of even such a monstrous cock – like a miniature cock itself. A metal saucer, like a collar, was bolted to the shaft at the corona of the glans. Each girl was roped by the wrists to a single metal cuff that slid up and down the shaft, but could not pass the obstacle of the saucer. She had, thus, a limited freedom of movement, being able to reach most parts of her body, but was unable to distance herself from her slave pole (as I learned the device was called) more than the length of her rope. She was also bound to her slave pole by a simple chain, passing through clamps – called nipple vices – on each of her bare nipples, and padlocked to the sliding cuff.

The girls were placed so that they could not reach far enough to touch each other. They looked at me with downcast heads and dulled expressions. The dungeon was low ceilinged, and 30 feet by 60. All around the walls were posts, trestles and frames, garnished with cuffs and straps, that I knew to be correctional stations. The place stank; there was no sign of a toilet, and I felt a pressing urge to dung. I couldn't help it; crying with shame, I felt my dungs plop from my anus, soiling my ropes and splattering the straw beneath my pussy. The dungeon tinkled with girls' snickering laughter. Exhaustion overcame my shame and my terror: my head lolled, and I must have fallen asleep.

Whap!

'Ahh!'

Whap!

'Ahh! Stop!'
Whap!
'Ahh! Please! No!'
Whap!
'Oh! Oh! Ohh!

I awoke to a frightful sound, and an even worse sight. Oh, Trudi, I thought, what have you gotten into? Is this what you wanted, in sweet, snowy New England . . .?

Whap! Whap! Whap!

'Ahh . . .!'

The nude body of a black girl writhed in a cat's cradle of ropes, between two flogging-posts. The strokes of a bullwhip, to her bare back and buttocks, slammed her ripe dugs and shuddering ribcage against the wall. The candles framing her body illuminated her, but not her whipper, whose thong snaked from shadow. Her legs were stretched wide, and sheathed in knots up to the knee, lifting her ankles a foot from the straw, which was gleaming with her piss, and – I gasped – a drip of come from the swollen dark lips of her cunt. Her arms flared upwards and sideways, similarly bound, up to the elbow. Only her hands and feet were free, and flapped in time with the anguished squirming of her bottom, vivid in the candlelight, and with the deep welts of the whip on her back and buttocks etched in shadow.

Her breath came in hoarse, groaning pants, and, as she was flogged, the naked black girl's plaited hair whirled like a nest of snakes. The other girls gazed, sighing, at the whipping, and I saw that those with unbound hands had their fingers between their thighs, and were masturbating. To my shame – but not, I bitterly realised, to my surprise – I sighed too. My own cunt was moistening as I watched the bare black flesh dance under the leather thong, and I needed suddenly to masturbate. I began to wriggle, until I was lying on my belly and could get my clitoris against the straw, then began to pump my loins to put pressure on the throbbing nubbin. Yes, I answered my question, this *is* what you wanted, Trudi, long ago, in Plattsburgh . . .

The louder the black girl's screams, the deeper the welts on her large ripe buttocks, now squirming madly in their agony, the wetter and wetter my come flowed from my cunt, writhing against the dung-splattered straw. I didn't care: I wanted to *be* that girl, helpless under whip, and I felt myself approaching orgasm, as I knew I very soon would be. That's why a sub girl will always masturbate at the sight of another sub punished: she anticipates her own turn. A little sleep had done wonders for my morale. I relished my bondage, my helplessness, and the awareness of imminent, merciless punishment. The leather whistled and flashed. Whap! Whap! Whap!

'AHH! OHH!'

The girl's jerking head suddenly slumped forward, and hung between her massive breasts, as though she had been whipped to unconsciousness. Perhaps she had; at any rate, a pail of water splashed, drenching her, and she stirred once more, moaning and wailing, with choking sobs. The water was thrown by a slab-muscled black male, over six feet tall, and nude, who stepped from the shadow, with his black cock swollen to a massive erection. Around his forearm coiled the bull-whip: it was he who had flogged the girl. His head was completely shaved, but I didn't care to look at his face, when the hugeness of his shiny tool, with its gleaming dark helmet, had me in thrall. I wriggled my cunt basin harder on the floor, bathing in a pool of my own come, sliming the straw along with my piss of earlier, and feeling my orgasm fluttering closer and closer. My clit was totally throbbing, and swollen. I was disappointed the whipping had ceased, but sensed that hard black cock was no accident, and that further events would bring me off.

'Oh, how *could* you, Miss?' the flogged girl whimpered. 'However *could* you . . .?'

Miss? Into the light, beside the whipper, stepped a white woman, holding a clipboard and pen. She wore a business suit similar to Miss Kuhl's, except that she had no blouse or bra underneath her single-buttoned jacket, which exposed her big bare breasts almost totally, straining against the fabric, her upper titties beaded with sweat.

'Jehanne Farragut,' she said. '50 lashes plus one. It says so here, quite plainly. Are you disputing the dungeon mistress's order?'

'Why, *no*, Miss Clatterbuck . . .!'

'Then why did you bleat just now? And wriggle like a carp on a hook when Weaver was attending to you? Childish, at best. I've a new slut to break in, so I can't waste time on you, though if you give any more trouble, you'll ride your pole for two hours, *in the anus*, *this time.*'

'Oh, no, Miss! I won't give any trouble!'

'Give me the whip, Weaver, and finish Jehanne's treatment,' said the white woman.

The whole chamber seethed with excitement as Weaver – I never did know if it was his first or last name – grasped Jehanne Farragut by her hips, and pulled her wide-stretched buttocks down the necessary few inches to impale her on his cock. The swollen glans stroked the lips of her juicing pussy for several moments, until it shone with her oil, then moved to the writhing pucker of her anus bud. The black man's buttocks jerked, and his cock-meat penetrated the girl's anal shaft. She squirmed wildly, lips bubbling and frothing with drool. She stifled a scream – and that was when only the glans had penetrated her hole. Weaver lubricated his shaft with come from her dripping cunt, then sank the bulk of his cock, right to his balls. The flogged black girl let out a long, despairing wail, and her head sank again over her breasts, only to jerk back, as Weaver grabbed her plaited braids and wrenched her mane towards him.

Tears wet her face, but her swollen cunt flaps dripped with come. She groaned, her voice rising to a shrill, and Weaver's bare ass began to pump powerfully as he buggered her. His cock rammed her anus with the force of a piston, the black shaft disappearing completely between the writhing globes of her buttocks, with his hips slapping her wealed bare ass loudly at each thrust. I looked round to see that all the inmates of the dungeon clung to their slave poles, writhing up and down on the shafts, while masturbating their clits. My own belly surged with want – I squirmed faster and faster on the straw, feeling its prickles against the exposed glans of my rope-twined clitty, and my flood of come soaking ropes, straw and my threshing thighs.

Weaver's cock was a dark, shining blur as he buggered the helpless black girl, yet now her buttocks responded to his thrusts, thrusting out to meet his tool, as he withdrew right to the glans, then plunged his cock fully into the anus once more, penetrating the anal elastic in a single savage stroke. I wriggled my own buttocks, imagining that massive cock penetrating me, splitting my asshole, and spunking right at my root ... Electricity surged up my spine, my cunt was awash with come, and I began to whimper, then yelp, as I heard the black male grunt, and saw his creamy, copious spunk froth at the cleft of Jehanne's jerking fesses. My belly and cunt glowed hot, as I moaned, gushing come down my thighs, in a searing, pulsating orgasm.

Whap!

'Ahh!' I screamed.

Miss Clatterbuck's bullwhip lashed me right across the roped buttocks, hurting dreadfully, even through my knots, and smarting like fire on the portions of bare skin uncovered by rope, where my naked flesh felt the impact of the leather thong. Whap! Whap! Whap! The awesome whip spun me over like a top, cutting me on the titties, on the thighs, feet and cunt, snaking everywhere on my roped body, as, one by one, the knots burst open at the force of the flogging. I began to whimper, then scream, as more and more of my bare skin was exposed to the leather, and, finally, only my wrists and ankles were bound in restraint: yet my whipping by Miss Clatterbuck continued, this time on my fully exposed buttocks and breasts.

It smarted beyond endurance; I couldn't help pissing myself, so copiously that the woman snarled my piss had spoiled her whip. Quite seriously, that evacuation was the only thing that kept me from fainting as her awful bullwhip lashed my already striped flesh. My titties quivered as each stroke slammed, with its dry, thudding crack, into my still-tender weals. My buttocks clenched and jerked like automata, and my eyes streamed; I saw Miss Clatterbuck had dropped her clipboard from under her arm, and it had fallen into my pool of pee. I had blurred glimpses of her jacket button breaking and her massive titties bursting free, the huge strawberry nipples pointed and erect like helmets; the snarling, hissing mistress with her mini-skirt pulled right up, and her exposed vulva dripping come on to my jerking flesh, as she masturbated while whipping me. Her bush was fully grown and untrimmed, a tangled wet mane of black cunt-tendrils that hung swaying beneath her swollen cunt flaps as her hot come sprayed my body. Whap! Whap! Whap!

'Ahh! Ahh! Ahh!'

I heard a voice in the distance, howling in agony, shrill to inhuman: it was my own. My whipping seemed to have no beginning and no end; my whole naked body was one jerking tendon of raw meat, my very weals screaming in their agony. The bullwhip's thong seemed never to leave me before landing in another stroke, coiling me in its embrace before the leather lashed my naked skin once more. I felt branded with red-hot iron.

'Oh ... please ... please ...' I heard mysef stammer, forming the words against pain that seemed to crush my larynx. *'I didn't want this ... Stop! Stop!'*

Suddenly, my flogging stopped. A hand thrust brutally into my quivering cunt, poked my pouch, and withdrew.

'What *did* you want, *bitch?*' snarled Miss Clatterbuck. She smeared my own come across my lips and nose: my pussy was soaking wet under the lash.

'Oh . . . *no!*' I sobbed.

It was too late; rough hands pinioned me to the floor, with a foot under my cunt and belly, so that my ass was raised.

'No . . . no . . .' I moaned, the words bubbling through piss-soaked straw; I knew – *craved* – what was to happen.

Weaver's glans was, incredibly, as stiff as wood as he nuzzled my gash flaps, to oil it with my come, then stroked my perineum with his pisshole before thrusting it into my anal pucker. I screamed again at the hugeness of the thing and the pain in my anus. As he had done with Jehanne, he fingered my cunt to get a palmful of come, oiled his cock, then penetrated me in a single, easy thrust. Yes, it *was* easy: I relaxed my sphincter, sobbing in the giddy, joyful shame of my submission, so that my anus relaxed fully to take in the hot flesh, before tightening again to suck his monstrous tool inside my asshole.

He slammed his glans tip hard against my root, sending spasms through my belly; then withdrew slowly, teasing me, his cock squelching from my clutching anus with the delicious tickling of a big dung. I felt my pussy flood with come. He penetrated me again, and repeated the slow withdrawal, then again, and again, his thrusts getting faster and harder. Suddenly, my hair was wrenched upwards, causing me to squeal, and my face was jammed between Miss Clatterbuck's thighs, right to her pussy, which was wet and swollen and gushing come. As Weaver buggered me, I began to tongue and chew her swollen clitoris (it was one of those abnormally extruded clits some women have), and she pulled my hair by the roots, until I obliged her by swallowing her come instead of letting it drool down my chin on to her skin. I gulped the salty liquid and the pain in my hair eased somewhat, but my squirming buttocks did not stop clenching and jerking, trying to trap – or escape from? – the monstrous black cock that buggered my asshole, seeming to fill my whole belly with my pain and the male's dominance.

Frantically, I tongued Miss Clatterbuck's cunt, as though that would lessen the agony of my buggery; she grunted, the flow of her come so copious that it was hard to swallow it all. I knew she was close to spasm. Weaver's cock began to tremble and buck, independently of his thrusts, and I knew, as every fucked or buggered woman does, that he was going to spurt. I squeezed his cock with my anal elastic, slowing his withdrawal and making his glans spend longer and longer at my anal root, which I twitched, to ream his pisshole, and that made him tremble even more violently. I felt the first drop of hot cream, then gasped into Miss Clatterbuck's cunt, as my asshole was flooded with a scalding gush of spunk that filled me and dribbled out hot and frothy on to my pulsing thighs. My teeth took hold of Miss Clatterbuck's clitty, and I bit savagely; I heard her yelp, felt her shudder, and she pressed my head into her cunt so hard, I could scarcely breathe. Weaver touched me just once, nipping my own clitty between his fingernails: a hot flood of pleasure filled me, and as my asshole drank the black man's spunk, and my throat gurgled with the woman's salty come, I felt my own cunt writhe and shudder, in a huge, gushing orgasm.

I lolled on my filthy staw, exhausted; did not stir, as I heard hammers and buckles and locks, and felt my hands roped, my nipples clamped in nip vices, and the unresisting nude package of my sub's body was fastened to my slave pole. I opened my eyes. Dirty straw had been replaced by clean, and at my loins lay bowls of water and food, that smelled of fish. I sniffed the food: it was Purina Cat Chow. That was the beginning of my three weeks' breaking in, as an inmate of the dungeon. It was so terrible that I can't think of it today without shuddering. I can't think of that whipped, buggered, tortured girl as *me*, so I must write as if she is someone else. *Me* couldn't possibly have endured such training ... and gladly done everything that followed. Yet, I suppose she must have.

Every place of confinement, however bizarre or terrible, has its own rules and social order, and the dungeon was no exception. It contained 13 girls, with Trudi Fahr. Their names were: Diorna Badd, from Elgin, Illinois; Saskia Beare, from Fort Richardson, Alaska; Kina Cushunt, from Duplessis, Louisiana; Xandra Dubet, from Minot, North Dakota; Petal Etchegui, from Vallejo Beach, California; Jehanne Farragut, from Ontario, California; Nathalie Farthquat, from La Harpe, Kansas; Ruth Fleisch, from Waukesha, Wisconsin; Pearl Garbeau, from Peach Grove, Kentucky; Marilyn Humble, from Xenia, Ohio; Belle Pettigrew, from Clearwater, Florida; Patsy Tushingham, from Evansville, Indiana; and Kissy Widener, from Spokane, Washington. Trudi learned fast that as a newcomer, and the only girl from the northeast, she was lowest in rank.

Talking was forbidden amongst the dungeon girls, on pain of instant bare-bottom caning of 15 strokes from Miss Clatterbuck's three-foot yew rod, but that rule was mostly honoured in disobedience, despite the risk of punishment. The girls were mostly away from the perpetual twilight of the dungeon itself, being occupied from the dawn waking bell with arduous physical exercise and tasks, idleness or failure being punished by the whip or cane, from one of the custodians. Miss

Clatterbuck, from Scottsdale, Arizona, was senior custodian, and under her served three juniors: Melanie Gortz, of Redding, California, Catilin Suplicy, of Albany, Oregon, and Angel Nogues, of Miami, Florida. Those girls, all the age of Trudi, or Darla Perkins, wore jackboots and clinging leotards, cut high at waist and low at breast cleft, all in matt black rubber, with their abundant manes swept back in pony-tails; Miss Clatterbuck appeared in her breast-baring business attire, or, outdoors, in custodian's costume, peach or yellow in colour, with her cane painted to match.

The day began with three hours of aerobics, followed by a communal ice-cold hosing, and return to the dungeon, for breakfast; then, three hours of harder gymnastics, followed by a second hosing, and lunch; after that, three hours in the yard, a glade, the size of a football field, where high prison walls enclosed blue sky, and where the girls practised rock-breaking, tree-climbing or diving, obliged to swim underwater for long periods in the green, algae-covered pond. One of the walls reflected cold sunshine on to the bodies of the girls working, or under lash; it was a dark mirror, and none dared gaze at it for too long without incurring the rod. Rumours quivered amid the bruised girls, as to who exactly was watching from behind the one-way mirror: movie producers, senators, the state governor . . .? Girls were taken singly, or in pairs, for buggy training. Trudi's first time, Angel Nogues led her and Pearl Garbeau, roped nude together, through underground passages, until they came up in desert, yet still within the stable's perimeter walls. There, they were bound in full horse's harness, with blinkers and iron horseshoes. The reins were fastened to nipple vices and cunt clamps, and they pulled a cart round and round a track, their nude bodies whipped on by their driver. That lasted two hours, until the girls' skins were patchworks of dark blue whip weals. Trudi afterwards partnered other girls, and was once flogged around the track, pulling the cart alone, by Miss Clatterbuck herself.

One of the lighter tasks was straw duty, the fouled straw being replaced, and the floor hosed, twice a day; another was chow service, the food being distributed to girls who took their meals fastened to their slave poles. At no point in the day were Trudi's ears free of the sound of whip cracks, or her bare buttocks unsmarted from the custodian's cane, since all activities were accompanied by the public thrashing of one of the girls. Sometimes, the dark body of Weaver would straddle a girl just flogged and bugger her while the others watched. Girls at labour were not only permitted but actively encouraged to masturbate, especially if Weaver was tooling, but no girl was permitted to masturbate another.

For masturbation, the girls were permitted to pause in their chores, so Trudi quickly followed the others, masturbating herself to orgasm a dozen or so times during the working day. Less rock-breaking was done than masturbating. If a girl was only play-acting, and did not bring herself off properly, she received a bullwhip flogging on both shoulders and buttocks, her body strung nude and upside down, with her head inches from the slimy pool's surface, or, on occasions, beneath it, with the miscreant helplessly bubbling, as her naked flesh writhed under whiplash. The girls remained nude throughout the day, except when obliged to wear punishment dress, consisting of: the hobble, the bit and harness, the yoke, the brank, or the twin prongs of an unpolished oaken dildo, strapped tightly to her waist. Encumbered by such painful apparatus, she had to work as fast as in the nude, and received a whipping if she failed.

As the exhausted girls slumped at their slave poles in sleep, they might be awoken at any time of night by an unannounced punishment, or by Weaver's cock penetrating them in either hole. 'Riding the pole' meant that a girl's vulva straddled the giant dildo atop her slave pole, the sharp edges of the saucer designed to chafe her thighs and spread her legs for maximum discomfort. Once, Trudi rode the pole in cunt for an hour, ordered by Melanie Gortz; once, in anus, ordered by Louella Clatterbuck herself, and during her anal punishment she received 25 strokes on the bare from Miss Clatterbuck's cane, which made her writhe, swivelling like a top, as the glans rammed her anus root and the saucer bit her thighs.

Punishments unearned were given at random, or by rota, so that the flogging of Jehanne Farragut had not been due to any misdemeanour, but simply because Miss Clatterbuck had picked her. Trudi was from the first singled out for the most vicious punishments, and, as she wept, clutching her smarting red shoulders or buttocks, she could not decide which of the custodians hated her the most or was the most jealous of her body. Such vanity was slowly and surely whipped out of her. During the day, it was rare that Trudi enjoyed the freedom of nudity, running the gamut of punishment dress right from her first day in the open. She was still shivering from the ice-cold hosing, when Melanie and Angel suddenly clamped her face in a brank, and yoked her, with her arms spread painfully above her shoulders. Like this, she had to carry rocks balanced on her yoke, for an hour, goaded by cane-strokes on the bare bottom, and with the promise of full whipping if she dropped any of her cargo.

Sometimes she was hobbled, and wore bit and harness, strapped with huge dildos that were agony in her asshole and cunt; with Catilin holding her by a lariat, or reins, she was pushed into the slimy pond, to flail, helplessly, in the muck, until the custodian deigned to pull her up, gasping for air. A day of hard labour in the nude, accompanied merely – *merely!* – by a whipping or caning of 30 or 40 strokes seemed luxury. Each custodian had her favourite implement: Miss Clatterbuck and Angel Nogues favoured the cane on bare bottom; Catilin the bullwhip, and Melanie Gortz a twelve-thonged rubber whip, the thongs two feet long. Trudi bare-skin tasted one or even all of those implements on an average day, during that first week, and she longed to return to the comfort of her straw and slave pole, even if she did receive nightly buggery from the tireless Weaver.

He, too, seemed to have singled her out for his most brutal attentions, rarely buggering her for less than 40 minutes, and often not even coming to his own spasm, although he frigged Trudi's cunt so that further orgasms were added to her daily tally. Trudi became used to the silky feel of his body atop rubbing her, the acrid tang of his sweat and the unyielding majesty of his cock, as painful in each buggery as in the first. Yet she found herself awaiting him, hoping for him, and masturbating her cunt to the wetness before orgasm, to be ready to receive and please him. Jehanne was the first inmate who befriended Trudi, having been early accomplices in the ordeal of buggery by Weaver. Trudi understood the brutality, and unending pain, designed to shatter a submissive girl's remaining independence, but not the licence to masturbate so copiously. It was Jehanne, on chow duty, who explained.

'They want to addict us to the whip,' she whispered, 'and addict us to masturbating, too, so we can never disassociate one from the other. That's why we play footsie, night times. We can't stop. I'll foot you tonight, girl.'

'Why do those bitches hate me so much?' Trudi asked. 'And that monstrous Weaver . . .?'

'They like you,' said Jehanne. 'Don't pretend you don't like them in turn . . .'

Trudi sobbed, for it was true: she loved her torments, and her tormentors. She was a sub. That night, in the absence of any custodian, she felt a warm toe tickle her clitoris, then gain entrance to her moistening pouch: it was Jehanne's. Trudi stretched her own foot into the darkness, and found Jehanne's buttocks, then her cunt. It was just possible for tall girls to fully stretch their bodies and achieve contact in this way. The dungeon was alive with quivering legs as girls foot-fucked. Trudi got her toes into Jehanne's quim and brought her to a quick flow of come, then felt the black girl's cunt flaps tighten around her foot as her body thudded the straw, and she orgasmed. Trudi's own come quickened, and she gasped as Jehanne got the whole of one foot into Trudi's gash, with her big toe into her anus; she, too, climaxed rapidly.

The girls had time to masturbate twice more, before Catilin Suplicy made her patrol and selected a girl in the far corner for an instant caning on the bare, of – Trudi counted – a full 30 strokes, which the girl took with only a whimpering sob throughout. At the tap-tap-tap of the cane on naked skin, Trudi masturbated herself to another orgasm, realising that every inmate was doing the same. There were no explanations, no hints what the future held once – if – released back to the stable. The masters of the stable were addicting her: to submission, to masturbation at another girl's agony, to her own nature. She had just gotten used to it, her whole life reduced to beatings, muscle-wrenching work, and humiliation beyond her dreams, when Miss Clatterbuck woke them before dawn and ordered her custodians to unfasten the girls from their poles. They were hooded, blindfold in rubber catmasks, roped together with wrists behind their backs, and shackled together in hobble bars. The trussed girls endured a long hosing, which swept the dungeon clean of fouled straw, and drenched their shivering bodies in icy water. Their wet buttocks slapped at random by the canes of Melanie, Catilin and Angel, they filed out of the dungeon until they felt daylight on their faces, and heard the dungeon slam shut behind them. Miss Clatterbuck said tersely that they were going to another place.

13

Housebroken Girls

Trudi thought, as her catmask was removed, This is American gothic run riot. The old plantation house was festooned with creepers, mosses and giant funghi; its boards were peeling off its frame, windows smashed, frames and doorways awry. The naked possé of girls, shackled at the ankles, picked their way over the rotten boards of the deck, wrinkling their noses at the stench, any stumbling or hesitation rewarded with a cut to the bare nates from a custodian's cane. They entered the vestibule, grey with spiders' webs, dust and the stink of decay, and scuttling with beetles, lice and roaches. The place was so awful, it was too much – like a stage set or a movie. Miss Clatterbuck announced that this was to be their home, and that they had a week to make it look like a new house. Everything must be cleaned and fixed up, outside and inside. Still shackled, the girls were taken around the house by their custodians, lithe in jackboots and rubber suits. There was power, cold running water and two rooms packed with repair equipment. They would sleep on rusty steel bunks, side by side, in a loft under the eaves.

Each bunk had cuffs at base and head and a rubber restraining corset dangling midway; Miss Clatterbuck announced that the restraints would be used as punishments, if needed. She did not say how or when they

185

might be needed. From the loft, slit windows looked over dank lawn and undergrowth, ending a football field's length away, with the same walls that had ringed their work yard, and the same one-way mirrror staring over them. In front of the house stood six whipping-frames in a row, in the form of double gallows. Trudi shivered, thinking that this was her New England fantasy come true – with Weaver to play harlot-whipper. The air was unusually dank and humid for the dryness of Nevada, and Miss Clatterbuck revealed why.

Behind the house was one outlet of the hot springs upon which the stable was built. She led them through dense undergrowth to a pond of bubbling, steaming crystal water, about the size of a whirlpool, and told each girl to place her fingers in it. Each did, and recoiled. Miss Clatterbuck sliced the nearest girl on her bare – the tall flaxen-haired girl from Spokane, named Kissy Widener, who later became Trudi's friend – and told her to put her hand in until ordered to remove it. Kissy did so, biting her lip, her eyes crinkling in pain. After a while, her breath became easier, but her body was flushed from the heat. Miss Clatterbuck said that long immersion in the hot pool was just one of the new punishments the girls must expect. The girls winced; the custodians laughed, and Miss Clatterbuck said that if they hated the hot tub, they were welcome to the freezer cabinet in the basement.

The first task was not, as Trudi and the girls hoped, fixing up their dormitory. They were split into two gangs, one to repair the outside structure and yard, the other to clean and repair the inside. The girls were unshackled for their tasks, and had to work in the nude, but the outside gang were issued with heavy rubber boots, like a diver's, along with rubber pads for knees and elbows, that protected from scrapes, but made running impossible. Insiders were less protected. Stretched flat and wriggling in a mass of soapy lather on the cleared kitchen floor, with sponges strapped to her waist, thighs, shoulders, cunt and breasts, Trudi winced, and stifled a yelp, as Angel's cane took her with a stinger, right in the ass cleft.

'For the encouragement, bitch,' Angel Nogues rasped, in her *Calle Ocho* Cuban sing-song, and followed the stroke with two more, to each of Trudi's haunches, making the girl's eyes water at the smart.

I wish they issued ass pads, she thought. There was an itchy ache in her cunt; she longed to masturbate. Perhaps, having accustomed us to masturbate, they are punishing us by preventing it, she reflected, trying to get some friction between her padded cunt and the soapy floor, but with little effect. Damn, damn . . . Beside her, Jehanne Farragut, spreadeagled, performed the same task, with Miss Clatterbuck's boot on the small of her back, pressing her pubis to the floor as she writhed, a human sponge. Her bare black bottom gleamed dull purple with cane weals, through the foam of soapsuds, where Miss Clatterbuck's cane had marked the straining fesse-muscle.

Each girl had to jerk like a crab across the floor, then jackknife her body to wring the sponges dry into a gutter before repeating the operation. Splinters from the bareboard floor nicked their nipples, bellies and cunt flaps, making them wince, each grimace followed by a slap from the cane, either on the bare buttocks or else on their upturned soles. Trudi jumped as a giant roach rushed passed her and scuttled between her thighs right into her cunt. She shuddered, pressing her gash flaps tight to squash the bug, then opened her bladder to piss the debris away. That earned her four stingers on the top buttocks from Angel Nogues. She gasped at the agony that seared the tender skin of the upper fesses, and as tears blurred her eyes, gazed at Jehanne, who smiled: the slap of Melanie's and Catilin's whips, from outside, indicated that no girl was escaping 'encouragement'.

By the end of their first day, the girls collapsed on to their ragged horsehair mattresses, too exhausted to masturbate, or to notice they had spent a whole day without diddling. They slept nude, for the house was sultry from the hot spring, but ticks, bedbugs and the spiky horsehair meant that no girl slept tranquilly. In the pitch dark of the night, feet padded from bed to bed, and the whimpers of girls, free at last to masturbate, whispered through the windless loft. Trudi raised herself from her mattress, seeking Jehanne's bed, to be flattened by the sensuous friction of silky black teats squashing her back. She pretended to resist; Jehanne had her locked in a wrestler's hold, her cunt at Trudi's mouth and her own tongue probing Trudi's gash folds for the clitty. Trudi moaned, as Jehanne found her nubbin, and began to chew, then broke off, to take her whole vulva into her mouth and suck it, clit and all, like a lollipop. Each girl stroked the other's caned buttocks, fingers tracing the day's welts, and rubbing the cleft, before finding the anus bud stretched open. They gamahuched each other thus, two fingers in each other's anus, and mouths locked on quims, sucking the throbbing swollen gash flesh, and swallowing the copious come that flowed hot and oily from their cunts, until neither could delay her orgasm much longer. They climaxed together, and as Jehanne's whimpers and gasps faded, she suddenly shrieked.

Trudi shrieked too, both girls crushed by the nude body of Weaver. His loins threshed as his erect cock sought entrance to Jehanne's anus; he penetrated her easily and began to bugger her while she still lay pinioned on top of Trudi, who gasped for breath. Weaver pressed Jehanne so hard to the bed, with his cock sliding just above Trudi's face, that his balls were within her tongue's reach. Trudi extended her tongue, and began to lick the man's balls as he buggered Jehanne, who moaned, squirming. Trudi's fingers crept to her own cunt, and she began to masturbate, her

188

mouth now reaching up like a sparrow's, to clasp the whole thrusting ball sac in her lips. Jehanne, too, masturbated her own clitty, as her ass shuddered under the pounding buggery of the giant black cock, her buttocks spread wide, stretching the flesh of her perineum and cleft to a drumskin. Trudi sensed a second come approaching, when suddenly, Weaver withdrew his balls from her mouth and his cock from Jehanne's anus.

His arms enfolded the two girls, flipping them so that Trudi's ass was now on top, facing the erect male. Without a sound, he nuzzled Trudi's open anus bud with the tip of his rock-hard glans, allowing her to thresh and moan in protest, before penetrating her. Jehanne's tongue was busy again at Trudi's clitoris, drinking the hot come that flowed from her writhing cunt slit, and Trudi had her nose buried inside Jehanne's own wet pouch. She gasped, as the cock penetrated her anus in one hard thrust, right to her root; felt three or four rapid thrusts, and knew that she would come soon; heard Weaver grunt. There was a hot drip of spunk from his pisshole; then his cock bucked inside Trudi's clinging anus and he disgorged his load of hot creamy sperm until it frothed from her anal pucker and dripped on to Jehanne's waiting lips. As soon as he had spunked in Trudi's anus, Weaver withdrew his cock and sprang from the bed, to disappear into the darkness. At once, a flashlight shone on the girls' naked embrace. It was Miss Clatterbuck, breasts bare under her unbuttoned suit jacket, and nipples erect; her hand was under her mini-skirt at her exposed pubic jungle, beneath which her red cunt lips were wet and swollen. She resumed a vigorous frotting of her clitoris, until her bared belly fluttered, and she spasmed, grinning at the two prisoners.

'Gamahuching?' she said, her breath still hoarse from her own masturbated climax, which had copious come sliming her stockings. 'That means restraint.'

189

Each girl, lying face up on her own bed, cinched her rubber restraining corset as tight as it would go, at the custodian's order, until her flesh was pinched and her face bright with pain. Then Miss Clatterbuck cuffed their wrists and ankles to the bed corners.

'Followed by double whipping, in the morning – *Kuhl's dirty bitches,*' she added.

The outside girls had made some impression on the jungle before the house, first clearing the space around the row of whipping-frames. Each frame was two gallows sharing the same spine, with the gibbets and footboards at a wide angle. Upon these, roped by wrists and ankles, hung the nude bodies of Trudi and Jehanne, stretched defenceless in the X position of public flogging. Dawn broke, and the pink sky was cold as the custodians prepared to carry out sentence before an audience of shivering naked prisoners, all hobbled, but with hands free. Miss Clatterbuck had told them they should expect to make up for a day's lost masturbation, as they watched their friends' bare skin weal. The whipping-gallows were high, forcing every muscle of Trudi and Jehanne's backs, thighs and buttocks to strain, quivering, as each tall girl just managed to balance on tiptoe. Trudi glanced to her left, to see herself and Jehanne reflected in the glass of the one-way mirror. Their heads were held high, each girl strung by her hair to the pole of the gibbet.

'I'm so scared,' Trudi whispered.

'Me, too,' said Jehanne. 'Damn that Verri Kuhl . . .!'

'She tricked me! Kevin, too . . .'

'*Yeah!* Doesn't Clatterbuck *know?* Calling us *her* bitches?'

'Does it matter whose bitch you are, Jehanne? *Now?*'

'No, Trudi. I guess that's the whole point . . .'

Vap! Vap!

'*Ahh!*'

'Ahh!'

Both girls screamed, their bodies jerking and their croups clenching, as the first strokes of the double flogging lashed them on the bare buttocks. Those strokes were from canes of green bamboo, six feet in length, half an inch thick, and split to a foot's length at the tips, which snaked around the girls' haunches and fesses in a sinuous, sucking embrace, before hissing off the wealed bare flesh for the next strokes. Melanie and Angel wielded the canes, with Angel and Miss Louella Clatterbuck standing aside, Louella bearing a bullwhip, and Angel a rubber flail of 13 thongs, each of whose four-foot thongs, knotted at the three inches, carried a silver nugget encased in the tip. Trudi and Jehanne's sentence was 40 strokes of the cane on the bare buttocks; 20 lashes of the bullwhip on the shoulders; and 20 lashes of the scourge on back or buttocks, at the choice of the miscreant. For a flogged girl, writhing in the agony of her welts, to be obliged to choose the instrument of her final whipping, was subtlest cruelty.

Vap! Vap!

'Oh! Oh!

'Ahh . . .! No!'

Vap! Vap!

'Ahh! Ahh!'

'Ahh! Please! Oh . . .!

Trudi and Jehanne jerked like marionettes on their whipping-gallows, after only three strokes from each cane. Already, there were coos of appreciation from their audience, whose hands began a gentle rubbing of their bare quims. Every muscle of the flogged girls' bodies pumped, straining, against her bonds, as if to escape the deadly whistle of the rods. Vap! Vap! The bamboo canes lashed again, striping each bare bottom with its perfect weal. Vap! Vap! Trudi and Jehanne moaned, sobbing, and their buttocks clenching madly, as the wood worked its way from top to bottom fesse, across the haunches, slapping the naked skin until black girl and white girl were united in the crimson of their naked bottoms, darkening slowly to purple, and the canes flogged remorselessly on. Vap! Vap! Vap! Vap!

'AHH! AHH!'

'AHH! AHH!

It seemed to Trudi that she had never known, nor could ever know, such agony. At the first strokes of the green bamboo, she had regretted her desire to call herself submissive – vain and foolish fancy of a pampered girl, when this horror was the *reality* of submission! Now, such regret was a distant luxury. There was only the agony of her caned bare bottom, filling her with white heat, that seemed to have neither beginning nor end. She did not know where she was, nor why, only that her whole being was in her whipped nates, her tenderest essence flogged raw. She heard screams, in her own voice, but they could not help her. They came from a distant world: Trudi's world was pure pain. Yet, there was salty wetness in that pain; at each jolt of the flogging tool on her naked flesh, desire grew inside her pouch, her clitoris hardened like a weal, and moisture seeped from her swelling gash flaps, as they writhed, squelching and throbbing, in time with her seared buttocks. The caning came to an end. After a moment, in which the flogged girls sobbed, trembling, the bullwhip was raised. It was worse than the caning, the heavy leather slamming their bare backs with 20 merciless strokes, like hammer-blows.

After their bullwhipping, the drooled bodies of the nude white and black girls hung shivering together, backs and buttocks whipped purple. They could not form the words to choose where their scourging should be applied, so Angel decided to flog their buttocks, strokes to be delivered to each croup in turn. Thwap! Thwap! The dull, dry impact of the rubber scourge belied the agony its 13 thongs imposed on the already raw fesses of the two victims. Their cries became deep, gurgling shrieks, as Angel's flail expertly caressed the shaking ass flesh, each stroke delivering 13 lashes, and covering the entire expanse of bare buttock. The young whipper took her time, savouring and allowing her vigorously masturbating watchers to savour the wriggling of the two bare croups, and the visible deepening and darkening of the weals already in place. The one-way mirror on the wall of the compound flickered, as the girls' naked bodies writhed, in the sinuous dance of their masturbation; above them, the slapped, quivering nudity of Trudi and Jehanne, heads pulled high by the hair and titties shuddering at each stroke of the rubber flail to their buttocks. Each girl's thighs were streaming with come, gushing from her pussy, to sparkle pink in the rising sun.

Trudi and Jehanne were unfastened from their bonds, and taken down, their faces numb and glassy. Trudi was insensate, her eyes closed, as light gave way to dark, the day's gathering warmth to chill, and the freshness of the wakening glade to the odour of surgical sterility. Her back and buttocks seemed alive, crawling with white-hot worms of pain, until, suddenly, those worms grew still. Trudi opened her eyes, and looked up, to see whiteness, tinged with blue, all around her. She lay on her back, on a table at waist height from the crystalline floor. All around her hung stalactites of frost; her table was a slab of ice. She sighed, as the cold numbed her pain, and began to breathe deeply, her gasps slowing to mellow breath. A white sheet draped her, up to her neck, and her neck, wrists and ankles were fastened with copper cuffs bolted deep inside her ice slab. She could not move; her arms were at her side, but her legs were spread wide, exposing her vulva and ass cleft. She lay, breathing in the frosty air, and sighing, as the pain stilled. Gradually, her limbs began to shiver, and her bare feet, protruding from the drape, were turning pale blue. Trudi's teeth chattered, and her wrists pulled, uselessly, at her cuffs. Her hot whipped buttocks seemed melded to the ice, and themselves turning to ice . . .

The door opened, and, dark against the sombre glow of the chill cabinet, the nude body of Weaver padded towards the shivering girl. He whipped the drape from her body, and threw it aside; Trudi gazed down and saw that the tips of her nipples and cunt flaps were rimmed with frost, and that her body glowed blue. Weaver was erect, and grinning, his eyes hooded and without expression. He clambered on top of Trudi, who lay perfectly still, since threshing was obviously a waste of her draining energy. She was ready to let events take their course. She felt Weaver's hand in her pussy, masturbating her. The pouch was dry and cold, but the pummelling of the black man's balled fist had Trudi's cunt basin and ass writhing, as her pussy warmed and began to seep come. She saw the giant black cock loom above her belly and instinctively relaxed her sphincter, for the butt-fucking she expected. Weaver's glans approached her bush, fringed with icicles, and swept it aside, touching her swollen clitoris as he did so; Trudi realised that her clitty was throbbing, and the knowledge made her cunt juice faster.

The glans stroked the inner labia before venturing an inch inside her pouch, right to the corona, for Weaver's prepuce was drawn fully back. Trudi shivered, in desire for that cock, and in desire for the man's heat: her body was cooling rapidly on the ice slab. Yet she feared the cock in her narrow vulva; in anus, it had been painful enough, but her heart thudded in the terror that its hugeness would split her tight cunt right open. What, to other males, had been thrilling tightness, would to Weaver's hugeness be more like an obstruction to be burst. She smelled his raw, acrid maleness; thrust her loins up to meet his cock, and with a single thrust, he penetrated her cunt, slamming his massive glans right to her womb-neck. Trudi shrieked, as her cunt walls gave

194

way to the massive penetration, which filled her pussy to bursting; groaned, flailing in her bonds, as the black man slid up and down her belly, getting her left nipple between his teeth and biting savagely, while arching his back in order to cunt-fuck the frozen girl.

Her gash juiced more and more copiously until the hot, stiff cock was bathed in a torrent of her fluid, and sank so easily into her tight cunt that she had to squeeze the shaft with rapid clutching caresses of her pouch on the glans, especially the sensitive frenulum and pisshole. Yet she did not want him to spurt in her too soon, and worked to still his thrusts momentarily, by arching her own back, thrusting her buttocks up, and clamping his cock with her cunt, its narrowness already fitting him tight as a glove.

Weaver shifted his teeth from teat to teat, biting each one, then sucking the whole breast into his mouth and forcing it against her, with his chin on her ribcage. Her nipples were rigid buds, as the man sucked and bit; Trudi saw his muscled ass pump up and down as his cock slammed harder and harder into the defenceless wetness of her cunt. Trudi's belly fluttered as she felt his cock tremble in preparation to spurt; she kicked, and found that her ankle-cuffs broke free of the ice, which had melted under the heat of their fucking. Joyfully, she threw her legs around Weaver's back, and, clamping him with her thighs and calves around his shoulders, began to buck her cunt and belly against his balls. His body pushed against hers, as if he hadn't expected her thighs' embrace, and wanted her to stay still, but it was too late. His cock was trembling as his balls prepared to deliver her cuntload of spunk. She groaned as his first spurt of cream rushed orgasm upon her, and as Weaver's balls emptied their sperm into Trudi's jerking womb-neck, she howled in climax, her own come flowing to melt runnels in the ice, like hot piss, before freezing in a pondlet.

Trudi's ears rang at the roar of the chainsaw, which Weaver held, blades whirring, inches from her breasts. She screamed, and hot piss flowed from her cunt in her new terror. The piss flowed, briefly melting the ice, before it too was frozen in the puddle of her own come and Weaver's frothed spunk. He guided the chainsaw over her titties, and began to carve at the ice slab, until Trudi fell to the floor, with her wrists still cuffed and fastened to a single block of ice three feet on each side. Weaver motioned her to precede him up the stairs, and she had to carry the burden backwards, hopping one step at a time, as the block of ice dribbled behind her. She slid the block across the clearing, past the flogging posts and behind the house, to the hot springs, from which Melanie and Catilin were hoisting the crimson, broiled and shackled body of Jehanne Farragut. The black girl's face poured with sweat, and her whip weals steamed in the open air. Trudi gasped helplessly as she neared the hot pool, then stood, poised on the brink, under the eyes of the other dozen girls, who no longer masturbated, but looked scared.

Miss Clatterbuck told Trudi that according to the air temperature from the local weather station, and thermal readings of the hot spring, her block of ice should take precisely one minute and 36 seconds to melt, sufficiently to release the embedded handcuffs. With that, Catilin, Angel and Melanie pushed Trudi into the scalding water. The ice crashed after her, and she plummeted down until she reached the bottom. Kicking her way above the ice block, she floated, until her head was inches from the surface. Her chilled body began to thaw as she fought to hold her breath. The heat penetrated her, and she felt her weals awaken and begin to throb once more, the pain growing more and more hideous, as the scalding water reached her core. She longed for breath, as her frozen tissue erupted into a glow of whipped pain, and she bobbed helplessly, cuff chains taut above the imprisoning ice block. She somersaulted and dived, to see if she could pick the copper bolts from within the ice, and began to chip at the rapidly melting block.

As she did so, her bare nates bobbed above the water's surface, and she stifled a scream as three quickfire strokes from the bamboo cane lashed her bare. She lost her grip on the ice, and, bottom smarting, let her head float once more to the surface. She pulled – her head spun, as her breasts heaved, striving not to lose precious air from her lungs – until, with a rush, the ice gave way, and she shot to the air, gulping furiously. The custodians pulled her from the water, while Miss Clatterbuck observed that the weather girl deserved a spanking, as her one minute and 36 seconds had proved to be one minute and 41 seconds. It was time for breakfast, and more housework. Trudi smiled, as she ate beside the recovered Jehanne, crouching like the others, with their clamped breasts on a leash, and their food and water in dog dishes. Whipped nearly to death, then frozen, then nearly drowned and scalded – Trudi got *respect*.

At least, that's what I imagined – I *had* to imagine it, because the thought that what happened to me wasn't meticulously planned to tame me was too horrible, and still is. That's why I wrote about the girl called 'Trudi' who was tortured. But I'm Trudi again now. After my ordeal, everything was easy, if not painless. Kissy Widener asked me in a breathy kind of voice how my 'slab job' had been – that's how I got to know her – and I thought she meant my ordeal in the hot springs, but no, she meant my fucking by Weaver. I told her he had fucked me in the cunt for the first time, and it was pretty good. I mentioned my fear of bursting, as I had such a tight pussy, and that made her curious, and just a tad jealous! She joined Jehanne and me in masturbation threesomes, and had a lovely golden body, with a rosebud cunt that I could get entirely into my mouth, for sucking purposes, although her extra-hairy cunt fuzz got in the way some. I envied her pointy titties, which were not quite as big as mine, but jutted more. She was Dutch, and said there were a lot of Dutch up in Washington state. She liked Jehanne, and said she had never had lesbian sex before, and never sex with an African-American, before Weaver. Jehanne and I laughed, and said we weren't lesbians, but extreme submissives. That made her feel OK.

It was three weeks of training in all, and the more we got that house gussied up, the looser rein we enjoyed, to mutually masturbate, and other stuff. The canings and whippings *never* ended, I must emphasise, nor did the attentions of Weaver's tool, and – as you can imagine, by that time, none of us *wanted* our submissive addiction to end. Jehanne and two other girls were treated to a slab job, but not Kissy Widener. I think she was miffed at being left out of a cunt-fucking, though I did my best to console her in our nightly sessions, fist-fucking her while she tongued Jehanne's clit and masturbated me. She liked that combination. But whatever our masturbatory pleasures, we were all addicted, and all tamed. A girl who becomes addicted to solo masturbation will adore multiple masturbation and accept any fantasy scene thereafter, because in multiple masturbation you are already part of other people's fantasies, and inhibitions melt, like ice . . .

Weaver's role was important: he was our only male, and, as we girls tongued and frotted each other, for want of tool, we longed more and more for real cock, so that by the end we were *begging* him to fuck us in the ass. Verri Kuhl, Louella Clatterbuck, or their superiors, had designed our programme perfectly, I guess like the Marines or Green Berets: a week of total degradation, and a week of back-breaking housework and punishment, gradually boosting our morale, followed by a week of training in *special skills* – you'll see what they trained us *for*. We made a fine job of that house! And then, the next crew of subs had to mess it all up again! I wonder who is in it now.

14

Nevada Popcorn

It was my first experience of a slave mart. I had never dreamed such things existed in the United States, but here it was; moreover, I was one of the slaves at auction. It was thrilling and scary at the same time: scary, for while a sub dreams of slavery, on achieving it, she is generally not far from her normal world, so has a possible escape if her master proves too hard. I was a slave somewhere in the middle of the Nevada desert, and all I knew was there was a weather station nearby. Some escape! Yet it was thrilling because of the delicious uncertainty and helplessness: any of the powerful, wealthy males ranged in front, to inspect me like some piece of meat, could purchase me – *all* of me – if he liked the beef. That's why enslavement, to a sub girl, is such a compliment. A slave is not the same as a bondservant. A slave has no rights at all, no way out, no voice. She can be bought and sold as livestock. At the same time, she has no responsibilities. Her training, feeding, and well-being, or its opposite, are entirely the duty of her master. He buys a female animal as a complete package, has chosen her with one practised look that takes in her eyes, her body, every little detail of her comportment, in a few seconds. So he is confident of his choice, and confidence is real power; it is the greatest turn-on to any girl, sub or not, that a male wants her completely, because, at one glance, he *knows* her.

My thrill was that the slave mart coincided with one of my earliest fantasies. I felt I'd already experienced something of the New England whipping-post, and now I found myself in my 'Queen of Sheba' fantasy. I guess most girls have those, with lots of lovely clothes and sherbet and male slaves, but perhaps without the whipping part. I was the Queen of Sheba, or Cleopatra – somebody like that – with total power over my court of adorable young men and totally hunky soldiers, and I could make them do anything I wanted. Of course, I got them to peel me grapes and suchlike, but I also made them wrestle nude, and the winner had to fuck me . . . then it was the winners, plural, who got to fuck me, one after the other, and then my muscly bodyguards joined in, and I just wore them all out because I was so insatiable. I'd have each lover whipped or caned naked, after he'd pleasured me, and while the next one was at his task. I'd take cocks in the asshole and cunt at once, while sucking off a third . . .

So far, so good. I mean, most girls can probably relate to that. But my sub's fantasy changed, halfway through. The personnel varied. I mean, there were girl-slaves in there too, tonguing my cunt or licking my buttocks or feet, and jostling with the young studs, whether the epicene or hard variety. I've mentioned my rosebud cunt, which is so suitable for a total tonguing, that is, where the fellator [or fellatrix!] gets the whole vulva into the mouth, and sucks and sucks, really hard: clit, lips, hair, everything. That drives any girl wild, especially when she gets a spongeing – the whole face wiped repeatedly up and down her cunt, anus and perineum, and with the tongue in the anus and the nose stuck into her pouch, sniffing her come. That makes me *super*-wild. The funny thing is, some men are frightened of hurting us by sucking our cunts too roughly. I guess they imagine that a cunt is as delicate as their own fragile little orbs, or the delicate masterpiece of a cock. Or they have to show off their artistry, probing with just a delicate tongue-tip in search of our clitties, when all that's needed is carpet-bombing, as it were. A vulva can take a lot of mauling and chewing, and sometimes girls understand that better than men, so I included girls in my mouth-fuck fantasies.

Somewhere in my dream, there was a dispute, among girls and men, while I was in a particularly submissive position, being double-tooled, while both sucked and sucking. Somebody said that no queen would submit to such disgrace, and that I wasn't the queen at all, but some impudent slut of a slave-girl who had kidnapped the queen and taken her place! Of course, with my mouth full of cock, I couldn't reply, and it wasn't long before I was strung up for a terrible naked back-whipping, with metal rods, then bent over for a bare-ass caning, while still obliged to suck an endless succession of cocks, and with laughing girls pissing on my face and breasts.

Torture after torture forced me to admit that I was no queen, but a slave-girl, and at that, I was sent up for public auction. My auctioneer demonstrated my prowess by binding me in tight ropes and hanging me by my breasts from a gibbet, then whipping my naked body all over to make me spin like a top, while customers stopped my whirling to probe my cunt, breasts, even my asshole. At last, I was bought, by this fabulous prince, who outbid every other in order to save his queen from slavery, but it turned out he was a total sadist, and I was only at the start of my torments! Until this other prince rescued me, in a daring kidnap, at night, but it turned out *he* was even *crueller* . . .

Teen romance, I admit, but I had never dreamed it would come *true*. It had. I was roped to all the other girls, nude, and in the wings of a stage like one of those infomercials, with a kitchenette and a sort of workspace for power tools, and a whole A-frame full of suburban junk crammed on to the one stage – except that this suburbia contained several whipping-posts and pillories. We were to put on a floor show! First, we must don provocative costumes and perform our tasks, slowly shedding garments, until we were entirely nude. After we had demonstrated our prowess, the males in the crowd could inspect us, feel us – ask for *anything* – before bidding. We had to demonstrate our special skills we had learned over the past week of training, you see. Whoever bought me could take me back to his quarters in the stable, as my absolute owner.

The stage was in a giant marquee, and outside the door was open desert, so I had no way of knowing if we were within the confines of the stable, or out in the open. We had been led through a warren of passages, roped and blindfolded, without knowing if our nude bodies were observed. Escape was unthinkable in either case, and I believe I speak for all of us when I say that none of us desired to escape. We *wanted* to be bought, and further degraded. Training had made us hungry. The buyers surprised me by looking so normal, as far as I could see them in the shadowy marquee, away from the stage's glare. I'd been expecting rhinestones and cowboy boots, and Arab sheikhs with gold watches, and corny displays of wealth like you see in Vegas, but of course seriously rich men attract attention by *not* looking rich. You have to peer closely to see how fine their clothes are, and that's power – making you look at *them*. A really powerful man doesn't even wear a watch: *he* makes the time.

Verri Kuhl had taken charge of us with Darla Perkins, smirking nastily at me, and wearing a gorgeous [I had to admit!] little French maid's uniform, with frilly apron, stilettos, peekaboo bra, fishnets and everything. On her, it looked trailer-park slut, of course, but emphasised the magnificent body underneath. Miss Kuhl took the register from Miss Clatterbuck, who said we were all accounted for, but Miss Kuhl made us sign our names again, for the voters' list, after she had called the roll: 'Badd, Diorna! Beare, Saskia! Cushunt, Kina! Dubet, Xandra! Etchegui, Petal! Fahr, Trudi! Farragut, Jehanne! Farthquat, Nathalie! Fleisch, Ruth! Garbeau, Pearl! Humble, Marilyn! Pettigrew, Belle! Tushingham, Patsy! Widener, Kissy!' Each of us cried 'Miss!' and snapped her heels, though we hadn't been ordered to. I was so proud to hear *my* name there! It seemed that the stable was almost the majority population in this sparse county, and aimed at taking control of the whole county government. So, we would go and vote – after our training, our docility was assumed! That's one of the interesting things about the west, and which I never imagined in New England, where everything seemed to have been fixed in stone, centuries ago. Out west, people and places are so changeable: towns go boom and bust. A century ago, Vegas, or even LA, scarcely existed, and so on. Some call the west rootless; I like to call it versatile.

Miss Kuhl was surprisingly nice to us, and after we had said goodbye to Miss Clatterbuck, Melanie, Angel and Catilin, invited us to call her 'Verri'. She wore her usual business attire, but now no blouse like Clatterbuck, and I saw how big and firm her bare tits were, thrusting against the single restraining button. I just knew it was to tease Clatterbuck, in her similarly revealing top, for her tits were slightly smaller, though not by much. Louella Clatterbuck carried her usual cane, but Verri had a coiled bullwhip *and* a cane. Verri said that the rule was, *she* wasn't allowed to inspect us during our breaking in, but training staff weren't allowed to see us afterwards, as sold slaves. Now it was time for or costuming, our floor show, our auction, and our fates. We all embraced each other, like we had been in the war or something. Even though we hardly knew each other, we felt we did.

'You understand that a slave sold at auction is still subject to stable rules,' Verri said, 'but is otherwise at the master's whim. Moreover, there is no time limit on your purchase, or resale. We do not regulate the market.'

We all nodded yes, and hugged each other some more. Then it was time to get into our costumes for the floor show. Verri scrutinised written notes from Louella, concerning our attitude and accomplishments. She murmured orders to Darla, who began to hand out costumes: sluttish, frilly, intricate, trad sexy or downright bizarre. All were designed to easily bare the vulva and nates. She raised an eyebrow and actually smiled when she came to read my notes. My costume was the most bizarre of all. Girls have an irrepressible desire to dress up, but they also have an urge to expose themselves, and tease, and when a group of girls are putting on any show, a kind of communal electricity seizes us. Even a straight girl will do things on a stage that she might not do elsewhere, and the 14 of us, naked, shamed and whipped into submission, were a long way from from straight ...

I wore a costume all in black latex, with its curious dusty perfume. My face was covered by a mask, buckled around my nape, which didn't really cover much as it left my eyes, mouth and nose bare, and my mane to swing free. I had a peekaboo bra, more of a string, which clamped my exposed nipples quite painfully, so as to force them out and up. The same for my crotchless pube-string, pressing my pussy so as to enhance the swelling of my gash flaps. It stuck tightly into my ass cleft, so that my bottom was pretty much bare. My generous [!] pubic fleece was entirely exposed, which always gives me a special thrill. Men really get turned on by big pubies. I had stilettos, so high that I could hardly walk, and I might as well have been in a hobble bar; above them, stockings of 15 denier latex, very sheer and shiny, and supported, though they clung anyway, by a garter belt and straps, also in black rubber, with a nice whorled pattern, like little lace beavers. I also had what looked like a tail, hanging from my belt, just at the nubbin of my spine, but it wasn't a tail: it was a rubber tongue, coated in adhesive, and just the length of my 'fertile crescent', that is, from my spine, round my cleft, perineum and vulva, to the top of my pubic bush. In addition, Verri ordered me to coat the inside of my pussy and my asshole, using an entire jar of Vaseline. It was a lovely squelchy feel, but I wondered uneasily what awaited my greased holes.

For starters, we all lined up and bared our bottoms, if they weren't bare already. We had to touch our toes, making our ass cracks, hence our genital apparatus, visible to the buyers. Those who wore panties of any kind, except me, had to lower them to their ankles. My tail dangled beneath my legs, and my moons were as near bare as to make no difference to a whopping. We each took a small whopping, just 12 strokes of a hardwood cane, delivered by Verri Kuhl, but she certainly made them hurt. We had to take our strokes absolutely still, without a sound or any quivering, not even clenching our fesses, an automatic reflex which you can stop only with great difficulty. Clenching dissipates the pain, or seems to flatten it, so to take the cane on bare ass globes and not even clench made the strokes hurt twice as much. I wasn't the only one who had to swallow that terrible rising of the gorge, or feel hot tears sting her eyes. The swishy whistle of the cane split the air at intervals of a second, then stung our bare bottoms with a full set of 12. I was done towards the end: the most terrible part was listening to that vip! vip! vip! getting louder and louder as the cane approached me. There was not a murmur in the marquee, but you could hear the men breathing heavily, and our own harsh gasps, especially at the last stroke of the set, which Verri made an upender, slicing vertically, right on the anus and cunt lips. I almost *screamed* at *my* upender, it smarted so terribly, and the thin rubber thong of my panties offered no protection – my bending over shifted it slightly, to one side of my cleft, so that the caner had a clear view of my intimate meat. That sounds gross, but that was the purpose of the exhibition – to show us future slaves as so much docile girl-meat. We all had to assist in each other's roles, if no more than stripping a girl of her clothing.

For example, I helped strip Marilyn, who wore a kitchen maid's costume, while she cooked at a stove in the stage kitchenette. A lot of our display had to do with housework and kitchen stuff, because that's part of a slave's duties in any dom/sub relationship – such as traditional marriage [*sorry,* Mom!]. Marilyn was cooking breakfast, which is the only meal American men really like, and she was a terrible cook. She couldn't make flapjacks properly, and got more and more of her flimsy clothing soaked in dough and water, so we had to strip her – I mean, we *ripped* the clothes from her, tearing them, and throwing the shreds of cloth on to the floor. Poor Marilyn, her bared bottom already glowing crimson with cane stripes, had to endure the shame of our fooling, as we splattered her with eggs and milk, until she was soaked. We got all her costume off – a strange levity took hold of us – and we vied to see who could do most to distract Marilyn from her task, like wiping her cunt with her panties soaked in pancake batter, or flicking her breast tips with a hot skillet. The great part was when she had to fry bacon, a whole lot of bacon! It popped and sizzled, and must have come from the fattest pig in America, for Marilyn jumped and winced and gasped in pain every time a hot splatter of bacon fat plopped on her tits or belly.

Then we began licking the congealed bacon fat off her skin, while she still worked. Some of the grease found its way to her cunt, so we made sure to get our tongues into her slit and give her clitty a good licking, to make her wet, and drop her frypan in her excitement. I pretended there was bacon fat in the crack of her ass, and got my tongue up her anus, which was quite nice, though different from bacon fat. Xandra Dubet got the whole of her tongue into Marilyn's pussy, and licked her to an orgasm that was quite real, and did indeed make her drop her frypan, splattering the rest of us. That earned her a spanking, of course; we took it in turns, one of us to pin Marilyn's head to the floor, while another spanked her bare bottom. Petal Etchegui collected handfuls of spilled hot bacon and crammed them into Marilyn's pussy, making her howl. That gave me a shiver, and you'll see why. I wedged a lot of rubbery scrambled egg into her asshole, which wasn't quite so uncomfortable, but looked funny. Verri made a comment or two, praising us, every so often. The buyers applauded.

They applauded more when we all had to get down on hands and knees and scrub the floor clean, most of us with sponges and brushes, but Diorna Badd with her mane. Yuk! Pearl Garbeau had to lift her cheerleader's skirt and take off her panties, and, holding her panties in her mouth, dry the floor with her cunt bush. I was a teensy bit jealous because I hadn't been chosen, and her raven jungle was bigger than my own. But then, mine was blonde [spanks for snobbery, Trudi!]. Patsy Tushingham cleaned the electric stove plates with her bare titties – I could see her tears, but she didn't make any noise other than gasp, as her sweat steamed from the hot metal. Verri discovered 'sloppiness' in [I think] Ruth Fleisch, and she had to 'ride the stove' – like riding the rail, in the old west – straddling the hotplate with her bare cunt and ass pressed to it. Verri said calmly that if it was too hot, she knew how to cool it, and Ruth grimaced, sobbing, as she released a steam of piss over the stove, which, I guess, might have cooled it somewhat. That got applause, too.

Jehanne had to stuff her pussy with raw garlic cloves, and press them until the juice dribbled from her cunt flaps – then repeat the trick with her anus. The juice was added to a flour bake mix, and three of the girls masturbated so that their come dripped into the bowl, while others stirred the mix with their tongues. Verri told the buyers it was the best coating for red snapper. My own tour de force was as surprising as it was painful. Without warning, four girls jumped me and pinioned me to the floor, while Nathalie Farthquat heated four shallow pans of cooking oil on the stove, filling each with popcorn. I was upended, and held with my feet in the air. Jehanne held my thong aside and my cunt flaps open, her gleeful eyes belying her mouthed 'sorry', while Saskia Beare inserted a surgical speculum into my anus, forcing it open, wider even than Weaver's giant cock could make it. I gulped, gasped, swallowed, bit my lips and tongue – anything rather than shame myself with a cry of pain. Worse was to come.

When the oil was steaming but the popcorn not hot enough to pop, some other girls took the pans and shovelled the corn into my open holes. I can't even begin to describe how much it stung, though I hoped the Vaseline coating would keep my mucous membranes safe. Verri announced that the buyers were to see a display of old-time Nevada popcorn-making. I was placed on my feet, and Verri swiftly took my latex tail and strapped both my holes shut, the adhesive clinging right across my cleft and covering my whole pubic fleece. I had to rub my crotch and my thighs together – in effect, masturbate vigorously – so that the heat of my cunt and asshole would pop the corn. I began to masturbate, and in fact the silky latex across my cunt made me want to do so. My pouch and asshole were filled to bursting! I masturbated my cunt with wide pressing strokes of my palm, while grinding my anus and clenching my sphincter. I guess it must have looked like the bumps and grinds of a striptease dancer – at any rate, I got a whole lot of applause throughout the performance, which spurred me on. Things were getting pretty wild by now, and I saw many of the other girls openly masturbating, with Verri beaming in approval. There was a loud pop! Then another, and another, and I gasped, as the corn popped inside me. I'd thought I was filled to bursting, but a girl's holes are more elastic than she imagines.

When the final pop had sounded, Verri ripped the adhesive latex strip from my pubis, and it took several of my pube hairs with it, the adhesive was so strong. That was when I almost screamed again. All the girls knelt, and began to swallow the popcorn that overflowed from my holes, dropping all down my thighs and scattering on the floor. There was an ocean of the stuff, and the pressure of all those tongues on my cunt and ass bud, coupled with the fact that my pussy was already gushing from my masturbate, made me go all the way. I gushed and gushed, my come making the popcorn damp, and heaved in a fabulous orgasm, just as the last bit of popcorn disappeared down Jehanne's gullet. I still wonder if I am the first girl in America, at least from outside Nevada, to have gotten off on popcorn.

Things got raunchier: girls were masturbating each other, with beavers and asses thrust provocatively at prospective buyers, to their delight. There was a pause, to calm us down, Verri said wickedly. That meant crouching with our bare butts high, to take another dozen, but this time with a rubber quirt of several thongs, of the type favoured by Melanie Gortz. The whap! whap! whap! of that accursed quirt deepened my existing cane welts. I won't go further, save that I had never experienced such agony as my naked buttocks were flogged with efficient savagery by Verri, and that all previous beatings faded. That, however, is the beauty of submission – *every* beating is the worst ever. After loud applause at our purpled croups, there was a wrestling contest, between Saskia and Nathalie. Each girl was oiled, Saskia by rubbing a huge greasy ham all over her nude body, and Nathalie, by rubbing come from several girls' cunts as they masturbated over her. The contest lasted 15 minutes, and Saskia was declared the winner, 'on points', Verri decided, rather mysteriously, for both girls were so livid with bruises after all the kicking, scratching and hair-pulling, that it seemed a draw.

All of us lined up, crouching again, as though for a beating, but in fact for a game: 'seize the cheese'. A mousetrap lay beneath each of our cunts, with a piece of cheese balanced rather than pinned to it. The idea was to seize the piece of cheese between the cunt flaps without setting off the mousetrap. Any girl who hesitated or shied would receive a further 12 strokes of the cane, on the bare, of course. I knew I'd never manage it, so shut my eyes and plunged. God! The mousetrap slammed right on my flaps and clit, and hurt me to tears. Three girls shied, and got their canings, and only Jehanne was able to seize the cheese. Verri laughed and clapped, for that got her into a worse mess. She had to kneel, arching her back to expose open cunt, while girls stuffed her pouch with Cheez Whiz. In came Darla Perkins, nude but for a snake wrapped around her tits and belly, its tail rattling in the crack of her ass, and its tongue flicking at her nipples. I guess in the trailer park a fully grown diamondback rattler, six feet long, is as normal as breakfast. It probably *is* breakfast. Verri explained to the buyers that the diamondback is the deadliest snake in America, but this one had had its poison sac removed. Suddenly, half a dozen mice rushed across the floor, and we all shrieked, in genuine horror, which the guys loved.

The fastest mouse got to Jehanne's open cunt and dived into the cheesy goop. Darla released the snake's head and it shot across the floor after the mouse, at which the other mice sensibly fled. The hungry one was stuck in the Cheez Whiz. At the last moment, as the snake's jaws opened, Verri plucked the mouse from Jehanne's cunt – you get political correctness even in Nevada – and the snake's head, carried by momentum, disappeared into her pouch. Jehanne's eyes were rolling, but she didn't shriek, as I would have. Meanwhile, Darla had the rattle of the snake inside her own cunt – it was a tug of war, each girl writhing and spinning, and clamping the snake inside her with her cunt muscle, while trying to topple the other – and both girls' thighs wet with come, as the snake's tongue flickered inside Jehanne's gash and the rattle vibrated Darla's. At last, Jehanne toppled Darla, who retreated, pouting, having wrapped herself in her snake again. I think she was sulking, because Jehanne got a come from the snake's tongue and Darla didn't. If I remember right, there was a kind of rodeo after that, where we rode each other, with the steeds trying to unseat their riders, who had short crops and spurs – we were all nude for that. I think I got more weals on my ass from a succession of girls' crops than I did from Verri, but it was fun anyhow. There were a few more shows like that, and we were caned again – Verri Kuhl is as tireless as she's excellent, as a caner – and then it was time for buyers' inspection, and the auction.

15

The Cost

We had to shower and clean up before the buyers had a chance to inspect us, because all of us were dirty, smelly and bruised. We were in the nude for the inspection, and Verri led us round the marquee, roped together at the waist. She paused at strategic spots, so that the men could paw and grope us, often quite intimately. My titties felt raw after being squeezed by so many fingers, and my ass and gash the same. If a buyer's hand spent too long inside a girl's cunt, Verri flicked the rope, and moved us on. The men weren't allowed to address us, nor could we speak to them, and all questions had to be asked of Verri. Mostly, they were about our caning prowess and punishment history – did we weep easily, and so on. Both Verri and the men referred to us as 'it'! It was gross and humiliating beyond belief – at least, that's what I *would* have thought, less than a year before. Now, it seemed quite normal.

After inspection, we went back on the stage, and a spotlight played on each girl as she was auctioned. The buyers were in shadow, so no communication was possible, like winking or smiling at one we liked. We had to keep stone faces. Little talking was done, as the bidding was mostly by waves or nods. The bids started at one, and in every case reached double figures. Verri called out 'Trudi Fahr, a young but willing animal, with great tolerance of whip or cane', and I was eventually knocked down for 28; it could have meant $28 or $2800, or $28 million – or, for all I know, 28 cents. Jehanne went for 25, and some others, like Marilyn and Kissy, went for 35 or 36: Verri had described them as weaklings, who cried easily, and were frightened of the whip, and I learned some dominants like such girls as an ego trip. Buyers of my kind, or Jehanne's, either enjoy the challenge of a hardened bottom or want to try their caning arm, or else, like my new master, were too cheap to buy the more expensive 'whimperers', preferring to win them at gaming.

It turned out that my own first buyer was really interested in trading up at the gaming table. He was young, raw-boned and soft-spoken, but exuded an aura of inherited wealth. When he took me by the dog leash, supplied with all sold slaves, and containing her entire sales and disciplinary history written down, and fastened in a zipper pouch, he ordered me quite casually: 'Follow me, cunt.' I couldn't believe what he said, and he slapped my face to make me move – not angrily, just as you would kickstart a motorcycle. He called me 'cunt' all the time he owned me, which was about three weeks. His name was Mr Reynolds. A slave has a right to know her owner's one name, but not more, unless he wishes.

He never caned me during his ownership of me. He chastised me by slippering, or spanking, with an aluminum softball bat – which stings an awful lot worse than it sounds – or with a device he claimed to have invented, a spanking glove. The glove was made of hard rubber, and extended on a spring worn on the wrist, so that he could spank a girl's bottom without the smarting of the spanker's palm, normal during manual spanking. My routine chastisements were three times daily, with additional ones whenever he felt in the mood. Confined to one room and the adjoining toilet, which I had to lick clean every single day, I heard the sounds of beating from other rooms, so knew he had more than one slave. I was a stake slave – a backhand compliment – a beauty, whose ass he left fresh of weals, so as to stake her in the gaming room to win other slaves, that he *did* cane. [I heard them scream.] My own beatings were long and vicious, the softball bat being the worst tool, and I took up to 500 whops with it. He explained he wanted to harden my ass without leaving weals, so that when he came to gamble with me at poker, my buttocks could stand a very hard and long caning.

He occupied a fancy penthouse apartment, and, although I wasn't allowed to look out the window, I managed to peek a few times when his back was turned. I saw a maze of rooftops, like medieval Paris, in that movie about the hunchback of Notre Dame. Somewhere in that maze were Jehanne, and my other dungeon comrades. I was kept chained and crouching, like a dog, at all times, and had to sleep curled up on the floor by his bed. At night, he would play poker – this was Nevada, after all – and, though I wasn't allowed to speak, he told me that when I was 'prime', it would be my turn – to be gambled, that is, with the girls as stakes, the bets made on how many cane-strokes a prize's bare bottom could stand, without her breaking down or fainting. 'Prime bare' is the highest compliment a stake slave could receive, and was the aim of my spank training from Mr Reynolds. He wasn't into fucking, much, and only fucked me twice, both times in the cunt, from the rear, and once he made me tongue his tiny cock. It was awful! I really hate a guy with a tiny cock. It's degenerate! Call me prejudiced, if you like.

He smoked big Cuban cigars and made me masturbate with them moist from his mouth or from my own pussy – unlit, to my relief, or, *perhaps,* chagrin. I offered to smoke one with my cunt, which I had learned at Miss

215

Clatterbuck's house, but he said he'd seen enough of that. I masturbated a lot, though, which he liked to watch, but he wouldn't use a whip or cane, even though my bottom longed for a proper bare-ass caning! He refused to mark me. I looked forward to the poker game, and hoped he would lose me to another, cane-loving master [preferably hung like a horse!] who would give me what I deserved. Mr Reynolds wasn't a bad master, really, but I wanted to be thrashed properly, and getting called 'cunt' was a novelty that wore off, because he seemed to relish the sound more than the meaning. I mean, every girl has a cunt. 'Bitch' or 'slut' are more satisfying appellations, for then the guy is serious. Maybe Mr Reynolds calls his other slaves – his whimperers – bitches or sluts, when he canes them. I realised later that he was cheap, and found whimperers too expensive at auction.

I was taken down to the gaming room at last. I was nude, bound at the wrists and hobbled at my ankles by a sliding hobble, and wore a rubber pixie hood with the eyeholes and mouth zippered. Mr Reynolds led me by some roundabout route to the gaming chamber, going down a number of staircases so that I had no clue where I was. While he walked, and I hobbled, he explained the rules of stable poker. It was all about money in the long run, but each poker chip represented a cane-stroke to a girl's bare backside, as well as a multiple of dollars [how many, I still don't know, but it was a big multiple].

Verri Kuhl, as stroke mistress, stood behind the stake girls with a cane. As a player bet – 'raise you five', for example – she would give his slave-girl five on the bare. If a girl cried out, or even whimpered, her owner lost his stake at once. Too much whimpering, and he might withdraw from play, to exact real vengeance on her bare ass, and Mr Reynolds said politely that I wouldn't enjoy such vengeance at all. Anyway, hard-ass subs like me have had our pride beaten into us, and are inured not to cry out. The winner scooped the pot, but also, his

216

cards represented cane-strokes: number cards, that number of strokes; jack, 11 strokes, queen, 12, king, 13. So, he could choose to cane the loser's stake girl by the numbers in his cards – a full house, tens on sixes, for example, earned a girl 48 strokes on the bare ass, and a royal flush, 47 strokes [ace counting one], but royally doubled to 94. Or he could demand cash for his chips. If the loser was cash broke, he forfeited his slave. A winner might choose to whop an opponent's stake girl, rather than cash his chips, to weaken her for the next hand, when she'd be sure to whimper, and he could bet high, with his own girl unmarked. Mr Reynolds aimed at a cane-off, girl versus girl, where the two slaves were thrashed until one of them whimpered, and the winner took both girl and cashpot.

I smelled male sweat and excitement, and fear, emanating from a number of female bodies. Like the other stake slaves, I was left hooded and my bound body draped over a wooden flogging-horse, with my slide hobble extended fully, spreading my thighs quite painfully, so as to maximise exposure of my cunt and ass cleft; I was fastened by hobble and wrist ropes to the base of the flogging-horse, with the parted cheeks of my bare ass held high, but my chin braced to hold my head up, in case of fainting under cane. It occurred to me that the best hand of all, four aces, would score a lousy four strokes, and figured that couldn't be right. I didn't have much time for thinking, though, once play started.

The first player said he'd stake five, and at once I heard five sharp stripe marks delivered to a bottom only two girls away from me. She didn't cry, just gasped a lot. Mr Reynolds said that he would venture to raise by six, and I jumped, clenching my buttocks, as they smarted under six searing stingers from Verri's hardwood cane. I panted, clenching hard, as the wood striped my bare flesh, and suppressed my tears and my rising gorge, for this was only the start of a long night.

Another player said he'd raise ten, and this time the strokes went to the girl right beside me. Vip! vip! vip! the cane whistled, and there was that awful tapping slap, as wood lashes bare ass flesh, followed by the shocked gasp and the body's shudder; after the fifth stroke, I recognised the gasping as Jehanne's.

There was no way we could communicate: any vocalisation was classed as a whimper, though sobbing was permitted, being unavoidable, as the night, and the dreadful game, wore on. Mr Reynolds kept upping his raises: I took sets of eight, 11, and even 15 strokes, my ass squirming like a rag doll, and my whole body straining and shuddering in my bonds. My feet were bare under the hobble bar, but no amount of wiggling my toes could dissipate the frightful pain of Verri's caning. Not being allowed to cry in pain was acceptable, but not even being able to talk, to empathise, was worse. Girls know that half the pleasure of any event, fucking, or even caning, is talking about it afterwards, or during. There were two players, and a raise of 18 strokes, and I listened to the lash of the rod on naked skin, sensing something was going to break. It was the girl: after 16 strokes – only two more to go, you stupid bitch! – she screamed, and started to wail, sobbing. A chuckle rose above her moans, as the winner scooped the pot, and the chuckle was familiar.

'Pair of threes,' he said, slapping down his cards, although the rules didn't require it.

'Damn you, Weaver!' said his opponent. 'I had aces on queens!'

'I'll take the *bitch,* if you're *short,*' sneered Weaver.

'Fuck you! Miss Kuhl, unstrap my slut, please! There's plenty of night left to thrash that hide raw! She won't have an ass left to whip, by the time I'm through . . .'

'*No! Please . . .!*' wailed the flogged girl, and now I knew her: it was Marilyn, sobbing, as her owner led her away to exact painful vengeance.

I was helpless to do anything, and am ashamed to admit I soon forgot her as my own torment increased. Mr Reynolds and Jehanne's owner were major players, and our bottoms were the most whopped. Even when not in play, my naked croup threshed and clenched unceasingly, trying vainly to ease the dreadful smarting of Verri's cane, and I could hear from Jehanne's movements that she was doing likewise. I didn't resent Verri. No, she was just doing her job, *the sadistic fucking bitch . . .!* There. As time passed, players left the game, unharnessing their sluts, bitches or cunts and taking them along. Weaver was still in, as was Mr Reynolds. My bottom was agony, every cane-stroke hurting worse, as the stakes rose. Suddenly, there was a shriek; a girl had to take a thrashing of 20, but could not control herself after the 14th. I heard the splashing of piss, and smelled the acrid fluid as she cried. It was Kissy Widener. Weaver chuckled.

'You lose,' he said, with a sound of chips gathered in.

'Damn you,' said the loser.

'Win it all back, dude,' said Weaver.

Mr Reynolds chuckled too.

'OK,' growled the loser, and the next hand was dealt. This time, the stakes were dangerously – for me and Jehanne, agonisingly – high. We were thrashed in sets of 15 at least, at each raise. *Hurry up and call*, I thought, through my tears, as my flaming bare buttocks squirmed. There was a lot of cash, or caning, on that table. Jehanne's owner folded, and so did Mr Reynolds.

'You going to call, or fold?' Weaver sneered.

'Damn you, Weaver. She's my last slave. I call,' muttered the loser.

'I got a lousy pair of threes,' Weaver laughed. 'You get your money back after all . . .'

'*No . . . !*' hissed the man.

'Pair of *deuces?*' cried Weaver, in mock horror. 'So *you* were bluffing!'

219

'You'll take my marker, won't you, Mr Weaver?' the man pleaded. 'I'm good for it . . . just need a few days . . .'

'Uh-uh, dude,' said Weaver, with the sound of his chair pushed back. 'Can't see a man down. I'll take your *bitch . . .*'

'*Oh! No! NO!*' wailed Kissy Widener.

'Shut up, whore, or I'll bet *real* high,' growled Weaver; Kissy shut up.

I was faint, and wished Mr Reynolds would hurry and win Jehanne, which seemed to be his aim. However, he seemed to be getting into the same cash shortage as the loser that Weaver had creamed. He was called, by Jehanne's owner, and showed a straight flush in spades.

'Too bad,' said Jehanne's owner, slapping down his cards.

'*Four aces!*'

'Cleans you out, huh?'

'My friend, why not cane the *cunt* instead?'

'Four itty-bitty strokes?'

'Don't dick around,' said Mr Reynolds, agitated now. 'You know four aces means more than caning.'

'Glad you know the house rules, mister.'

After four ferocious cuts from Verri's cane, I thought it was over: but no. I screamed, because my anus was suddenly penetrated, then split to bursting, by a naked cock as monstrous as Weaver's, hurting me dreadfully, and without benefit of lubrication. The winner chuckled as he buggered me, tooling me so powerfully that despite my weals, my cunt started moistening. As the thrusts grew harder, his cock slimed by my ass grease, he withdrew right to my anus bud before ramming the shaft in again, to my root. My gash was dripping come, and I felt my clitty tingle and his belly slapping my buttocks as he ass-fucked me. I longed to masturbate. I heard myself moan in pleasure; drool dribbled on my chin and smeared my nipples and tits, as come poured from my writhing cunt. I knew I was going to come. He had such *power*. I felt that huge cock tremble, and the first hot drop of spunk slime my anal root, then the cock shuddered and bucked, and a jet of hot cream, more powerful even than Weaver's, spunked into my bursting asshole, filling me completely, and spurting out to dribble down my thighs and into my come-soaked gash hairs. I gave way and, my belly twitching and my clitty throbbing, cried out, as a cunt-soaking, searing orgasm clutched me, and left me gasping. I knew who I wanted for my new owner – not least because I might share that cock with Jehanne. The next hand started. Mr Reynolds was angry, and an angry man doesn't play good poker. When I was sure he had staked his last chip, and Verri was just beginning to flog me a set of 20, I made sure to scream several times, and piss myself noisily and stinkily.

'You damn whimperer!' Mr Reynolds cursed. 'Shit! She's even got piss on my shirt!'

'Then I'll take the *cunt* off your hands, Mr Reynolds, so you can cover your laundry bill,' said my new owner, in a velvet baritone.

He sighed.

'No matter how hard-ass they think they are, *my* bitches *always* whimper . . .'

He ordered me unfastened, and Verri bent to his will.

'Good luck, girl,' she whispered, her voice strangely tense. 'I . . . I'd hoped you'd be spared. Remember you're on your own, now. Nobody'll know where you are. Few enough Americans know where *Nevada* is, apart from the weather people.'

Still blindfold, I was led alongside Jehanne, my sister slave. I thought Verri sounded melodramatic – *Jehanne* was OK, wasn't she? That fabulous ass-tooling had made me optimistic – any discipline would be acceptable, with such buggery as its reward! I mean, it was the most fabulous orgasm I could remember, my pussy just juiced and glowed and tingled, and wanted another, absolutely straight away! Our master might even allow us to converse, or mutually masturbate, as we shared punishment. We went through tortuous passages, ending up in the place which I can never forget. Once again, it is hard to imagine that a girl called Trudi Fahr submitted to these things . . .

The slave Trudi Fahr was assigned the number 25 on arrival at the penal chamber popularly called The Cost, as in, the cost of submission. Number 25's mask was removed, and she exclaimed in awe at the splendour of her surroundings, modelled on the Château La Coste, France. Though non-verbal, her exclamation was punished by her owner, with a cut of a rubber crop across her cheek, leaving a weal she was to bear for several days. Slave number 22, called Jehanne, warned her with pressed lips, and a frown, that communication was undesirable. That was confirmed by number 25's new owner, Mr Sextus Mach, who addressed his new acquisition. Mr Mach was tall, tanned, and sandy-haired, dressed western casual, in blue denim and cowboy boots. He reminded Trudi of Kevin.

'You may feel honoured, or ashamed, to be in the company of degraded whores and sluts, most of them here against their will, while you, like 22, were chosen for your *suitability,*' he said. 'I don't care what you feel, as long as it is pain. Lest you be tempted to express anything else, you will wear a tongue clip, like the others, which will prevent you from talking but not from eating the slop that is served to keep you alive. Kneel, 25.'

Trembling, the slave Trudi, now merely number 25, lowered herself to her knees and put out her tongue. Two slaves, completely sheathed in black rubber, with zippers at mouth and vulva, took hold of her mane and pulled her head back. The slaves had rings of spiked steel enclosing both neck, waist and ankles, over feet in rubber boots, with a rigid extrusion, in the form of an outsize erect cock, at each toecap. Their left breasts bore the stencilled numbers 2 and 3, respectively. Trudi groaned, as her tongue was enclosed in a hard rubber envelope, its open end sealed with a zipper and tiny padlock. She waggled her tongue, but could not even form silent words. Only swallowing was possible. Like Jehanne's, her feet were still hobbled and her wrists bound behind her back; Mr Mach ordered both girls freed, and held by their manes, which the rubber-sheathed slaves twisted tightly in their gloved fists. Trudi gazed upwards at the baby-blue rococo ceiling, adorned with plaster nymphs, naked, agonised, and whipped by erect satyrs.

'Prisoners remain nude at all times,' said Mr Mach, 'save when in exemplary bondage, or punishment dress. You may expect several whippings a day, at my whim, or that of my trusties. Punishment, not rehabilitation, is our goal here, and you shall be exhibited to other slaves as a warning against recalcitrance. Since Château La Coste is a prison, not a training dungeon, do not imagine your punishments lead to anything but further punishments. There is the *remote* possibility I may choose you as trusties, like two and three here. First, you must hate your punishment, hate the château, and, above all, hate *me*, and wish to avenge your shame on the flesh of other girls.'

The two rubber-sheathed slaves thrust their croups at Trudi, showing cutaways in their sheaths, which bared a circle of skin on each deeply scarred buttock. The left buttock bore the letter S, the right an M, both coloured dark crimson. Both letters were tattooed indelibly in the flesh.

'SM,' said Mr Mach, 'means the art of sado-maso-chism. It also stands for *Sade, Marquis*. Château La Coste was the Marquis de Sade's ancestral home, and the site of his most interesting experiments on female bodies. It also signifies my own name, Sextus Mach.'

Trudi followed Jehanne's croup through a doorway, leading to the cell block, a low chamber, slightly bigger than the dungeon, but warm, bright and airy. Thirty-six barred steel cells, all visible to each other, were ranged in a circle, around a central dais, beside which stood pillory, gibbet, whipping-post and a fish tank. The tank was a glass oblong, taller, just, than a human, and contained a human. A nude girl floated, suspended by her mane, from a top bar, with her legs bent backwards, spreading her cunt and thighs. Behind her, her wrists and feet were locked in a hobble. The tank swarmed with fish, crustaceans and eels, wriggling on her body. An air mask enclosed her mouth and nose, leading by a tube to the surface. Eels snapped at her anus and nipples, while a crab crawled into her vulva. Her eyes were slits of pain.

Three other trusties, in the same rubber uniforms, numbered 4, 5 and 6, patrolled the area. The sliding doors of two adjacent cells stood open, and into them Trudi and Jehanne were thrown. Jehanne was locked in, while trusties 2 and 3 followed Trudi to the corner of her cell. As Mr Mach watched, they took turns at using the rubber dildos on their toecaps to lift or push her, proceeding to penetrate and ram her pouch. When sobbing Trudi's cunt was oiled with come, they slapped her titties, turned her, and applied their dildo toecaps to her anus, with one girl holding the buttocks spread, to let the other bugger her. Trudi was left, crying and naked, in a pool of the come, still dripping from her slit. Her cell door slid shut. She began to moan, as one hand crept to her throbbing clitty, and the other to her raw, whipped buttocks. Stroking her wealed fesses, she gasped as her thumb pressed the clitty and her fingers entered her pouch. Her index tickled her anus bud, penetrated, and thrust to the hilt, finger-fucking her own ass. She mewled, as if in protest at her own body's needs, as she masturbated herself to a wriggling orgasm, under the eyes of Mr Mach and all five trusties. Coming, Trudi imagined that huge cock that had newly buggered her to orgasm, and enslaved her in desire . . .

'Masturbation is your only freedom,' said Mr Mach, 'and is, of course, punished by whipping. So is failure to masturbate.'

The cells had bareboard floors; no furniture, other than cuffs, anklets and waist cinches, embedded in the walls. An aluminium hole in the corner served as shower and WC, and a shower of cold water sprayed it without cease. Other prisoners with their faces upended were in the shower, to drink. Outside each cell hung a leather drape, to be shut, Mr Mach explained, for cruel or unusual punishment.

'Your training in the dungeon enabled you to be competent slaves,' he said to Trudi, 'but a prisoner needs no training at all. She needs only to obey, and accept pain, on threat of worse – like the aquarium. There are other refinenents, other rooms, *and you shall experience them all, number 25!* It is day or night at my whim, so you may not even anticipate the comfort of darkness, to lick your wounds. I am that creature called a pervert – those you have met before were mere actors, and the only favour you may expect is to pleasure me in one of the many grotesque perversions at which I am adept.'

Trudi crouched, shivering, in the corner of the cell, staring at the handsome face leering benignly at her.

'You shall come to hate me, number 25, and hatred is the truest form of love.'

Trudi felt tears flowing from her eyes; Mr Mach clapped.

'I shall only do you one kindness, cunt,' he said, 'and that is to rob you of hope. You already think that even the recalcitrants' dungeon could not be worse than this.'

Trudi nodded.

'This is the recalcitrants' dungeon.'

Prisoner number 25 spent five months and 17 days in the recalcitrants' dungeon before she escaped. During that time, she endured frightful indignities and constant pain, of which whipping was the mildest cause. Her tortures became harsher as her skin hardened and her mind was numbed. As Sextus Mach had promised, she suffered every agony and shame the château offered. Food was soup, dripped twice a day from a wooden bowl fixed between the bars of her cell, out of her reach. Daily whipping robbed her of appetite for anything but sleep, of which there was never enough. Ten strokes of the cane, taken on the bare, bending over, was the signal of dawn. Then, backbreaking work in the yard, open to the sky, amid hgh walls: the work construction, or use, of instruments of supplice. Each girl, bolting together a whipping-frame, gibbet or treadmill, awaited her turn to be hung high for a bullwhip flogging, while Mr Mach dined off a whipped slave-girl's bare back. Trudi wept bitter tears on the occasions when Mr Mach chose to bugger her in full view of the other prisoners, for, unlike them, she came speedily and copiously to juice, and to orgasm. She wept in shame at her weakness and her desire for Mr Mach's cock in her anus. With Jehanne, Mr Mach preferred cunt-fucking; Trudi tried to make eye contact with her friend, but soon each girl's eyes were too dulled by pain, or hooded with lust for their master's cock, to perceive the other. Mr Mach never spunked in a girl's hole, preferring to laugh as she climaxed under buggery, or masturbated herself to orgasm while he throat-fucked her. Trudi thought he reserved his sperm for his five trusties, always hooded and sheathed in rubber; at first, she wondered who they were, then stopped wondering. All were equally brutal with cane or whip.

There were varied tortures: the treadmill, the aquarium, the roasting spit, the rack. At all of those, prisoners

226

helped to torture their sister slaves, and Trudi was no exception. Jehanne's howling, as Trudi basted her nude body with her own come as it turned over a charcoal brazier, left Trudi indifferent, although several prisoners masturbated openly as the trusties flogged the black girl's bare buttocks with wands of elm wood. A girl marching the treadmill endured cane-strokes from the other girls, eager to stripe her naked flesh as they knew their own would be striped. There was neither kindness nor honour among prisoners, and Trudi knew that was how a girl showed her mettle, to become a trusty. Whenever possible, she administered the cane to Jehanne's bare buttocks, hoping Mr Mach would notice her betrayal of friendship.

One room contained a birching block, at which a prisoner must kneel to have her wrists, neck and ankles roped down, for a birching on the bare buttocks: never less than 30 lashes, and sometimes 100. The floor stank, for few girls could take birching without losing control of their bowels. Trudi was birched at least once a week, and orgasmed by her tenth stroke, sometimes orgasming twice in the same flogging. She wept in shame at her own pleasure. The dungeon, and Miss Clatterbuck's harsh training, seemed a pleasant memory, now, although memories faded: Don, Elle, Marc, Peter, Kevin, Darla, Verri . . . all just names in a dream. She herself had to birch Jehanne to 80 lashes, during which Jehanne pissed herslf twice, and fainted three times, being revived by strong jets of piss from the watching, masturbating girls. Trudi masturbated too, as Jehanne's bare black buttocks shuddered in pain under the crackling caress of the birch, but when another girl was birched, she masturbated with the same cruel glee. Pain was her world; she must either feel, give or receive it, or masturbate over observed pain – as long as there was tortured, whipped girl-skin.

Displays of punishment were given to an audience of male guests, with their female slaves, on the dais in the centre of the cell block, and the prisoners strove to outdo each other in cruelty, so that the roped or bound slave-girls gazed wide-eyed at the punishments, clinging loyally to their owners, lest the same be visited on their own bodies.

Girls were knotted intricately in ropes, before whippings on cunt and teat; donned strap-on rubber dildos to bugger each other; whipped one another at pillory or gibbet. They wrestled nude: gouging, kicking and hair-pulling, sometimes fighting underwater in the aquarium. Girls unpunished awaited punishment with their holes held open, or penetrated, by a variety of speculums, forceps and other surgical implements. Every girl took breast-whipping, seated on a throne of penitence, with two huge wooden dildos set in the seat, and impaling her anus and cunt; while the buttocks, extruded through holes like toilet seats, were caned from beneath.

Trudi wielded a whippy little elm wand, one day – or night – on shuddering bare breasts she dimly recognised: looking at the face contorted in agony, she saw it was Darla Perkins, writhing on the throne of penitence. Beside her, the naked buttocks of a girl treading the mill squirmed under half a dozen canes, and the eyes twisted to look at Trudi. Trudi gazed dully at Miss Verri Kuhl, her pubic bush now fully grown, and dripping with sweat, piss and come, but continued to whip Darla Perkins' nipples, until the red nipple flesh bruised by the cane seemed to spread like jam over the entire firmness of the teat. Mr Mach told her to join the girls caning the new prisoner on the treadmill, and Trudi obediently applied her strokes to Verri's crimson buttocks. Mr Mach said he was pleased with her progress, and she would join him in his chamber that night, before her special honorary tattooing on the morrow. Prisoners 25 and 22, Trudi and Jehanne, were to become trusties, and their cunts would receive Mr Mach's sperm.

Roped beneath Mr Mach's four-poster bed, the nude Jehanne and Trudi took turns at sucking the giant stiff cock that protruded through a knothole in the bedstead. Their tongues remained zipped in rubber, as the master relished the feel of rubber in a girl's mouth. Above them, the air whistled with cane-strokes, then there were groans as Mr Mach's bound body was penetrated by the strap-on rubber dildos of each trusty.

'Yes, bitch!' he hissed. 'Bugger me deeper!' or 'Whip harder, monstrous whore! *Pain!* The new slut who drinks my spunk shall brand the other first!'

The girls together tongued the glans, licking peehole and corona, or deep-throating the shaft to the balls. As Jehanne expertly fellated the master, with his cock at the back of her throat, Trudi saw a window open to stars and rooftops; silently, she began to gnaw through her ropes. If Jehanne noticed, she gave no sign. Trudi took over fellation and felt the sperm trickle then spurt, from the cock of Sextus Mach, as the master writhed atop her, buggered and flogged by his rubber-sheathed trusties. Trudi swallowed all the spunk, and gestured to Jehanne that they should break for the window to escape: Jehanne shook her head, no. Her eyes stared wide. Trudi continued to lick Mr Mach's prepuce, as he moaned in pleasure, and the bed creaked as he was buggered by the females. Trudi made warning motions of marking on the buttocks; Jehanne bowed her head, nodding her accord. She *would* be marked. Trudi kissed her lips, squirting a mouthful of the master's spunk into Jehanne's mouth; then sprang to the open window, past the black rubber figures, dildos stiff, vigorously buggering and whipping the trussed master of La Coste. A rubber lariat snaked after her and just missed her neck: without pausing, Trudi jumped.

16

Juniper Berry

I was in the nude, running, and it was a warm desert
night. I realised it was now summer in Nevada, though
temperatures, and weather generally, are totally un-
predictable here. Low humidity, but still I was sweating
– in fear. Behind me, the sullen mass of the stable, like
a great rock of terror: ahead, nothing but desert, jagged
hills, dark under the stars. I couldn't *believe* I'd escaped
from it, or *if* I'd escaped from it, and this wasn't
another of Sextus Mach's games. The rocks hurt my
feet, and I didn't care, because I was gloriously barefoot, not hobbled or shackled. I ran for what seemed
like miles, my titties bouncing uncomfortably, breast
skin and erect nipples shining in the starlight, my lungs
aching, and suddenly I stopped. I'd run out of steam; I
was exhausted, thirsty, and I needed to pee. All alone in
that desert, I went behind a boulder, as if someone
might see! I squatted and pissed copiously, cupping the
hot liquid in my palms, and forcing my bladder to stop
when my cup was full. I raised it to my lips, and
poured the piss down my throat. I did that three times,
until the last drips of pee shook from my pussy. The pee
tasted acrid, yet nourishing, and took away the burning
in my mouth and throat. I wrenched at the rubber
sheathing my tongue, clawing, until I tore it, and got the
hateful thing off. It was fabulous to feel my tongue free,

after five months, though all I could taste was my own pee.

'I'm free!' I cried, to the desert night.

Yet, the beautiful thing was, I wasn't free. I was trapped in beauty, naked and alone and miles from help, in the most submissive situation of all. I stood and parted my legs, selecting a star to gaze at. I chose Mars, burning bright and red – not a star, really. But I imagined Mars as a delicious weal, lashed in the heavens by a celestial cane. My fingers found my clitty, already throbbing, and I was giddy with lust for the whole sky and desert, the prison that enfolded me, the night breeze caressing my nipples to rocks, as I began to masturbate. My cunt was already seeping juice, and before long, the seep was a lake of salty come, dripping, then flowing down my thighs and on to the desert floor. I thumbed my clitty, got three then four fingers into my pouch, and began to pummel my womb neck; crouching slightly, I parted my buttocks and oiled my other hand with come from my gushing cunt. I tickled and greased my anal pucker, sending that delightful shiver through my fesses and spinal nubbin, then poked my fingers into my anal shaft. Soon, I had two fingers poking the root of my anus, and began to finger-fuck my asshole really hard. My titties tingled with electricity, and I swept a hand up across my soaking pubic bush, from my cunt, to pinch and scratch my nipples, smearing come all over my titties and belly, and then my thighs, although I was so wet, I didn't need to do much there. I screamed with joy, as my belly and cunt pulsed in a glorious climax, that wracked my whole body in a spasm of delight. After masturbating, I at once curled up beneath the rock, and fell asleep in a fetal position, with my thumb in my mouth and my hand clasping my cunt.

I awoke in searing bright sunlight, with a boot kicking my crotch, and screamed. It was no dream; above me, in shadow, stood a figure in a wide-brimmed hat, holding a baton. I rubbed my eyes, and peered: it was a woman, wearing a brown skirt and shirt, with a star pinned to the breast. I had fallen asleep beside a highway, an empty ribbon of tar stretching into the hills, and beside me was parked a police cruiser.

'On your feet, and spread them, you bitch!' snarled the woman, in an accent I couldn't place.

I supposed it was a native Nevadan, a bit like Darla and her trailer-park voice. In fact, it was English, from England! But I'll get to that. At that time, I was too scared to care about accents. I was so shocked at being kicked between my legs, I couldn't move. She kicked me again, harder, and I writhed in pain.

'Move, you fucking slut!' she barked. 'Get over that rock, with your arms and legs apart.'

I struggled to my feet, and did as she ordered. I felt her gloved hands sliding up and down my skin, and realised, to my amazement, that she was searching me! I couldn't help laughing, despite the pain in my beaver.

'I've no clothes on,' I blurted. 'I mean, do you think I'm carrying a gun or something?'

Vap! The baton cracked against my bare bottom, and I howled. Most girls have never been spanked on the bare with a police baton, and they should know it's less than fun.

'Shut up, bitch,' she hissed, and put her gloved fist inside my cunt, spreading her fingers inside the pouch.

I trembled in shame, feeling my pussy begin to moisten. The woman began to stroke the walls of my cunt, making my come flow. Her other hand felt my ass cleft and anus bud, lingering, before patting the welts on my buttocks. She ran her fingers slowly and deeply down the criss-cross of ridges left by various canes and whips.

'What *is* this?' I gasped.

'Someone's taken quite a run at you,' she said. 'Or are you some kind of *pervert*? No *perverts* in *this* county.'

232

'Oh, yeah?' I sneered, which earned me another crack across my bare ass; with a choking sob, I said I'd escaped from a whole ranch of perverts.

She still had her hand in my pussy, and her glove was soaked in my come. I hoped she would give me another crack with the baton. The weals were beginning to throb and glow, and I remembered my masturbation, and hoped she'd give me a whole spanking with that baton. Honestly. The desert works magic on a girl's pussy and ass.

'I'm Deputy Sheriff Berry,' she said. 'I'm taking you in for questioning. Get into the car, bitch.'

'*Questioning?*' I cried, already stumbling towards the car, with the deputy's hand in my cunt. 'What *for?*'

'You'll see,' said Deputy Sheriff Berry, slamming me into the backseat cage, and sliding into the front seat.

I saw in the mirror that her skirt rode way up, over tan thighs, and that she wore no panties. Her auburn pubic bush was as full as my own, and was wet, with an oily sheen. I could smell its aroma, even from the back seat – full and tangy, as if she rarely washed her cunt. Her first name was Juniper. Deputy Sheriff Juniper M Berry gunned the cruiser towards the mountains, the powerful motor sending vibrations between my thighs that made my clitoris throb and my cunt wet. I wondered if I'd come before we reached the police station. My hands weren't cuffed, so I began to thumb my clit, just to make sure. I looked into the mirror again: the deputy sheriff was driving with one hand, while the other was plunged between the swollen lips of her hairy wet gash, as she masturbated herself. We both enjoyed the drive.

'Weather Station', the sign read. The letters were branded into the wooden beam above the police station. I'd never heard of a deputy sheriff in a weather station before, and, as Juniper hustled me inside, summoned up the nerve to say so. I wouldn't mind if she spanked my

233

bare ass again with that zinger of a baton. I felt intimate already – we had both masturbated to the thrumming of the police cruiser, up the craggy mountain road, and, looking at each other in the mirror, both came at the same time. That's pair bonding, of a kind.

'I have to do everything round here,' she said, her voice mellow. 'The county gives me practically no budget, so I have to moonlight as weather girl. Funny, yeah?'

I laughed dutifully, which put her in a good mood.

'See that?'

She pointed to a pylon with an antenna on top.

'I operate my own TV weather channel. It goes out by satellite, nationwide. Good money from subscribers.'

'Why would people pay to see the weather?'

'You'll see. Why, you'll help. My girls have to earn their keep.'

Alarm bells in my head.

'*My girls*, officer? Aren't you going to read me my rights?'

Vap!

'*Ah!*'

My bare ass smarted horribly, and I squirmed. Juniper gestured to the stunningly beautiful, and stunningly empty, lunar landscape beneath and around us.

'You really want me to? Who'd listen?'

We looked at each other, and the tip of her baton traced the curve of my ass cleft, and my gash flaps, still swollen and moist from masturbating.

'I . . . I guess not,' I whispered.

'I can use some home help,' she said.

'Now, wait a minute . . .'

It was big inside, more like a ranch house than a jail, but my cell was small enough. Juniper cuffed me for the first time, and locked me in, standing, with my cuffs looped through a bolt in the cell wall, above my head. I was uncomfortably aware that I was in whipping position. She lounged, ogling my ass and back, with

234

boots propped on her desk. I half expected her to chaw tobacco.

'You don't expect me to stay like this,' I said.

'Only until you see reason,' she said.

I shrugged.

'I see reason, Sherriff Berry,' I said, meekly; really, I was excited by my standing, spread nude in whipping position, as any sub girl is.

'You call me *deputy*,' she snarled. 'Sheriff isn't here.'

She paused, eyeing my nipples, already stiff.

'I intend to whip you for that mistake.'

I lowered my head.

'If it pleases you, Deputy.'

She spat. She *was* chawing tobacco.

'If it pleases *you*,' she said, uncoiling a braided leather horsewhip about four feet long, and unlocking my cell.

Juniper delivered a perfect whipping on my bare back and buttocks. By perfect, I mean excruciatingly painful. I didn't make a sound, though tears flooded my eyes, and my cunt was soaking in desire to be masturbated again. She gave me 25 strokes on the shoulders, and 25 to the ass, and had me gasping like a carp out of water. It did please me, and she knew it. It was a lovely whipping: deft, graceful, expert and extremely painful. I was whipped in a jail cell, just as in the old west, and my pussy was full of come, as I squirmed under Juniper's lashing. I was *tame*.

'You *are* a pervert,' she said, after the 50th stroke.

'Yes,' I sobbed, my body still shuddering in pain.

'Submissive.'

'Yes, Deputy. You've . . . you've tamed me.'

'Even better. I want you to be a housemaid. Wear uniform, serve me tea and things. I'm English, you see. You look English.'

'German, Deputy.'

'Same difference. You'll wear a proper maid's uniform, and serve me *Kaffee und Kuchen*. Get a spanking on your bare ass, any time you misbehave. Oh, and assist with the weather forecast, when I think you're ready. Deal, slut?'

'Deal, Deputy.'

Juniper M Berry released me from my cuffs and my cell. It was time, she said, for her morning coffee, and I was to serve her. On the deck outside her spacious lounge, overlooking the mountains and desert, I teetered on high heels, with a uniform of frilly apron, short skirt, a too-tight blouse with a cleavage that showed most of my tits in a scalloped uplift bra, lace garter belt and too-tight panties, which were little more than a G-string. She didn't spank me again that day, but made me do all the household chores, even those that seemed done already. Then I repeated the service, only with English afternoon tea, cookies and stuff. I didn't know what she did for dinner. I had a new cell to sleep in, with a mattress, but I was still locked in and nude, though not cuffed. I had to pee in a bucket. Yuk!

The next day, when I had finished morning coffee service, she said she must spank me. My whip weals still smarted, but I was pleased, and willingly bent over her thighs, to lift my skirt, pull down my tight G-string, and have my bare backside slapped to crimson. The sun was really hot, and she made the spanking leisurely. Smack! Smack! Smack! My naked buttocks wriggled like kittens as she spanked me. She said it was good for a German bottom to feel a good English spanking, and though I agreed, I pretended to protest. She spanked hard. Juniper told me that her middle name was Maybelle, and her something-great-grandmother was Maybelle Berry, the 'whupped woman' of Virginia City. She had made her fortune as a flagellant in the silver-mining days, and had attracted an English lord, who came to gamble and be whipped in the brothels of Nevada. America was a no-nonsense place – I mean, if you could pay for something, you got it, even if people didn't understand why a man would want women to cane his bare bottom crimson. Taken to London, Maybelle continued to shine in her career, though she discovered that while 'martinets' were plentiful – that is, girls of the servant class, who took naked caning – only a select few ladies knew how to wield the cane on the bare asses of the British aristocracy, which is what most of them wanted, it seemed. She had all kinds of gimmicks, like a flogging-frame that was also a torture rack, with a hole for the subject's cock and balls, which would be sucked by Maybelle's girl assistants, as she whaled some lord's buttocks with a cane.

Maybelle made sure her descendants kept US nationality, and a love of the rod, but Juniper was the first born-again flagellant to revisit her ancestral home. That was after an education at just about the most expensive girls' boarding school in England, where, she said, the 19th century had never gone away. Girls were punished by caning, on bare buttocks, and when a girl rose through the ranks to become a monitor, she had such a taste for the rod that she was glad to cane the bare bottoms of fresh miscreants. It took several days, and several spankings, for her to reveal more and more of the truth, and that she knew all about the First Amendment. After I was spanked, she liked me to masturbate her while she played with my titties, but did not let me masturbate myself. That I had to do in private, or when I watched her lithe, tan body in her pool, with her titties floating around her like big brown lily pads, while I waited with her fluffy yellow bathrobe. She didn't swim nude, but wore the bottom half of a peach-coloured bikini. There were cabanas all round the pool, and I hoped that if I behaved, I might get to have one instead of a cell. Her brown skin – the colour I had wanted to get, sunbathing at Lake Champlain! – looked stunning against the yellow. I had already seen her massive pubic fleece, and, like me, she did not shave under her arms. Her breasts and ass were the equal of mine.

'Grandma Maybelle discovered,' she drawled, on the hundredth or so smack of my morning spanking, 'that most men prefer to *be* spanked. Dominants like Sextus Mach are a rarity, though he's not as dominant as he likes to think.'

I said I could scarcely help her, as I was truly submissive. I didn't want to say just yet, that I knew Mach's secret love of being humiliated by his ladies in rubber.

'Americans, like the English, are puritans,' she added. 'They like to fuck, then be punished for it. You can *fuck*, I take it.'

I assured her I could.

'Jolly good show,' she said.

That night, I was summoned to sleep with her. She slept in a big brass four-poster bed, and it was glorious to sink into the scented sheets and pillows. They did not remain scented for long, for, when she went down on me – both of us nude – her oral sex was so good, I was wet in an instant, and my come flowed all over the bedsheets, her face and auburn mane. She shifted her belly so that her own juicing cunt squashed my face, and I tongued her cunt, with my nose in her pouch, and often getting my tongue an inch inside her come-greased anus. At the same time, we pinched each other's nipples, which she called 'dialling telephone numbers'. It was at such times that her cute British idiom showed through. We didn't speak – starlight gleamed on our slippery bare bodies, because it was too hot to caress under the coverlet. It went on until dawn, and I can't count the number of times I came, with my come flowing into Juniper's mouth, and hers into mine, and our teeth on each other's throbbing clits. There was no spanking, not even slapping, as though spanking was a formal ceremony for daytime – very English and proper. With the dawn light, I saw clearly her naked ass, that I had licked, bitten and stroked so many times. Into it were inked the letters S and M. Juniper grunted.

'I told you I knew about the First Amendment,' she said. 'I was Sextus Mach's first trusty. He enslaved me, quite beautifully. Another bloody German! From Milwaukee, actually. There's submissive in all of us, even me.'

I kissed her bare buttocks, pressing my nose in her cleft, to sniff her wet cunt.

'And the other trusties?' I murmured.

'School friends of mine,' she said. 'The price of my freedom. Man-haters, who haven't outgrown their schoolgirl passion for other girls.'

'*I'm* not really lesbian, Juniper,' I whispered.

'Neither am I, but we can enjoy each other until the right man comes along.'

'I guess so.'

'If only men weren't so stupid. This nonsense about caring and being sensitive ... If only they could understand us! Understand a female animal is happy when enslaved, well whipped and obedient. Mm ... Do that again.'

'OK.'

When I did get my morning spanking, Juniper was just as stern in her slaps and as teasing of my titties as ever, as if she'd forgotten our intimacy. Now that I had seen her branded buttocks, she swam in the nude, with her pubic hairs trailing between her pumping thighs and fesses like tendrils of seaweed. That went on for several days, until finally she said I could help with the weather report, and that I first must strip. Nude, I followed her to the weather room: inside, it was a miniature TV studio. Juniper pressed switches and there were hums and flickers from various computers and cameras and stuff. The camera was automatically controlled, and she did the editing later, to transmit an hour after the recording. It was weird. I had to stay out of sight, while Juniper sat in a swivel office chair, in her full deputy sheriff's uniform, and brown nylon stockings, with her legs crossed.

'Hello!' she said, exaggerating her cute English accent. 'This is worldwide weather network, and I'm Deputy Sheriff Juniper M Berry, bringing you the weather across the US, and the world. First, Idaho . . .'

Idaho . . .! She began to prattle about cold fronts coming in from Canada, and high pressure and low pressure and all, and told farmers in Idaho to watch out for their broccoli, and be sure and get some more Weaverbrite polarised plexiglass to shield their crops, 'just like the Weaverbrite I use right here in the Nevada sun, when I'm relaxing – uh, *completely nude!* – on my deck.'

Juniper smiled coyly, took off her sheriff's hat, and cast it aside with a flourish, letting her auburn mane cascade over her breasts, while undoing her necktie. Then she unfastened the top button of her uniform shirt, then the next button . . . She zipped from state to state, with stuff about convection currents in the Gulf of Mexico, or barometric pressure in Maine, and hints about this crop or that crop doing fine, or not so fine, and always the answer seemed to be some Weaverbrite product. Hurricanes in Florida? Power outages in California? You needed Weaverbrite storm windows, or hurricane lamps, or whatever. It was the same worldwide. The coffee crop in Brazil, diamonds in South Africa, Moroccan phosphates – the weather had some surprise, and investors should be careful, even if they couldn't get any Weaverbrite. All the time, Juniper was doing a striptease.

Her shirt came off, and she was down to her bra and skirt; that dropped, leaving her in bra, panties and garter belt, with big tufts of moist pube hair sticking out of her lacy G-string. She kicked off her boots, then slid off one stocking after another, and finally unhooked her bra, letting the cups dangle an inch from her bare teats before dropping it. The garter belt came off, after a tantalisingly slow unstrapping, and then she wriggled out of her panties – all the time keeping up her weather jargon. She lifted one foot on to the arm of her chair, completely exposing her beaver, and began to stroke the lips of her vulva and her visibly stiff clitty. She pawed the inside of her pouch until her fingers came out oily, for her to lick, winking at the camera. Then she began a slow, luxurious masturbation, though the flow of chatter never stopped, in that sing-song English lilt.

'Missouri!' she cried. 'Why, I'd almost forgotten *Missouri!* That's a *spanking offence!* Big ugly hailstorm coming your way, and if you don't know what hail-stones sound like . . .'

She beckoned to me, and I approached, to be bent smartly over her thigh, with my bottom high and spread. Smack! Smack! Smack! She began to spank me on the bare, which was still flushed from my morning hundred, right to the camera. Smack! Smack! Smack! I wriggled, in real discomfort, as she slapped my ass in quickfire rhythm, keeping up her chatter about how the only protection against hailstones was a Weaverbrite hail shield, otherwise, whatever they grow in Missouri, which I still don't know, was in big trouble.

'*That's* what hailstones sound like!' she declared, smacking my naked buttocks for the 80th or 90th time, 'and if this sinful girl was wearing Weaverbrite trailer padding, why, she wouldn't be squealing like a hog in heat!'

I realised that I *was* squealing. That spanking really hurt: my fesses were wriggling, and my cunt was oozing come. As she continued to spank me, Juniper raised her hand from my neck, and transferred it to her own gushing cunt, which she resumed masturbating. I was so hot and wet, I couldn't help using my own fingers to do the same. We both masturbated ourselves to climax, after which Juniper delivered a final spank, sneakily, right on my oozing gash flaps, and said that terminated the weather report. We exited the TV studio and returned to the lounge overlooking the pool. Juniper went straight to her computer and began to key.

'Got to trade,' she muttered. 'Let's see ... long position on broccoli futures ... orange juice ... coffee, sell short ...'

After a while, she pronounced herself satisfied.

'You use *weather reports* to play the *stock market?*' I exclaimed.

'Americans are in awe of weather reports and religion,' she said, 'and especially of naked women. I vary my act – use snakes, or lizards, or have little geckos crawling all over me. The message gets through subliminally. Should do handsomely with Idaho broccoli this year ...'

'Weaverbrite?' I gasped. 'Whatever ... ?'

'Company in Gary, Indiana,' she said.

'There was a man called Weaver –' I began.

'I know. He's the sheriff. I'm married to him, but what does *that* mean?' she snorted. 'It was Weaver who helped me escape from Sextus Mach.'

'I got a slab job from Weaver,' I said, faltering.

'Did you, indeed? He's a filthy slut – you don't look a bit like his ex. He must like you.'

'What *is* a slab job?'

'What do you think? Weaver hates his first wife – she still lives in Gary, Indiana. I'm whipping the hatred slowly out of him, so that he'll hate me instead, but he cries when I whip him. *I* hate *that.* Certain men like slab jobs, for revenge, or fantasy, because the women are ... shall we say, inert. I get a lot of clients for makeover girls – made up to look like their favourite movie queen, so they can show the video to the boys back home. Or else, like their ex, so they can send it to *her.* Men! Yuk. Mostly, clients are just normal subs, and want me to thrash and humiliate them.'

Before I could ask about these *clients*, a cabana door opened, poolside, and a black man, naked, with huge

242

cock dangling, emerged, carrying a nude black female. Her wrists and ankles were bound, and, peering, I saw she was not in fact African-American, but was covered from head to foot in mascara or something. Despite the colour, I recognised Kissy Widener.

'Weaver!' cried Juniper.

Snarling, Weaver hurled the bound girl into the swimming pool. At once, I rushed out and dived in to save her. But Kissy was already swimming. Her wrists and ankles had been bound with elastic bands. We embraced underwater, our two nude bodies intertwined, breasts and cunts pressed, until we had to come up and gulp air. An astonishing sight, if a familiar sound, greeted us. Weaver crouched, his bare buttocks high, with Juniper standing over him, wearing her peach-coloured bikini. Vip! Vip! Vip! Weaver's bare ass squirmed as Juniper thrashed him with a hickory cane.

'I warned you!' she hissed.

'Bitch wouldn't lay still!'

Vip! Vip! Vip!

'Ahh . . .!' Weaver screamed.

'I warned you . . .'

Vip! Vip! Vip!

'Oh, please . . .'

Vip! Vip1 Vip!

'Please, what?'

'Please, Mistress . . .!'

Vip! Vip! Vip!

In the pool, Kissy and I embraced. I stroked her spine, then lingered at the crack of her ass, while her fingertips teased my cunt lips. A seep of oil drifted from my gash into the clear pool water, and Kissy, too, began to juice, our come mingling as our slits opened to show pink. I had so much to tell her, about Mr Reynolds, and Verri Kuhl, and Sextus Mach, and Jehanne, and everything. It seemed the most natural thing in the world for us to mutually masturbate at the sight of a male caned

243

bare, and squirming, with his cock stiff. Especially as it was *Weaver*. We finger-fucked, pretending it was with Weaver's tool.

That was months ago, and it's the end of summer, now, and still scorching hot. I proved myself useful to Juniper in many ways, as Kissy did. She has a dominant streak – it is she and Juniper who whip the rich dudes that fly in to grovel, while I've made makeover my specialty, in the submissive role I like best. I like dressing up – demure English schoolgirl, pigtailed German *Mädchen,* complete with yodelling, Japanese geisha, you name it – then undressing, for my beating. Lots of times I get a photo kit to study, so I can be the girl of the guy's dreams, like, the prom queen he never dated, or a movie star, or something like that, out of his reach, you know?

It gives me a thrill, too, to be someone else. I do a slab job, sometimes, and you get used to it. I make sure Juniper gives me a sound spanking first, before my ass goes on ice, and I always piss, just after the guy comes, to surprise him – like his fabulous tooling has woken up his princess. Imagine my surprise when one of my clients for a slab was Peter Murchy and – I had to make myself up as *myself.* Yes, as the plaything from Plattsburgh. I could hardly remember what I looked like back before my body was golden and all, and I had to use white makeup to disguise my all-over tan. Peter had a thing for me because I reminded him of his bitch ex-wife, and at first he didn't realise I *was* his plaything from Plattsburgh. I was eager for gossip, but one of the rules of a slab is no talk. It was a good fuck, though. He did me three times in two hours, once in the cunt, once in the throat, and once in the ass.

Juniper lets me go barefoot, and nude, too, but she never lets any of us forget who is boss, and can hobble, bind or shackle us at her whim. She whips us, too. Weaver doesn't get to do that, as he needs all his energy for fucking us, when he is absent from his duties at the stable. Kissy said there is nothing so fabulous as being boned in the ass by a black stud, and I told her not to be vulgar, then giggled, for that was a little bit of New England resurfacing in me. Actually, Juniper makes him fuck me in the cunt from time to time, and makes sure to watch that he gives me all his spunk – then thrashes him for doing so, while I masturbate with Kissy.

Turned out that Juniper herself is the stable mistress and controls the souce of the hot spring. She sends instructions, again at whim – that was why Verri and Darla got sent to Sextus Mach, to remind them that fate is a turning wheel. I wish she'd do something to Kevin. No, I don't, really, he was only doing his job, in seducing me, and he was a fabulous fuck. I heard a rumour that Elle, or maybe Cher – maybe both, now I think of it – had, ahem, double-dated Kevin, and become slave-girls at the stable. It wouldn't surprise me. I know they'd be happy as slave-girls – the bitches! As it is, I get more fucking than Juniper or Kissy, so we three pleasure each other, three in a bed, when we don't have Weaver's cock to play with, and I tell them all about the cocks I've had inside me. I like the weather reports, too, especially when I get a spanking, or – special treat – have little geckos crawling all over me, on my nipples and into my pussy, which makes me all tingly. Sometimes, Juniper lets Kissy spank, or even whip me, while she gets on top of Weaver. I think Weaver will probably help a few more girls to escape from Sextus Mach soon – ones with that dominant streak, because there are *so many* powerful men who want to be whipped raw by a woman!

Juniper had a whole bunch of quirts sent from New England – devil's club, poison oak, vine maple, and of course, birches. That's what men like best, being birched by a woman, preferably in dominant costume – black rubber, like Mach's trusties. I get off on watching, as

Kissy or Juniper birches them, and I masturbate, which adds to their pleasure. After all, they are paying for it. I wouldn't be surprised to see Sextus Mach crawl in here, begging for thrashing, after seeing what his rubber vixens were doing to him the night of my escape. Heavens, I wouldn't be surprised to see good old Donkey Don Funicello, with one of his yellow ribbons tied round his cock, getting his bare ass whopped. Anything is possible here, out west, and nothing is surprising. Juniper keeps her secrets, and that's OK. I don't know her relation with Sextus, although there must be one. Maybe *she* sports rubber costume and whips his ass at bedtimes back at his, omigosh, *château?*

That's about all there is to tell. I had the stuff from my New York apartment sold at auction, which is ironic. I sometimes wonder what happened to Marc and Helena, and all the people who helped tame me, but I guess they can look after themselves. Things come and go, in the west, all under a big sky. People are less complicated. I still think of Jehanne, and the others, and Jehanne's gorgeous silky ass. I have plenty to shiver about already, though. Right now, Juniper's just freed me from a hobbled hogtie. I took 60 on the bare, with her cane, and boy, does it smart! The sun's coming up over the desert, all crimson, like my bottom. Weaver likes me that way. He's going to fuck my ass again soon, and my pussy's wet just thinking about it. I like it here, out west. I really do.

NEXUS BACKLIST

This information is correct at time of printing. For up-to-date information, please visit our website at www.nexus-books.co.uk

All books are priced at £5.99 unless another price is given.

Nexus books with a contemporary setting

ACCIDENTS WILL HAPPEN	Lucy Golden ISBN 0 352 33596 3	☐
ANGEL	Lindsay Gordon ISBN 0 352 33590 4	☐
BEAST	Wendy Swanscombe ISBN 0 352 33649 8	☐
THE BLACK MASQUE	Lisette Ashton ISBN 0 352 33372 3	☐
THE BLACK WIDOW	Lisette Ashton ISBN 0 352 33338 3	☐
THE BOND	Lindsay Gordon ISBN 0 352 33480 0	☐
BROUGHT TO HEEL	Arabella Knight ISBN 0 352 33508 4	☐
CAGED!	Yolanda Celbridge ISBN 0 352 33650 1	☐
CANDY IN CAPTIVITY	Arabella Knight ISBN 0 352 33495 9	☐
CAPTIVES OF THE PRIVATE HOUSE	Esme Ombreux ISBN 0 352 33619 6	☐
DANCE OF SUBMISSION	Lisette Ashton ISBN 0 352 33450 9	☐
DARK DELIGHTS	Maria del Rey ISBN 0 352 33276 X	☐
DISCIPLES OF SHAME	Stephanie Calvin ISBN 0 352 33343 X	☐

DISCIPLINE OF THE PRIVATE HOUSE	Esme Ombreux ISBN 0 352 33459 2	☐
DISCIPLINED SKIN	Wendy Swanscombe ISBN 0 352 33541 6	☐
DISPLAYS OF EXPERIENCE	Lucy Golden ISBN 0 352 33505 X	☐
DISPLAYS OF PENITENCE	Lucy Golden ISBN 0 352 33646 3	☐
DRAWN TO DISCIPLINE	Tara Black ISBN 0 352 33626 9	☐
AN EDUCATION IN THE PRIVATE HOUSE	Esme Ombreux ISBN 0 352 33525 4	☐
EMMA'S SECRET DOMINATION	Hilary James ISBN 0 352 33226 3	☐
GISELLE	Jean Aveline ISBN 0 352 33440 1	☐
GROOMING LUCY	Yvonne Marshall ISBN 0 352 33529 7	☐
HEART OF DESIRE	Maria del Rey ISBN 0 352 32900 9	☐
HIS MISTRESS'S VOICE	G. C. Scott ISBN 0 352 33425 8	☐
HOUSE RULES	G. C. Scott ISBN 0 352 33441 X	☐
IN FOR A PENNY	Penny Birch ISBN 0 352 33449 5	☐
THE LAST STRAW	Christina Shelly ISBN 0 352 33643 9	☐
LESSONS IN OBEDIENCE	Lucy Golden ISBN 0 352 33550 5	☐
NURSES ENSLAVED	Yolanda Celbridge ISBN 0 352 33601 3	☐
ONE WEEK IN THE PRIVATE HOUSE	Esme Ombreux ISBN 0 352 32788 X	☐
THE ORDER	Nadine Somers ISBN 0 352 33460 6	☐
THE PALACE OF EROS	Delver Maddingley ISBN 0 352 32921 1	☐

PEEPING AT PAMELA	Yolanda Celbridge ISBN 0 352 33538 6	☐
PENNY PIECES	Penny Birch ISBN 0 352 33631 5	☐
PET TRAINING IN THE PRIVATE HOUSE	Esme Ombreux ISBN 0 352 33655 2	☐
PLAYTHING	Penny Birch ISBN 0 352 33493 2	☐
THE PLEASURE CHAMBER	Brigitte Markham ISBN 0 352 33371 5	☐
POLICE LADIES	Yolanda Celbridge ISBN 0 352 33489 4	☐
SANDRA'S NEW SCHOOL	Yolanda Celbridge ISBN 0 352 33454 1	☐
SEE-THROUGH	Lindsay Gordon ISBN 0 352 33656 0	☐
SKIN SLAVE	Yolanda Celbridge ISBN 0 352 33507 6	☐
THE SLAVE AUCTION	Lisette Ashton ISBN 0 352 33481 9	☐
SLAVE EXODUS	Jennifer Jane Pope ISBN 0 352 33551 3	☐
SLAVE GENESIS	Jennifer Jane Pope ISBN 0 352 33503 3	☐
SLAVE REVELATIONS	Jennifer Jane Pope ISBN 0 352 33627 7	☐
SLAVE SENTENCE	Lisette Ashton ISBN 0 352 33494 0	☐
SOLDIER GIRLS	Yolanda Celbridge ISBN 0 352 33586 6	☐
THE SUBMISSION GALLERY	Lindsay Gordon ISBN 0 352 33370 7	☐
SURRENDER	Laura Bowen ISBN 0 352 33524 6	☐
TAKING PAINS TO PLEASE	Arabella Knight ISBN 0 352 33369 3	☐
TEMPER TANTRUMS	Penny Birch ISBN 0 352 33647 1	☐

------ ✂ -----------------------------

Please send me the books I have ticked above.

Name   ....

Address   ....

            ....

            ....

            .... Post code...................

Send to: **Cash Sales, Nexus Books, Thames Wharf Studios, Rainville Road, London W6 9HA**

US customers: for prices and details of how to order books for delivery by mail, call 1-800-805-1083.

Please enclose a cheque or postal order, made payable to **Nexus Books Ltd,** to the value of the books you have ordered plus postage and packing costs as follows:

UK and BFPO – £1.00 for the first book, 50p for each subsequent book.

Overseas (including Republic of Ireland) – £2.00 for the first book, £1.00 for each subsequent book.

If you would prefer to pay by VISA, ACCESS/MASTERCARD, AMEX, DINERS CLUB or SWITCH, please write your card number and expiry date here:

....

Please allow up to 28 days for delivery.

Signature ....

Our privacy policy.

We will not disclose information you supply us to any other parties. We will not disclose any information which identifies you personally to any person without your express consent.

From time to time we may send out information about Nexus books and special offers. Please tick here if you do *not* wish to receive Nexus information.   ☐

------ ✂ -----------------------------